My name is Barry Allen, and I am the fastest man alive. A freak accident sent a lightning bolt into my lab one night, dousing me with electricity and chemicals, and gifting me with superspeed. Since then, I've used my powers to fight the good fight, protecting my city, my world, and my universe from all manner of threats. I've stared down crazed speedsters, time-traveling techno-magicians, and every sort of thief, crook, and lunatic you can imagine.

With the help of my friends and my adopted family, I run S.T.A.R. Labs, a hub of super-science, and use it as a staging base to keep Central City safe from those who would cause it harm.

I've traveled to not one but two different futures, and I've seen the amazing heights to which humanity will soar. In the present, I do everything I can to help get us there.

I am . . .

THE FL

BY BARRY LYGA

ASH™

CROSSOVER CRISIS

THE LEGENDS OF FOREVER

AMULET BOOKS
NEW YORK

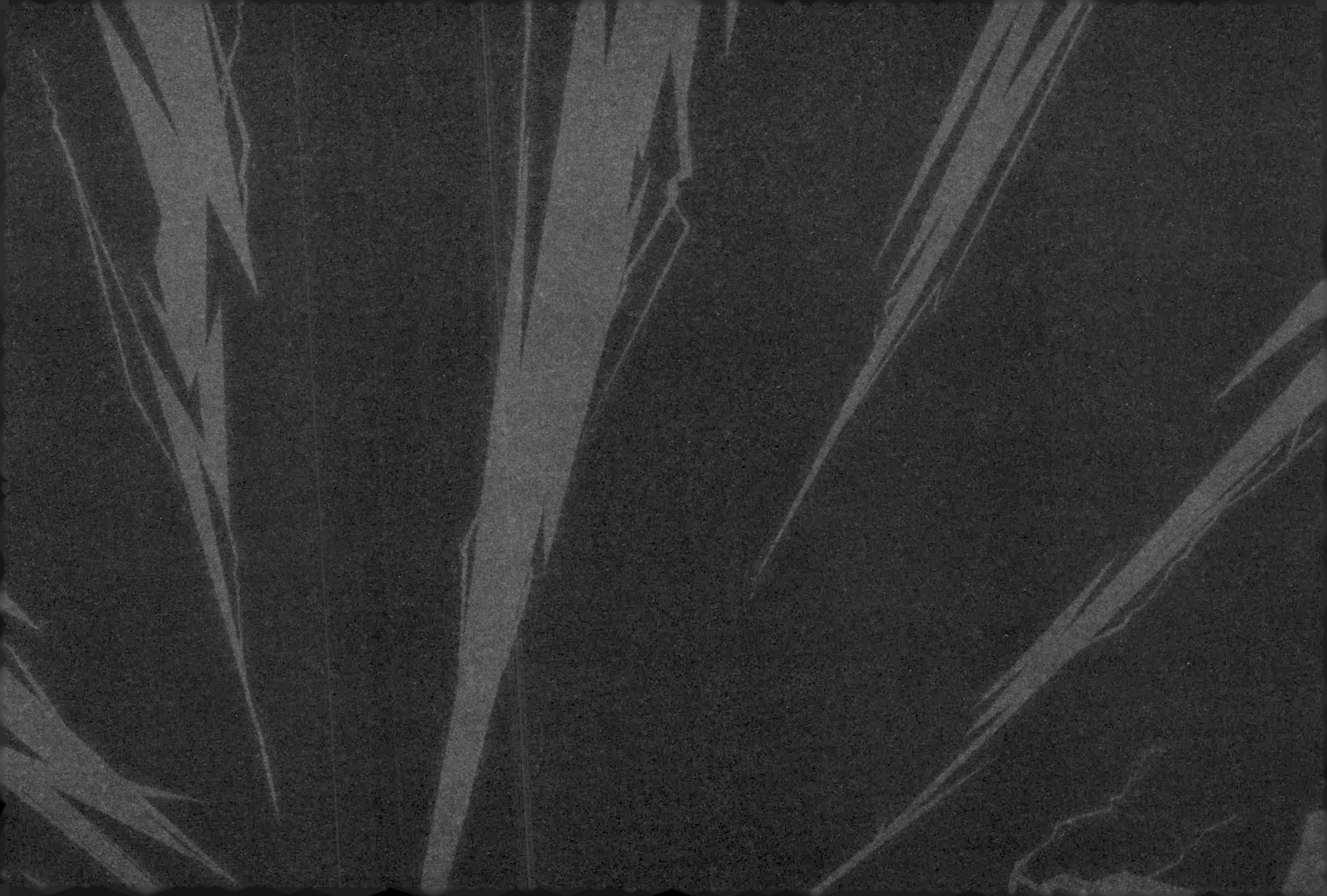

Cataloging-in-Publication Data has been applied for and may be obtained from the Library of Congress.

ISBN 978-1-4197-4686-4

Cover Illustration by Shawn M. Moll
Book design by Brenda E. Angelilli

Printed and bound in U.S.A.
10 9 8 7 6 5 4 3 2 1

ABRAMS The Art of Books
195 Broadway, New York, NY 10007
abramsbooks.com

PREVIOUSLY IN

It's not the end of the world—it's the end of the worlds!

The villainous Crime Syndicate of America has escaped from the destroyed Earth 27, wreaking havoc on Earth 1. And with them come ten thousand innocent refugees, each imbued with superspeed! In Star City, the quite insane Ambush Bug has pranked the city into paralysis and now plans to unleash a horde of robot bees.

On Earth 38, the Flash, Green Arrow, Supergirl, and Superman managed to defeat Anti-Matter Man, at the cost of Supergirl's powers. And now breaches have opened throughout the Multiverse, randomly catapulting people from universe to universe.

Thanks to the Martian Manhunter, our heroes know that their foe is at the End of Time. Now they just have to get there . . .

ROLL CALL

THE FLASH (BARRY ALLEN)

GREEN ARROW (OLIVER QUEEN)

SUPERMAN (KAL-EL/CLARK KENT)

SUPERGIRL (KARA ZOR-EL/
KARA DANVERS)

IRIS WEST-ALLEN

VIBE (CISCO RAMON)

AVA SHARPE

WHITE CANARY (SARA LANCE)

HEAT WAVE (MICK RORY)

THE ATOM (RAY PALMER)

MADAME XANADU

OWLMAN (BRUCE WAYNE)

PLUS:

SPECIAL GUEST STARS GALORE!

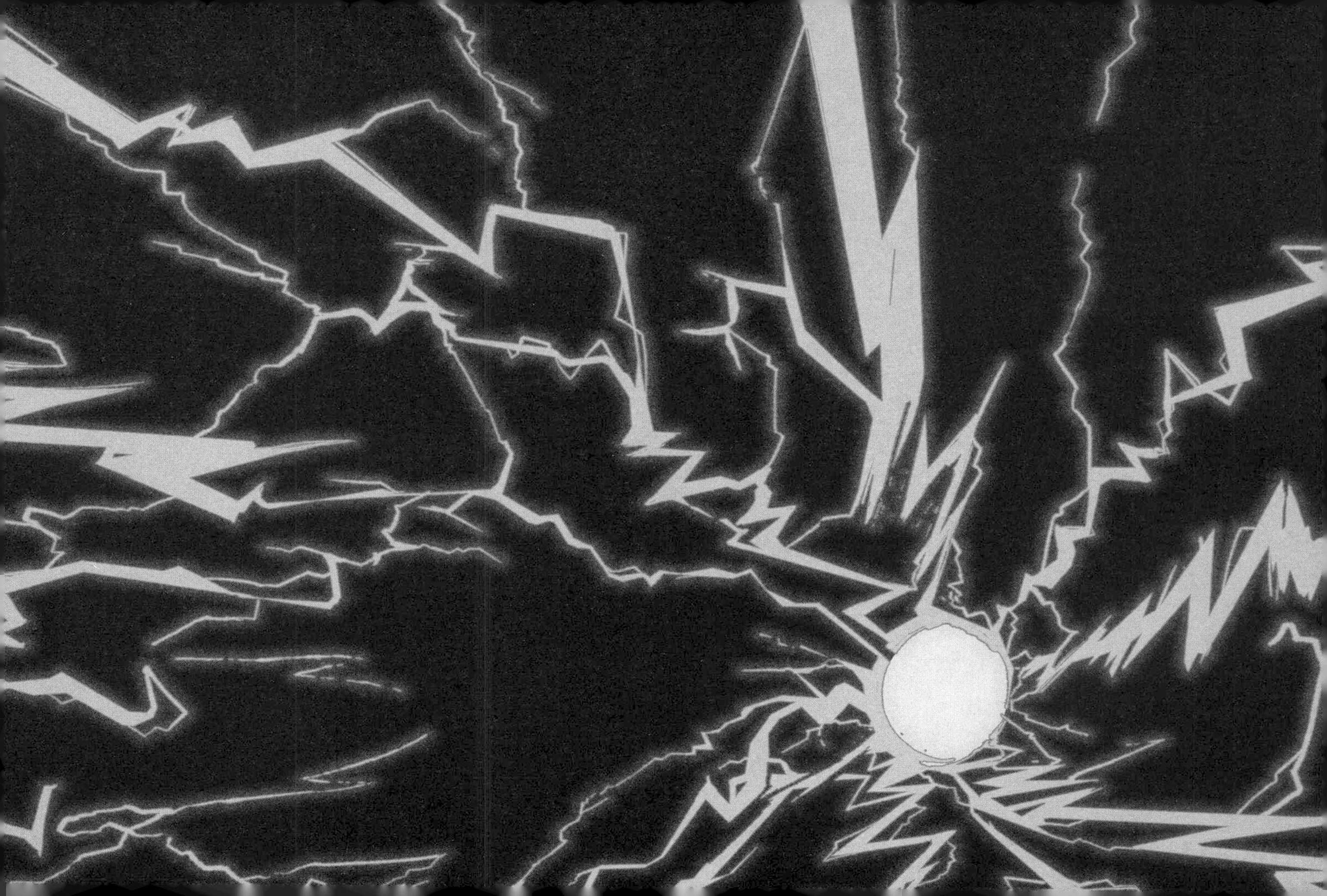

IN A PLACE AT A TIME

HELLO.

I have gone by many names, but I am most often and most familiarly known as . . . the Phantom Stranger. For untold years following interminable years, I have walked the world and the worlds, known to many, friend to none. I help those I can, sometimes through direct intervention, more often through the timely and prudent injection of information, of truth, of perception. Cursed to wander for all eternity, I do what I can to lessen the pain of mere living.

In my time, I have witnessed the rise of tyrants, the fall of empires, the glory of peace, and the horror of war.

Never have I seen impending doom such as I see now, spreading throughout the Multiverse from its origin point at the End of All Time. Fissures in the very fabric of reality have opened, and the barriers between universes—once fortified and difficult to traverse—have frayed. Ordinary people find themselves transported from one universe to another, many of them lost in worlds they cannot comprehend, at risk of losing their sanity or even their lives.

What of our heroes, you wonder? Surely their puissance is high enough to meet the challenge?

They, sadly, believe they understand the contours of their challenge, the perimeter of its dangers.

They do not.

Their foe is no ordinary enemy. Their foe perceives all of reality from the vantage point of its ending. All of history is at the enemy's command . . . and the threat is larger than anyone could imagine, encompassing not merely the reality of the book you hold in your hands, but the *other* reality as well!

The threat of Anti-Matter Man took almost all the power of our heroes to defeat. And he was merely the first salvo.

Worlds will live. Worlds will die. And the DC Universe—this one, at least—will never be the same again.

Perhaps you have heard these words before. Perhaps you scoff.

Do so at your own risk.

Now, Dear Reader, turn the page. For the story is about to begin. And end.

"Time's an enemy and a friend."

—BRUCE SPRINGSTEEN,
"Visitation at Fort Horn"

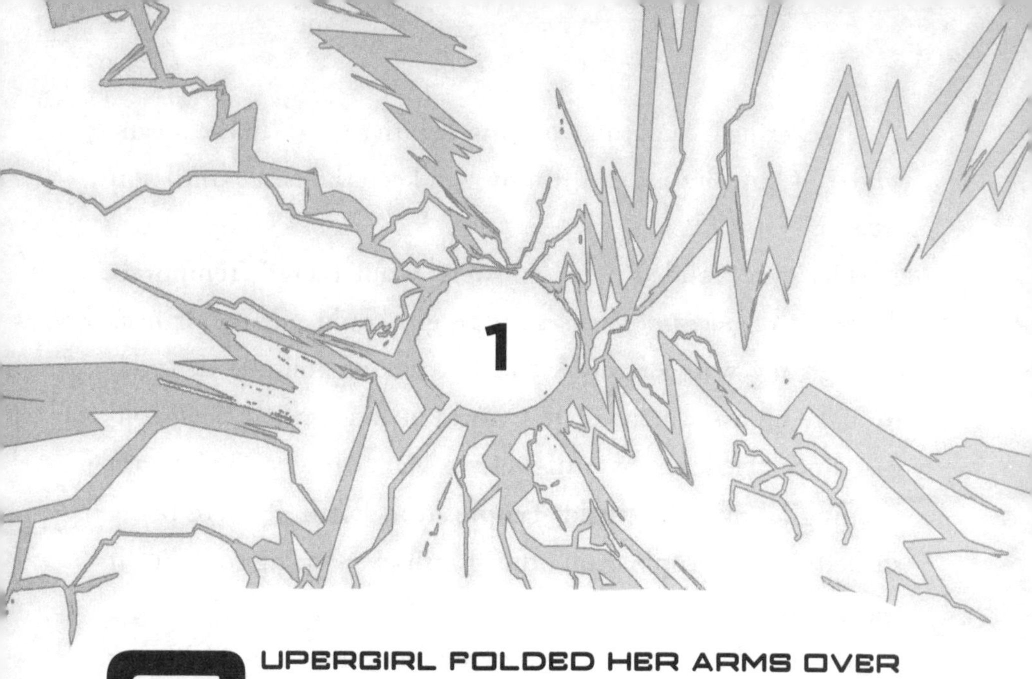

1

SUPERGIRL FOLDED HER ARMS OVER her chest as she sat up in the recovery bed at the Fortress of Solitude. "I should be the one going!" she complained.

Her cousin shook his head. "No," said Superman. "You're still recuperating from your battle with Anti-Matter Man. Your powers haven't even begun to return yet."

It was true. With the entire world on the precipice of destruction due to the corrosive powers of Anti-Matter Man, a synthetic life-form/weapon from the anti-matter universe, Supergirl had risked her life and sacrificed her powers. Channeling all her powers into a Super Flare, she'd funneled so much energy into Anti-Matter Man that the construct had exploded. The world was saved, but at the cost of Supergirl's powers. They would return . . .

Eventually.

With a frustrated groan, Supergirl sank back against the pillow. "Man, I *never* get to save the Multiverse."

"Next time," Superman promised with a grin. "In the meanwhile, J'Onn, Brainy, and Jimmy will keep the peace until you recover."

Her eyes clouded over. "How is it out there?" Temporarily bereft of her super-senses, Supergirl could not see or hear through the walls of the Arctic Fortress of Solitude in order to make an assessment of the world at large. She'd been told that since her defeat of Anti-Matter Man, breaches had begun opening all over the world. People from Earth 38 were being sucked in, and people from other Earths were being spat out. It was chaos.

But thanks to J'Onn J'Onzz's mental link with Anti-Matter Man, they at least had an inkling of how to stop things: Anti-Matter Man had been released from his prison inside the moon of Qward in the antiverse by a force at the End of Time. Her friend Barry Allen—the Flash—thought that he knew of a way to get to the End of Time, but they would have to return to Earth 1 first. Superman insisted on joining them.

"Between Flash and Green Arrow, they have speed, power, brains, and talent," Kal told her. "But I think they could use a little super-boost."

He was right, she knew. The Flash and Green Arrow and their respective teams had bravery, intelligence, and wits to spare, but their enemy in this case could project its power through the time stream, create breaches at will, and break open a moon. Speed and arrows could go only so far; Kryptonian strength and stamina would be a big help.

"Be careful, OK?" she told him. "I didn't blow myself up just so that you could go flying off to the End of Time and get killed."

Kal grinned. "Don't worry, cousin. Lois would never forgive me if I didn't come back. She's already read me the riot act. 'Go do your hero thing, Smallville, but don't forget you have two thousand words on the mayoral election due to Perry by Thursday.'"

Smiling, Kara allowed herself to relax. "I knew there was a reason I liked her. Good luck, Kal. Go with Rao."

He winked at her. "Enjoy the next twenty-four hours of bed rest. It'll be the only rest you get for a while, I suspect."

"Ever made the Multiverse transit before?" Barry asked the Man 7
of Steel.

Superman tilted his head this way and that, as though not entirely sure how to answer the question. "I've been places," he said.

They stood atop the DEO building in National City. Brainiac 5 had reverse-engineered the transmatter device Cisco Ramon had invented so that it could project a large enough breach for the Flash, Green Arrow, and Superman to travel to Earth 1.

"At the same time," Brainy said, "I believe I may be able to use this technology to begin closing breaches from other Earths to Earth 38." He paused. "But this is only theoretical at this point in time."

"And we still need to identify the strays from other Earths . . ." Alex Danvers put in.

"*And* track down the people from Earth 38 who've ended up on other Earths . . ." J'Onn added.

Gathered on the roof, the team exchanged a group look of exhaustion.

"Our best bet," Superman told them with a sunny confidence that seemed both out of place yet wholly earned, "is to track down the villain behind this and stop him."

"Or her," Alex said, fuming. "Women can be world-conquering, time-traveling, universe-distorting menaces, too, you know."

Superman nodded. "Point well taken. I apologize. Once we confront and stop him *or her*, the quantum breaches should halt. Then we'll have a finite number of Multiversal refugees to locate and return."

"Assuming we can identify all of them and figure out where they're supposed to be," Oliver said somewhat dourly. "It's a big, complicated Multiverse out there."

There were, so far as they knew, fifty-four universes: the fifty-two universes of the known Multiverse, plus the rogue Nazi universe of Earth X. All fifty-three of which were composed of positive matter.

The fifty-fourth was the antiverse, the anti-matter universe, including Qward, the world where Anti-Matter Man had been created. So far, no breaches had opened to or from that hellish place, but if they did, the current crisis would worsen beyond imagining—when positive matter and anti-matter came into contact, they destroyed each other, causing a cascading toxic chain reaction that had wiped out Earth 27 and almost eradicated all life on Earth 38 as well.

With breaches opening at random between the fifty-three positive-matter universes, it was, as Green Arrow had indicated, nearly impossible to track who had come from or gone to which universe.

Superman smiled. "I have every confidence we'll figure it out, Green Arrow."

"Your optimism is appreciated, if not entirely founded in logic," Brainy said. He grimaced for a moment at the tablet he held. "There is considerable interference at the quark level. No doubt a side effect of our unnamed foe opening so many breaches at once. The fabric between universes was never intended to suffer so many tears." He paused and looked up at them all. "You understand I'm using the word *fabric* metaphorically? There is no actual—"

"We get it, Brainy." Barry Allen—the Flash—bounced on the balls of his feet in mingled eagerness and frustration. Every second they wasted on Earth 38 was another second that his archenemy, Eobard Thawne, the Reverse-Flash, spent at the End of Time, using his speed to power the machinery that their mysterious foe used to wreak havoc on the present. Barry knew that they needed to get back to Earth 1 and use the Time Bureau's technology to head to the End of Time. End this once and for all.

"I just wanted to avoid any unnecessary confusion," Brainy sniffed. "Now, due to the recurring breaches, there is a slight chance that you may experience some limited chronal realignment during transit."

Superman's eyebrow arched as though to say, *Oh? Do tell.*

"'Limited chronal realignment?'" Oliver said. "What's that?"

"Time travel," Barry said with a slight shiver. "Come on, Brainy . . ."

"Very, very limited," Brainy promised. "No more than a day. I promise."

"Scout's honor?" Barry asked.

"I assume you refer to the oath of the Pangalactic Scouts of Zoon, the most holy oath in the galaxy. Yes, scout's honor."

"A day at most?" Oliver snorted. "Big deal. Been there, done that."

"That's the spirit, Oliver," Barry said, slapping him on the back. "We'll make you a mad scientist yet."

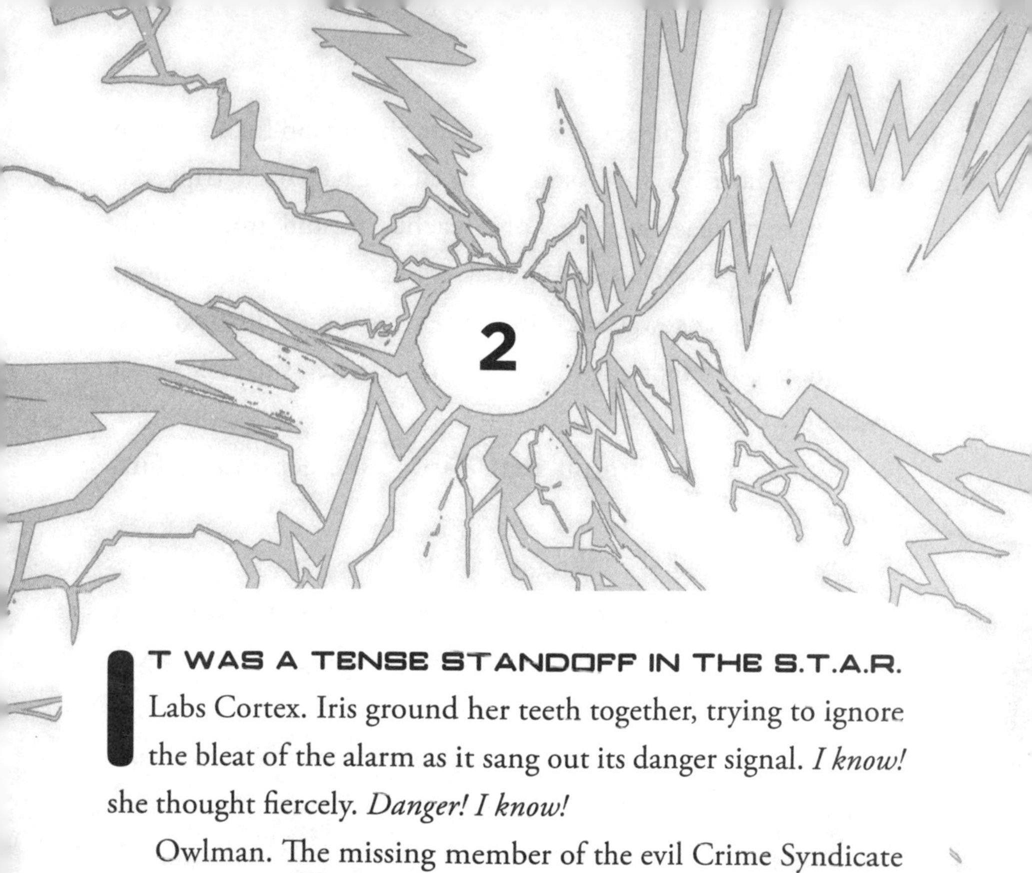

IT WAS A TENSE STANDOFF IN THE S.T.A.R. Labs Cortex. Iris ground her teeth together, trying to ignore the bleat of the alarm as it sang out its danger signal. *I know!* she thought fiercely. *Danger! I know!*

Owlman. The missing member of the evil Crime Syndicate of America from the now-defunct Earth 27. He stood in the doorway to the Cortex, holding a knife to the throat of Madame Xanadu. He'd shown up right after Team Flash managed to rescue Mr. Terrific and Cisco Ramon from the past . . .

That rescue that would go down in the record books as the shortest and least effective ever. Mr. Terrific—Curtis Holt—was fine: winded a bit and slumped in a chair, but none the worse for wear. Cisco, though, was nowhere to be seen. He'd emerged from the time breach with Curtis, only to be snatched almost immediately and yanked back through by . . . something. Something big. Something incredibly powerful.

As bad as all that was, it wasn't even the reason for the alarm singing its horribly shrill song. The alarm had been triggered by a sudden, massive surge of breaches to and from multiple universes. The Multiverse had gone Swiss cheese without warning, and Iris was standing there without superpowers, without her resident genius, and without her superspeedster husband.

"Can someone turn off that alarm!" she demanded. First things first.

Owlman leered. "Finding it hard to focus, dear?"

"I'm not talking to you yet," Iris snapped at him. "Some guy with a lousy mask and a baggy costume holding a knife doesn't even make my top ten priority list right now."

"Um, I think the keyword in that sentence is *knife*," said Felicity Smoak, hacker on loan from Team Arrow. "We seem to have brought bare hands to a knife fight."

"Just turn off the alarm," Iris told her.

Felicity slapped her palm down on a control pad. The alarm went silent.

"Can anyone else hear that ringing noise?" Caitlin Snow said very, very loudly. She'd gone temporarily deaf when she used some jerry-rigged equipment to bring Curtis and Cisco back from the past.

"Not now!" Iris told her.

"Iris! What's going on? Iris!" It was her father's voice, emanating from the big monitor at the center of the Cortex. He'd called to plead for help with his Ambush Bug case in Star City, and the webcam in the Cortex didn't show him Owlman.

"Dad!" she said, spinning to the screen. "We'll help you as soon as we can. But right now the world is falling apart and we've got more concerns than a bunch of bees in Star City."

"But—" Joe West began, cut off instantly as Iris disconnected the Star City team.

"Felicity! Mr. Terrific!" she barked in the tone of a woman who was used to being heeded *immediately*. "Start analyzing the satellite data on these new breaches. I want a report in ten minutes, along with suggestions for fixing the problem."

"In ten minutes?" Curtis's voice betrayed a wounded sense of the impossible as he shuttled his chair over to a workstation.

"Then do it in nine," she snapped, turning her attention back to Owlman. Folding her arms over her chest, she struck her most confident pose. "And you. You say you're here to save the world? Great. Put down the knife and get started."

Owlman pursed his lips. She could tell he was considering her previous jab at him and whether he could or should let it slide. He made her wait a moment longer before speaking again.

"I am indeed ready to save the world. But first: What's in it for me?"

Iris snorted. "How about having a world to live in?"

He shrugged, a movement that caused the point of his knife to indent Madame Xanadu's throat in a very unnatural way. "I survived things you wouldn't believe on Earth 27."

"An Earth that is now dead," Iris told him, as if he needed a reminder, "which sort of calls into question your world-saving bona fides. Now, tell me why I shouldn't just throw you in the Pipeline along with the rest of your twisted friends—or *stop.*

Wasting. My. Time." Those last words she hurled with as much venom and aggravation as she could conjure.

She had no way to deduce Owlman's motives or even his abilities. All she had on her side was what she knew of Earth 27. Owlman came from a world where good was evil and evil was good, where he ruled with an iron fist, his every whim a command to be obeyed instantly, or else. So maybe, just maybe, he wouldn't be accustomed to being dissed and dismissed. If she could keep him off guard, maybe she could stall long enough for a miracle.

"Tell them, Bruce," said Madame Xanadu.

"Bruce?" Iris said.

Owlman's upper lip curled in disgust and he opened his mouth to speak . . .

. . . just as a sudden wind erupted in the center of the room, bringing with it a lurid red light that hovered and throbbed in midair before coalescing into a familiar form.

Barry.

He stood there for a single second, not moving as his body vibrated into view. His costume, ragged and torn, revealed bruises and patches of blood. He stood between Iris and Owlman, but even with him turned three-quarters away from her, Iris knew her husband—his stance, his poise. It was him.

"Owlman?" Barry said, his voice tremulous and thready. "But that must mean . . ."

And then, as they all watched, he vanished just as quickly as he'd appeared.

Before anyone could react, a bolt of silver spun across the room, slamming into Owlman's jaw at top speed. The villain spasmed, dropping his knife as he collapsed to the floor, unconscious. A shiny ball of metal hovered in the air near Madame Xanadu's shoulder.

From his chair at a workstation, Mr. Terrific grinned. "Not exactly what I created the T-spheres for," he admitted, "but it got the job done, right?"

Iris tried to collect her thoughts even as Caitlin dashed to Madame Xanadu's side to support her. Felicity kicked Owlman's knife out of range.

"What do we do with this guy?" she asked, gesturing to him.

"Pipeline," Iris said. "Like I—"

She cut herself off as the room lit up again, this time with a familiar blue light. In an instant, there were Barry and Oliver, along with a man she'd never seen before, but who wore the very familiar and very welcome emblem of the Kryptonian house of El. She was used to seeing it on Supergirl, not whoever this guy was. But that was the least of her concerns right now.

"Is it really you?" Iris rushed to Barry's side and clutched him before he could vanish again.

"It's me," he told her. "I told you I'd come back. I think we were supposed to get here tomorrow, but from the look of things, I guess it's better that we got here when we did."

"Oh, I love it when you talk time travel shenanigans," Iris deadpanned.

They kissed.

"You gonna give me some of that action, Green Arrow?" Felicity asked.

Much to everyone's surprise—possibly even Oliver's—he swept her into his arms and planted a serious, deep kiss on her.

"You should travel the Multiverse more often," Felicity said when she could catch her breath.

Barry made introductions after whisking Owlman down to the Pipeline, where he joined the rest of the Crime Syndicate in a cell. Back in the Cortex, there was a confused babble of overlapping voices and stories for a moment before Superman stepped into the center of the room and, without speaking, commanded everyone's attention. Then, very calmly, he pointed to each person in turn and requested an update. Soon, everyone knew the status of each crisis.

They were all grim.

"And what's the deal with these visions of Barry everyone keeps seeing?" Felicity asked. When the collected heroes all groaned, she threw her hands up in the air. "What? Yeah, I know it's not the end of the universe, but it's *weird* and it has me freaked out, OK?"

Mr. Terrific stroked his chin, deep in thought. "It could be some kind of interuniversal quantum residue from Anti-Matter Man's incursion into a plus-matter universe."

"I know that was English," said Green Arrow, "but could you try it in English for fourth graders?"

"He's saying that Anti-Matter Man's transit from universe to universe was so violent that images from other universes might be bleeding through into ours," Barry said. He checked with Curtis, who nodded his assent.

“Yeah,” said Mr. Terrific. “With something that big and that violent ripping open the universe, there’s a good chance we’d see all kinds of temporal refractions and rebounds for a while.”

“Then it wasn’t really you?” Iris asked. “It was a Barry Allen from another Earth?”

“Or a possible future,” Mr. Terrific added. “Or the past.”

“Maybe even the TV world,” Barry speculated, shrugging.

“TV world?” Superman asked.

Barry quickly recapped for the Man of Steel the story of the other version of the Multiverse, the one in which Barry Allen had decided to change history. Now there were two entire realities, one in which Barry had changed history—the transuniversal version, or TV—and one in which he hadn’t . . . their own.

“Only Cisco can communicate with the TV world, thanks to his Vibe powers,” Barry finished. “Without him, there’s no way to be sure if this other Flash that people are seeing is from *our* Multiverse or somehow crossing over from the other one.”

“In any event,” said Iris, clutching Barry’s hand tightly, “it’s surely the least important of our problems right now.”

Barry nodded. “From what you said, it sounds like Cisco was kidnapped by our foe at the End of Time.” He suddenly cracked a grin. “Good thing we’re headed there anyway.”

“Oh?” Iris asked archly. “Are you planning to run there? Last time you got lucky and the Tornado Twins let you use the Cosmic Treadmill. What’s your plan this time?”

“The Time Bureau,” Barry announced, then, for Superman’s benefit, explained: “That’s a government agency here on Earth 1 that helps police the time stream. They have Time Couriers, which can transport you anywhere in space or time. They were no help in rescuing Cisco or Curtis because we didn't know where and when to look. But now we have a destination."

"The end of everything," Superman said solemnly.

The room went silent. For a moment, there'd been an incipient sense of something like relief, something akin to optimism. The Flash was back, and he'd brought an ally with the powers of a god! Everything would be OK!

But the End of Time . . . as Superman said, it was the end of *everything*. Who knew what dangers and evils lurked there? And any foe who could turn the Reverse-Flash into a living weapon was a true menace to be reckoned with.

"Iris, Curtis," Barry said soberly, "I want you two to coordinate with Brainiac 5 and J'Onn J'Onzz on Earth 38. Do whatever you can to start closing these breaches and tracking down the people who've fallen through them."

"What about me?" Felicity asked. "I'm more than just arm candy for the Emerald Archer, you know."

"You start working remotely with the crew back in Star City," Oliver suggested. "Give them some tech support in their hunt for Ambush Bug."

"All due respect, Oliver," Mr. Terrific interrupted, "but I'm a hometown boy and even I'm wondering if Star City is really a priority. We're talking about the sanctity and survival of the entire Multiverse here. One city's safety just doesn't seem to measure up."

Before Oliver could respond, Superman spoke: "Green Arrow is right," he said, his voice soft yet steady. "We don't just fight the biggest battles or the strongest foes. There's a wise saying: 'Whoever saves one life has saved the world.' I truly believe that. We can't turn our back on pain, suffering, or people in distress just because there might be something worse around the corner. Even if there *is* something worse around the corner."

Mr. Terrific nodded slowly, but still seemed unconvinced. "We just seem to be stretching ourselves pretty thin."

"Then we stretch as far and as thin as we need to," Superman said.

In the S.T.A.R. Labs medical bay, Caitlin Snow helped Madame Xanadu back into her bed. "I'm so sorry you had to go through that," she apologized. "We don't usually let super villains kidnap people who are recuperating. Or, you know, not even recuperating. We just generally try to avoid letting super villains kidnap people as a matter of policy."

"He did not kidnap me," Madame Xanadu said, settling onto the bed. "I went with him voluntarily."

Caitlin blinked rapidly, positive she'd misheard. "I'm sorry . . . What did you just say?"

Madame Xanadu gestured with both hands, her fingers inscribing complicated kaleidoscopic patterns of woven light in the air. Caitlin stared into the shifting, shimmering brightness, her eyes wide and unmoving, her jaw slack.

"It is time, Caitlin Snow," said Madame Xanadu. "And time is a trap."

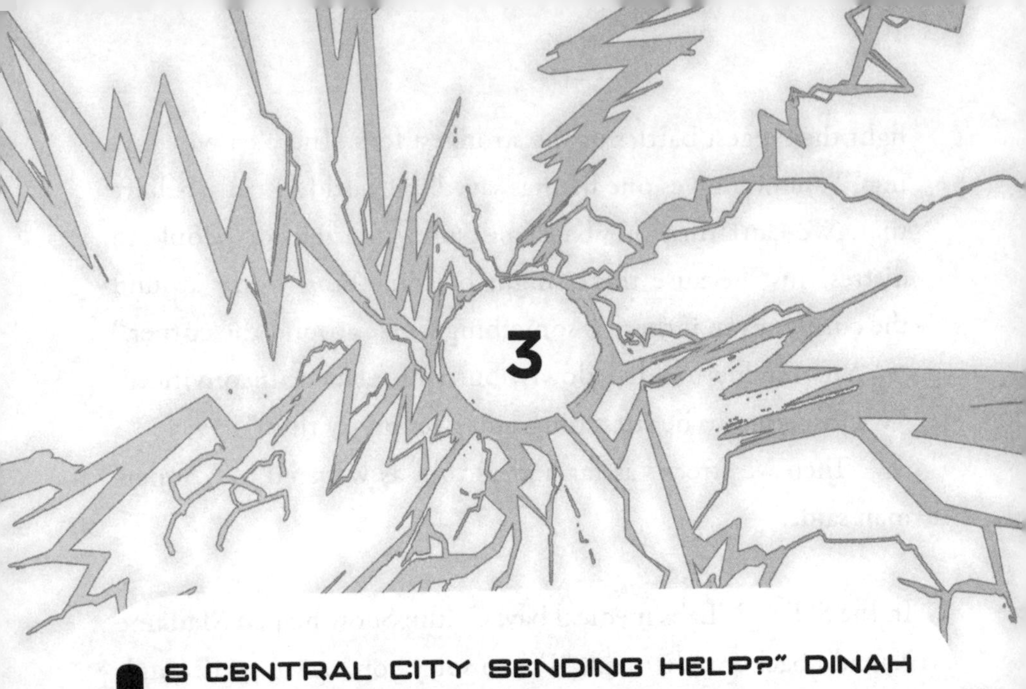

IS CENTRAL CITY SENDING HELP?" DINAH Drake asked. The situation in Star City had quickly degenerated from lunacy to outright panic. Ambush Bug was no longer just a demented pest—he was now an absolute threat.

Joe grimaced. He understood perfectly well why Team Flash couldn't afford to send someone to Star City to help out. The threats to the universe and the Multiverse *of course* superseded Ambush Bug's smaller-scale threat. But he still chafed at the wholly rational, utterly horrific calculus that meant the lives of those in Star City could, would, and had to be sacrificed in the name of the greater good. He wouldn't surrender. He wouldn't give up. Not for any reason.

If the universe died, then and only then would the people of Star City die. That was Joe's promise to himself.

"We're on our own," he said, sucking in his breath. "Felicity's gonna do what she can from Central City, but other than that . . ."

Wild Dog, Diggle, and Dinah took it about as well as he'd

anticipated. Dinah rolled her eyes and huffed out a breath, crossing her arms over her chest defensively. Dig shook his head and stared at the floor.

And Rene snorted in disgust and threw his Wild Dog mask against a table. "Are you kiddin' me, hoss? We got a psychopath ready to sting the whole city to death, and your posse can't spare five minutes to help out?"

Joe pondered how, exactly, to explain it to them. The breaches. The foe at the End of Time. The Reverse-Flash. It was all so enormous that it almost defied comprehension. The threat to Star City was so much easier to juggle.

"We can handle this," Joe promised with a confidence he did not feel. He used the big monitor to call up Bert Larvan, the Bug-Eyed Bandit's brother. He'd been helping Joe and the others anticipate Ambush Bug's moves and was working on a way to track the Bug using his intimate knowledge of his sister's tech.

"Do you have good news for me, Bert?" Joe asked when Larvan's face filled the screen.

"I've made some progress," Larvan said. He looked tired, his eyes bloodshot and sunken into purplish folds of skin. "We know he's using the bees as his teleport targets. I think I might be able to identify the bees as he uses them."

"What good's that?" Wild Dog scoffed.

Joe shushed him. "That means if he teleports away, we'll know where, right?"

Larvan cast a baleful eye through the camera, no doubt hoping his angry gaze would fall on Wild Dog. Rene, for his part, loitered against one of the Bunker's workstations, cleaning dirt from under his fingernails with a ridiculously large, sharp knife, not paying any attention at all to Larvan's glare.

"Yes, Detective West. That is precisely what it means. This Overwatch person you have me working with seems to think he can repurpose a weather satellite to locate the bees along Ambush Bug's path."

Joe permitted himself a small smile at Larvan's assumption that Overwatch was a man. Sometimes people's prejudices made keeping a secret identity easier. "Great. That will at least give us something. In the meantime, Bert, how many bees did he get? Can we calculate how long it'll take for them to swarm over the city?"

Larvan considered. "Brie designed the bees based on actual biological bee anatomy, but with enhanced stamina. Mr. Schwab received one hundred and thirty-seven of Brie's bees . . ."

"Great," Joe said. "We can start to—"

". . . but," Larvan went on, "he has Brie's schematics, remember?"

"What are you saying, Bert?" Joe said.

Wild Dog answered before Larvan could. "He's saying Ambush Bug can make more. Probably already has. Right?"

Larvan hesitated a moment, then nodded once, curtly. "It wouldn't be difficult. The bees are actually designed to assist in creating more. Given the proper materials, the swarm could double itself every six hours."

Joe buried his faced in his hands. "How long has Ambush Bug had these things?"

"Don't do the math," Dig advised. "It's too depressing."

"So," said Dinah, "what do we do now?"

Joe had no answer. None at all.

4

SARA LANCE WOKE, STRETCHED, yawned, and then remembered that she was in the thirty-first century.

Waking up in a different time period was not necessarily a new thing for her. As the captain of the *Waverider* and the leader of the somewhat snarkily dubbed "Legends of Tomorrow," Sara had roused herself in a plethora of eras. She'd been knocked unconscious and revived in medieval France, passed out and woken up in twenty-second-century Germany, and even groped her way toward awareness in the year 8892.

But this was different. Everything was different now.

The guest quarters she'd been assigned were spare, the walls polished silvery metal that curved and enclosed like living inside a large, rounded pyramid. A planter buoyed on antigravity disks hovered nearby, an array of purple and red and white flora spilling from it. Alien plants, she'd been told, from a world called Phlon.

Flan? she'd asked, imagining a quivering, gelatinous Mexican dessert. Only the first of many comedic and idiotic lingual collisions between her and the members of the Legion of Super-Heroes, her rescuers, her landlords, her guides through the new world of the thirty-first century.

The bed itself was a cloud. Floating a couple of feet from the floor, it was pure white and felt like silk, cotton, and pudding whenever she climbed into it. She'd been skeptical at first—the thing didn't look to have the structural integrity to hold a teddy bear, much less a human body—but it was the most comfortable bed she'd ever slept in. It wrapped diaphanous yet sturdy and supportive clots of cloudy material around her, conforming to her body in such a way as to obviate the need for blankets or pillows.

Welcome to the future.

She rolled to her side, and the bed accommodated by opening a little niche for her to swing her legs out. "Gideon, what's the weather today?" she asked the air.

A small panel of yellow light swimming with orange bubbles throbbed along the wall. "*Breep!* Captain Lance," said an almost too-soothing voice, "I've told you before that you need not use a trigger phrase to activate me. I use a phonemic processing algorithm along with voice timbre analysis and psychohistorical data to determine if you are speaking to me or to a biological. The weather has been programmed for sun with winds from the northeast at roughly three miles per hour. A nice breeze. Temperature will vary between sixty-two degrees and seventy-one degrees Fahrenheit. Also, my name is Computo, not Gideon. *Breep!*"

The Legion headquarters' built-in AI was a million times more sophisticated than the Gideon AI that Barry Allen had developed/would develop at some point in her past/his future. It automatically spoke to her in what the Legionnaires called "ancient English" (a tongue in which they were all fluent, thank God), and even converted thirty-first-century measurements from something called the Coluan Standard Measurement Scale to things like miles, hours, and feet for the benefit of her cave-woman self.

As miraculous as this technology was, though, there were certain things it could not do.

Levering herself off the bed, she did a couple of quick squats, just to get the blood flowing. And then she asked the question she'd asked every morning since arriving here in the thirty-first century more than a month ago:

"How's Zari?"

Sara thought she detected a momentary hesitation before Computo responded to her question. A pause of compassion? Or just a rare, microsecond-long glitch in the AI? No way to tell.

"There has been no change in Ms. Tomaz's status," Computo announced. "*Breep!* According to telemetry from the medical bay and Dr. Gym'll's notes, she is still comatose. I can, however, inform you that Mr. Palmer and Mr. Rory are convalescing well and expected to make a full recovery."

Sara sighed heavily. Her usual morning workout routine suddenly seemed . . . pointless.

Over a month ago—on her own personal timeline—she and the Legends had been within the temporal zone, the "space" they used to travel through time on the *Waverider*. An alert had suddenly rung out, and they'd experienced a burst of tachyons from the far, far future. Something very powerful was moving backward through time at incredible speed. What, where, and why, they had no time to determine.

The next thing she knew, the ship itself was caught up in the temporal ebb tide of the tachyon burst. Trapped in a time bolus, the ship accelerated into the far future, on a collision course with some sort of barrier across the time stream.

Sara had had mere seconds to figure out what to do, to figure out how to save her crew before they smashed into the barrier at the speed of light.

When she closed her eyes to sleep at night, she could still remember Gideon counting down, the moments to impact. Could still hear Ray yelling from his seat in the cockpit . . .

She'd made the only tenable decision: At the last possible instant, she'd cut the *Waverider*'s time circuits completely, using a kill switch to shut off the ship's time travel abilities. Usually, the *Waverider* gently decelerated from time travel mode to space travel mode.

Not this time.

Killing the time travel circuits had jerked the ship out of the temporal zone and back into real space with all the violence of a greyhound running full tilt and then hitting the limit of its choke chain. The ship itself could scarcely handle the stresses of the drop into real time; it broke apart, exploding its remains and expelling its crew over a swath of time and space.

Sara and Zari had ended up on Earth's moon in the year 3005. Fortunately for them, the moon had been colonized by then and had a rudimentary atmosphere even outside the colony domes. Unfortunately, Zari took a serious blow to the head and had yet to wake up.

Ray had "landed" three days later on the Saturnian moon of Titan, where the local telepaths quickly located him. Mick had ended up farthest away, arriving two weeks later on the ruins of the planet Trom, where apparently the elemental structure was quite unstable and no longer suitable for habitation.

The Legion of Super-Heroes (and yeah, they actually called themselves that . . . although who was she to judge, leading a group called the Legends of Tomorrow?) had received various temporal alerts when the wreckage of the *Waverider* exploded out of the temporal zone and into real space. They'd scrambled teams across the galaxy to rescue the time-lost refugees.

But still so many of the Legends were lost, missing somewhere in time: Mona Wu. Nate Heywood. Charlie. John Constantine. All of them scattered across time.

Mick and Ray would recover. Even thirty-first-century science couldn't say what would happen to Zari. And the others? No one could say for sure. Sara knew they were "out there." Somewhere.

Slipping into her White Canary togs, Sara set her lips in a grim line. *I need a ship. And a crew. And then I'll find them. I swear.*

"Breep!" Computo chirped for attention. "Captain Lance,

your presence has been requested in the medical bay, if you don't mind."

Sara grabbed her jacket, threw it around her shoulders, and headed for the door. "On my way, Gideon!" she shouted.

"I mean *Computo*," she muttered under her breath as she stepped into the corridor.

5

CISCO WAS BEING TORN APART, shredded, disassembled.

Strangely, it didn't hurt at all. He observed as though from afar, as though watching on a screen somewhere. The laceration of his self happened on a level beyond the physical. Beyond even the metaphysical. It was, perhaps, something superphysical. Spiritual. His entire concept of self had been dissected, his history left bleeding in the open air.

There he was in school, with Jake Puckett dunking his head in the toilet until Cisco cried uncle and agreed to let his bully copy his homework. And there he was again, mooning after Melinda Tores, the love of his life, never to be with him after his brother, Dante, thought it would be funny to lie and tell her that Cisco intended to become a priest.

Days at school, working hard. Nights at home, poring over tech magazines and journals, wishing that someone in his family would bother to notice him, would look up from their worship of Dante and his magical fingers at the piano.

Flashing forward, strips of history and time flayed from the corpus of his life and were left crumpled and sodden on the floor of the past. College and his roommate, Sebastian. Graduating. The job at S.T.A.R. Labs. And then so much more . . .

Cisco saw it all in an instant, his entire life arrayed around him in an infinity of facets, as though he were embedded in the center of a jewel made of concentrated time itself. Each facet was stripped away, pulled from him, examined.

And then it all came together again, the jewel collapsing into him. With the return of his own history came the return of his physicality, the return of pain. He screamed in agony as every punch, pinch, kick, scrape, cut, bruise, and contusion in his life revisited him at once.

Every heartache. Every tear. Every moment of sadness and anger and self-recrimination. His soul swelled with pain.

And then it was over. He was intact and real again, collapsed on a rough metal floor rusted with age. Around him, an energy field crackled and spat blue-white sparks.

"Yes, you will do nicely, Cisco Ramon."

He managed to lift his head enough to look up. The perspective was wonky, but through the energy field, he spied a figure in a bedraggled purple cloak standing over him. A hood shrouded the face in utter darkness, and the voice from within grated, echoing along itself.

"You time-napped the wrong superhero, dude," Cisco said

with much bravado, in contrast to how he felt. He didn't have the energy to summon a breach right at the moment, but once he did . . .

"You are precisely the right person, Cisco Ramon. Indeed, in the whole of the Multiverses, you are the exact individual I require. One out of trillions."

Multiverses? Multi*verses*? Plural?

So it turned out this guy knew about the TV world, then. Cisco forced out a single, wry chuckle. "Shows what you know, buddy. There's an excellent Xerox of me out there."

The voice spoke again, lacking emotion, the syllables and phonemes sliding against one another. *"The doppelgänger you speak of surrendered his powers for a time, and their return has left him somewhat weaker. You are the sole possessor of the powers I need. And now you are mine."*

Cisco licked his lips. "You're lying." But deep down, he knew it was true. He'd tried to commune with the TV Cisco when he was trapped in the past but had felt no reciprocal vibe in return. TV Cisco was powerless—or at least, powered less.

Why? Why would he do that? Why would he render himself defenseless in the face of so much danger?

"Well," Cisco said with what he hoped was a muscular, defiant tone, "when my buddy Barry gets here, you're gonna wish you'd never heard the name Cisco Ramon. Ever been punched in the face fourteen thousand times at the speed of light? Maybe if you let me go, he won't run over here and pummel you into the dirt."

The voice emanating from the solid shadows within the hood did not so much as chuckle, but Cisco thought he detected amusement nonetheless.

"I am eager for your friend to arrive, Cisco Ramon. Indeed, I rely on it."

6

BARRY VIBRATED THROUGH THE walls of the Time Bureau and into Ava Sharpe's office. It was empty and dark, with a half-eaten ham sandwich abandoned on a crumpled square of wax paper in a cone of light from the desk lamp. Barry tapped his left ear to activate his comms bud.

"Superman? Do you see her?"

Hovering above the clouds in order to conceal his presence on Earth 1—the people here were used to metahumans, not godlike aliens—Superman spoke with a calm resignation. "I don't like to invade people's privacy with my X-ray vision, but I suppose these are extenuating circumstances. I see a woman matching your description in the northern stairwell. And Flash?"

Barry was already speeding in that direction so quickly that no one at the Time Bureau would be able to see him. "Yeah?"

"Be kind," Superman said.

• • •

As director of the Time Bureau, Ava found that privacy had become a rare commodity. The demands on her—pardon the pun—time were constant, intense, and unrelenting. Like endless hail. That was on fire. And bristling with sharp spikes.

The northern stairwell was one of the few places that afforded her a measure of privacy. No one used it because it was too distant from the central command theater. Plus, there were no bathrooms nearby.

So when she needed a moment to herself, a moment of humanity and vulnerability and mourning, she retreated to the stairwell and sat alone on the stairs. The cold of the concrete steps leached through the seat of her pants, and the cement walls echoed her tears back to her, but at least it was only her own voice, not the endless vocal demands of the agents of the Time Bureau.

She wept for Sara. Sara, the White Canary, the captain of the missing *Waverider*, and the love of Ava's genetically foreshortened life. Sara and her crew and vessel had disappeared without so much as a wisp of evidence or a byte of telemetry data to mark their passing or delineate their trail.

Without Sara, Ava had only work. As a clone, she had no family, no long-standing friendships. Her only relationships of any depth or import were with the time-traveling Legends of Tomorrow.

All of whom had vanished.

A red blur manifested itself along the south wall of the stairwell. At first, she thought it was her eyes playing tricks on her: tear-smeared light from the glowing exit sign. But then the blur, roughly human-shaped, resolved into a solid figure.

"Director Sharpe—" began the Flash.

"I'm so sick of you super-people," Ava growled through her tears. "I'm sick of your costumes and your powers and your code names. Your secret identities and your archnemeses and your hidden cities and your customized weapons. I don't want to live in a world of wonder and splendor and marvels if the price of it is losing the woman I love. I want to live in a boring world with boring people and boring clothes and a boring job in a boring house with my boring girlfriend, do you hear me?"

The Flash said nothing for a moment. Then, "I'm very sorry."

They did not speak. The Flash crouched down next to her. Ava decided that if he took her hands in his own, she would scream bloody murder and bite his nose right off his face.

Fortunately for the Flash's future olfactory delights, he did not even feint in the direction of touching her. Instead, he pressed his hands together as though praying, focusing every bit of his attention on her as he spoke.

"I know things look bad. I know things are chaotic. But we think we can find the person responsible for the breaches. And it seems like too much of a coincidence that all of this happened right when the *Waverider* disappeared. If we find the person who started all of this, I bet we'll also find the *Waverider* and Sara and her crew. Please, Director Sharpe. *Ava*. We can't do it without you."

He gazed at her so intently with those ridiculously needy eyes behind that ridiculous cowl that she sighed heavily, then knuckled her tears away, and said, "What do you need?"

7

CAITLIN WALKED WITH STIFF LEGS and nearly motionless arms down the empty S.T.A.R. Labs corridor toward the Pipeline.

She was not hypnotized or mind controlled. Not precisely. The best description for her condition was *numb*. She could still control herself and she could have shaken off Madame Xanadu's orders . . . but she just couldn't be bothered.

Fully aware of where she was headed and what she was about to do, she could not bring herself to resist. Madame Xanadu had not commanded her, precisely. Instead, the seeress had . . . suggested Caitlin's course of action. And Caitlin—knowing it was insanity, knowing it was dangerous—instantly understood that she would comply nonetheless.

In the Pipeline, she ignored Superwoman and Ultraman as they hooted and cursed at her. Johnny Quick dozed in the corner of his cell. Power Ring had curled into a ball, knees to his chest, rocking back and forth and weeping.

She didn't care about them at all. She cared about the cell at the end of the corridor.

"Did you mean it?" she asked Owlman. "Did you mean it when you said you would save the world?"

Unfolding himself from the floor, where he sat cross-legged, the villain from Earth 27 stood to tower over her.

And smiled a smile that spoke many emotions, none of which were mirth.

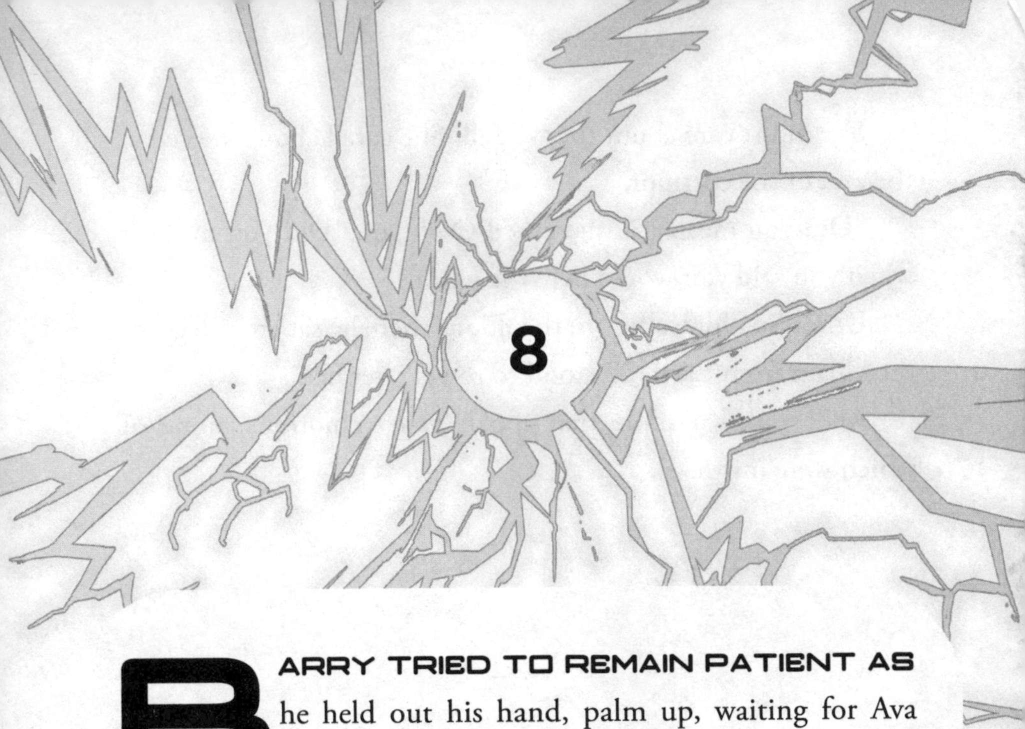

BARRY TRIED TO REMAIN PATIENT AS he held out his hand, palm up, waiting for Ava Sharpe to give him the Time Courier. It seemed to be taking for*ever*.

"And you promise you'll bring it back?" she asked.

"For the third time," Barry said solemnly, "yes."

She hovered it over his palm, pausing. "And you're sure this will help you find Sara and the others?"

Barry sighed with exasperation and dropped his hand to his side. "I can't be sure of anything, but it just makes sense. I promise you—if we get to the End of Time and defeat our enemy and that *doesn't* turn up the Legends, I will spend however long it takes searching the time stream for them. I *will* rescue them, Ava. Now . . . please?"

He held out his hand again and nodded to the Time Courier. It was a chunky black bracelet with a slightly thicker bulge where a watch face would normally be. And it could take him anywhere in time or space. Just what he needed to get to the End of Time.

With a firm nod, as though convincing herself of something, Ava dropped the Time Courier into his hand. "Just one thing, Flash: The Legends have been to the End of Time. There was nothing there. Certainly no enemy. There was once a group called the Time Masters who had a headquarters there, but they're no longer, uh, extant."

Barry considered this. That someone had already been to the End of Time hadn't occurred to him. "Well, we'll report back once we get there and see what's what," he told her. "Maybe the whole thing's a wild-goose chase. But the Martian who got us this intel has really reliable telepathy."

Ava goggled. "Martian? Telepathy?"

With a shrug and a grin, Barry gave her a thumbs-up as he darted toward the door, ready to phase through the Time Bureau headquarters and dash back to Central City. "Don't worry, Director Sharpe," he called out. "We've got the team and the talent."

Much to the surprise of everyone in the Cortex, Owlman strode in as though he owned the place, with Caitlin Snow at his side. Mr. Terrific and Felicity were at workstations, while Iris and Green Arrow stood nearby. With a smug, satisfied grin, Owlman planted his fists on his hips. "Let's try this again, shall we?"

Green Arrow spun around instantly at the sound of Owlman's voice, drawing and nocking an arrow in less than a heartbeat. He aimed unerringly at Owlman's head. "If you so much as blink in a way that makes me nervous," Oliver Queen said, his voice steady and low, "I will put this through your eye."

Owlman chuckled but—crucially—did not move. "How skittish are the proponents of truth and justice on this Earth," he said. "You have me outnumbered, on an unfamiliar playing field, and yet you identify as the prey, not the predator."

"We've heard enough about you from the Earth 27 refugees to respect your abilities," Iris said. "Oliver, can you disable him?"

"Define *disable*."

"Guys!" Caitlin shouted, and stepped between Oliver's bow and Owlman. "He's really here to save the world. Or at least, that's what Madame Xanadu says."

Iris folded her arms over her chest as Green Arrow shifted

his feet slightly, repositioning himself. If necessary, he could fire the arrow over Caitlin's shoulder, ricochet it off the wall, and clip Owlman in the ear. Not fatal, but it would distract the villain long enough for Oliver to prep another arrow and get a better vantage point.

"Madame Xanadu?" Iris asked. "What do you mean? He had a knife to her throat."

Caitlin shook her head. "That was *her* idea. She knew we wouldn't trust Owlman if he just walked in here, so she offered herself up as a hostage in order to give him time to explain."

"Why didn't *she* just tell us herself? Why all the trickery?"

"Because you people need to be duped into doing anything remotely effective," Owlman sneered.

"You talk like you think you're the good guy," Oliver said. "How deluded are you?"

"Deluded? No, I'm precisely as you understand me. I'm the hero of the story—not weak-willed and incapable of making the tough decisions, like you lot from Earth 1. I'm the hero who gets things done. And yes, sometimes people die." He thought for a moment. Shrugged. "A lot of times, actually. But look at it this way—the refugees were all on Earth 27 and they'd all be dead now anyway."

"He's got a point," said Mr. Terrific.

"No, he doesn't," Oliver said, seething. "You think murdering people makes you a hero? Trust me, it doesn't."

Owlman inclined his head, scrutinizing Green Arrow. "You know something of killing, don't you, archer? Too squeamish to keep pulling the trigger, though, eh? I've seen it before. It's always sad when the superior man allows himself to be neutered by the concerns of weaklings."

"It takes more strength *not* to kill," Oliver informed him.

"We could debate ethics and philosophy all day," Owlman said airily, "and you'd still be wrong. The point remains: You can cling to your absurd morality or you can opt for pragmatism. Which will it be?"

"What, *exactly*, are you offering?" Iris asked him.

"It's quite simple—I'm brilliant. I figured out how to open an interdimensional breach from my world to yours, working with substandard equipment under very dire circumstances. I can help you take the battle to the End of Time . . . and defeat the enemy that awaits us there."

"What do you know about this enemy?" Oliver asked, narrowing his eyes. He had been holding his bow at full draw for several minutes now and showed no signs at all of weakening.

“Madame Xanadu told him. And me,” Caitlin said. “The enemy is a creature at the End of Time. We have to—”

“Didn’t I already put you in the Pipeline?”

It was Barry, returning from Washington, D.C., and the Time Bureau. Just as he phased through the wall of the Cortex, Superman swooped in through the doorway and hovered in the air just over Owlman.

“Hh,” Owlman grunted, looking up. “I know someone just like you.”

“Bruce?” Superman asked, confused.

“Give me one good reason why I shouldn’t lock you up again,” Barry said.

Caitlin clenched her fists and screamed at the top of her lungs. “Will you all just *listen* to me?” she shouted. “I just watched my best friend get sucked into a breach after we moved heaven and earth to rescue him from the past, and now *this* guy says he can help and Madame Xanadu vouches for him, and I believe her, so can we *please* stop arguing and get a move on before Cisco gets killed?”

“I’m sorry, Caitlin,” Barry said soberly. He remembered everything the Earth 27 James Jesse had said about Owlman. The crimes he’d committed. The horrors he’d visited upon the people of that Earth. “I just can’t trust him.”

Owlman grinned. “You’re a fool.” But he held out his hands. “Back to the cell, then. I predict I won’t be there for long.”

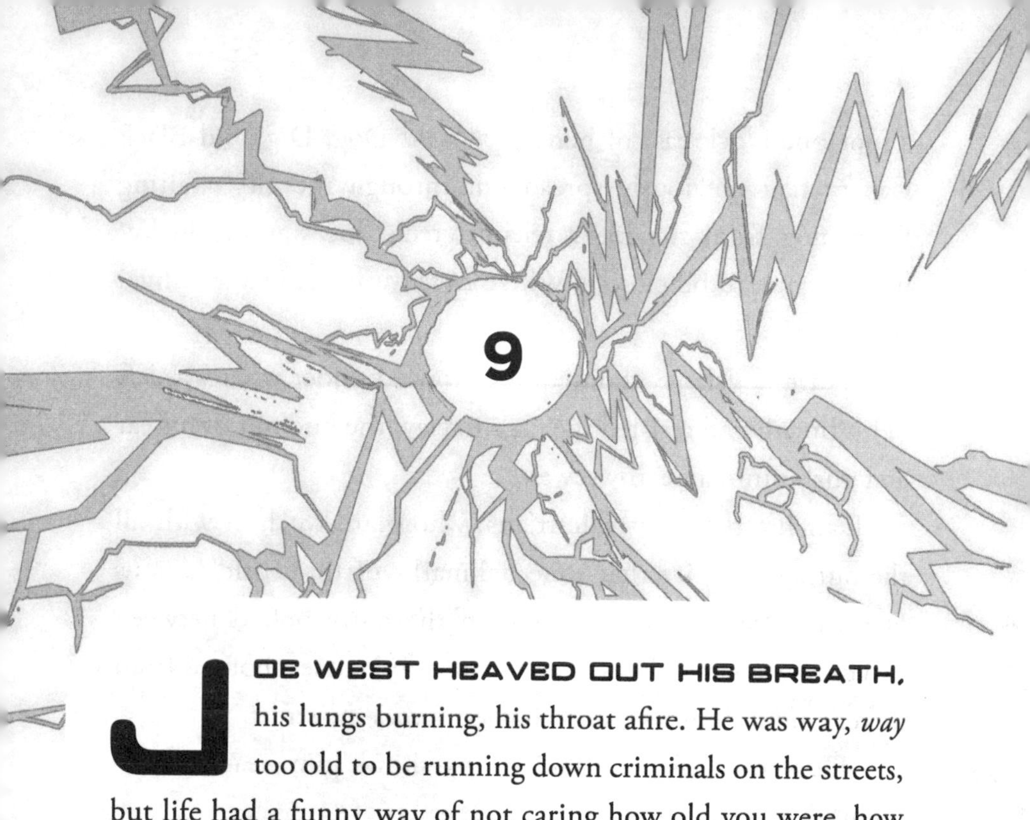

9

JOE WEST HEAVED OUT HIS BREATH, his lungs burning, his throat afire. He was way, *way* too old to be running down criminals on the streets, but life had a funny way of not caring how old you were, how much your knees hurt, or how hot the fury of that stitch threading up your side was as you ran.

"GPS has you almost in position, Joe," Felicity said over the comms bud he wore in his left ear. "Just one more block."

"Easy . . . for you . . . to say . . ." Joe panted. His tie flapped against his chest as he dug down deep for some more energy, slamming one leaden foot after another on the Star City sidewalk lining the north side of Hester Avenue. Why in the world was he still dressed like a detective? What madness had inspired him to leave on his suit jacket and tie in order to run like a lunatic through the city? He should have put on sweats and sneakers.

According to the S.T.A.R. Labs satellites and some convenient hacking by Felicity, Ambush Bug had just teleported to a spot one block east of here. Joe, Wild Dog, Dig, and Black Canary had previously spread out through the city, waiting for a ping from the Bug's teleport tech. Joe was the lucky/unlucky one to be closest. Where *closest* was defined as a five-block run.

"Hurry!" Felicity shouted. Joe growled under what was left of his breath and resisted the urge to claw the bud out of his ear and hurl it into a nearby sewer.

Dancing between pedestrians, who glared at him with all the outrage and ire that were hallmarks of the world-famous Star City "charm," Joe stepped off the curb, bolted between two cars—to horn blares of annoyance and curses shouted from driver's-side windows—and charged across the street.

"He's gone," Felicity said. "Ping shows him near the stadium. Anyone nearby?"

Joe pulled up on the sidewalk outside a bodega. "Hold on. Don't panic yet."

A woman came running out of the bodega, shrieking. Joe caught a glimpse of fur, then spun to watch her. A cluster of animals—three of them, he counted—snarled and snapped around her shoulders. The woman stopped just short of running into traffic, howling at the top of her lungs as the critters capered on her.

They were minks, Joe realized. Still catching his breath, he loped over to the woman and knocked one off. The little fur ball hissed as it dropped to the sidewalk, then skittered away down the street.

Managing to sustain only a couple of scratches and scrapes in the process, Joe wrestled the other two minks from the woman's shoulders. They came loose reluctantly, ripping out ribbons of her shirt, but Joe freed her, tossing the nasty little creatures off to one side, where they scrambled away toward a pile of trash bags.

"Are you OK?" Joe asked. Without waiting for an answer, he moved on to the question he really cared about: "Was it Ambush Bug? Did he do this to you?"

"I was just in there to buy a soda," she said, gasping, eyes wide. "I heard a *pop!* sound behind me . . . He . . . he was in green . . . I was wearing my coat with the fur collar . . . It's *fake* fur." She repeated it, grabbing Joe's lapels. "I don't get it. He said, *Fur is murder!* And then . . . And then he said, *Fur? Murder? I guess that's furder! I made up a word! I'm a writer, too, Lyga!* And then he stuck out his tongue, ripped off my coat, and dropped those . . . things on me."

"Let me guess," Joe said. "Then he just popped away into thin air."

"Joe," Felicity said in his ear, "he's already gone from the stadium. Wild Dog couldn't get there in time."

"There's crazy traffic on Smith Boulevard!" Wild Dog complained. "Ain't my fault!"

"Hang on," Joe said. He guided the woman to a nearby bench and helped her sit down. No doubt the Star City cops would be by to take her statement. In the meantime . . .

He slipped into the bodega, opening the door as narrowly as possible and closing it immediately behind him. There were no customers, just an employee at the register. Four rows of snacks, chips, and sundry household goods lay before Joe, ending at a wall of coolers resplendent with a rainbow of soda and juice bottles.

The guy behind the counter wore a plaid flannel shirt, a black cap, and a suspicious expression that relaxed when Joe flashed his police badge. It was the wrong city, sure, but no one ever looked closely.

"Ambush Bug was just here?" he asked.

"Yeah, but he's gone," the guy at the register said.

Joe twisted the lock on the front door. "Got any open windows or back doors?"

The man frowned with his eyebrows. "Nothing open. Why?"

Joe shook his head and waved his hand for silence. The bodega was quiet, the only sound the slight hum of street noise from outside.

"Joe, what are you doing?" Felicity asked. He pulled the comms bud out of his ear. He needed nothing obstructing his hearing.

Ambush Bug was gone, yes, but he'd teleported inside a building. There was a chance that the bee he'd used as his teleport target was still in the bodega. If Joe could find it and catch it . . .

A sound caught his attention. Jerking to his left, he spied a black shape cutting the air against a backdrop of yellow laundry detergent boxes. Flailing by reflex, he missed it entirely.

"Are you on something?" the guy behind the counter asked. He didn't sound overly concerned at the prospect, more amused than anything.

"Quiet!" Joe ordered. Arms held out at an angle, he turned a slow circle, ears pricked up, attendant for the telltale buzz . . .

When Iris and Barry were kids, Joe used to astonish them by catching flies out on the back porch on hot summer nights. Barry had been fascinated by bugs—budding scientist, even in single digits—and Iris had been afraid of anything that crept, crawled, slithered, or flew. So Joe took the opportunity to kill two birds with one stone: Snagging a fly out of the air let him examine it with Barry, and seeing it pick careful steps across his fingers without harm demystified the insect for Iris.

It had been a while, but he figured it was like riding a bike—you never really forgot how.

A sound to his right. Joe snapped out his hand. Clenched a fist. Came up with nothing.

"Dude, is this, like, performance art?" the guy at the register asked.

Joe hissed another order to be quiet while still turning in a slow circle. He could hear the muted buzz of the robot bee's wings as they thrashed the air.

"Because if it is," the guy went on, "it sorta sucks."

"Man," Joe said, exasperated, "what part of *be quiet* do you not understand?" To emphasize his point, he threw back the tail of his jacket to reveal his holstered weapon.

"Sure thing, Grampa—" the guy started to say, then jumped back in terror as Joe rushed at the counter.

The bee had landed on the edge of the cash register, right next to a plastic box holding a chain of lottery scratch-offs.

Joe pounced, bringing down his hand, careful to cup it so that he wouldn't smash the thing. The cash register let out a ring at the smack of his hand, and the drawer sprung open.

"Got it!" he crowed excitedly, more to himself than to the guy at the counter. Under his hand, he felt the bee shifting and testing its boundaries. Steeling himself for the inevitable sting, he turned to the cowering employee, who'd pressed himself back against a wall of cell phone chargers.

"Hey, man, go get me a box or a cup with a lid or something."

The guy flattened himself further against the wall. A couple of chargers fell off their pegs and clattered to the floor.

"Come on, man. Get a move on."

Licking his lips, the employee sidled away from the counter, toward a soda machine. There, he grabbed a clear plastic cup, a lid, and—amusingly—a straw. He set them down on the counter near Joe and backed away.

Joe grabbed the cup with his free hand and moved quickly, slapping it into place as he pulled his other hand out of the way. The bee buzzed and clicked angrily against the side of the cup. For a heartbeat, Joe expected it to break through the thin plastic, but the cup held.

He put the lid on before the bee could escape.

It looked like a normal bee. Joe would have worried that he'd wasted his time, but when he put his eye right up against the cup, he could just barely make out the glint of metal along the bee's antennae. This was a Bug-Eyed Bandit special, all right. Modified by Ambush Bug himself.

Joe felt around for his comms bud and slipped it back in his ear. Dig, Dinah, and Rene were all calling out to one another as Ambush Bug pinged around the city.

Aware of the presence of a civilian, Joe was careful to use Felicity's code name. "Overwatch, this is Joe West. I have a bee." His chest swelled with pride, and he could not hold back a self-satisfied smile.

"Good for you, dude," the guy at the counter said without a trace of sarcasm, and lifted a thumbs-up as Joe headed out the door.

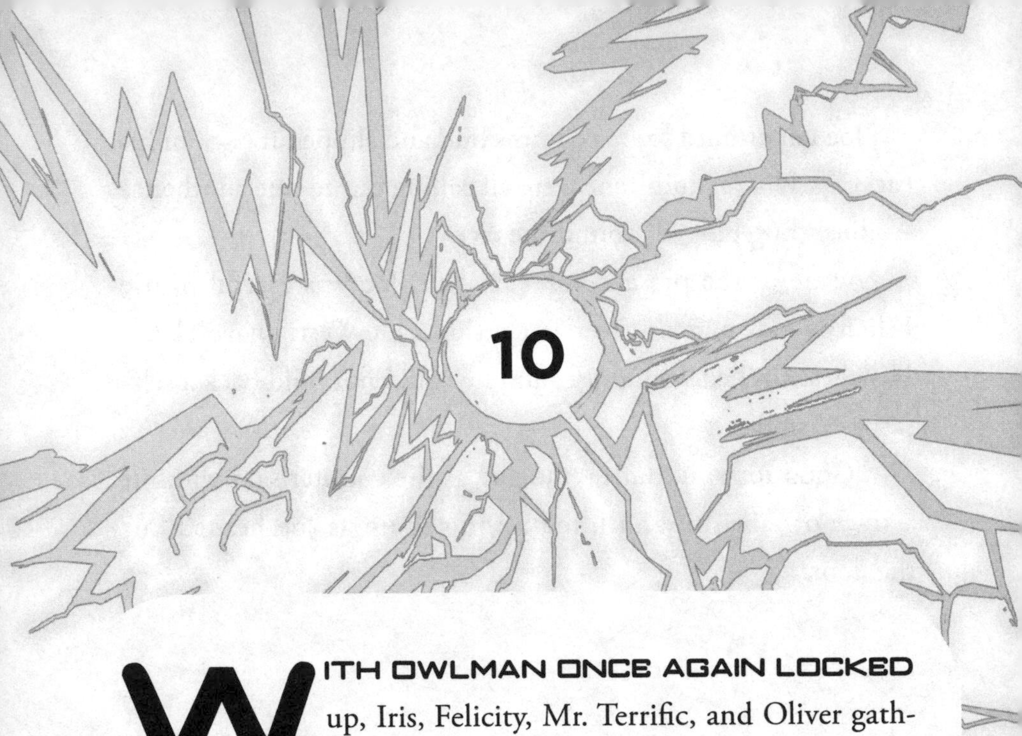

10

WITH OWLMAN ONCE AGAIN LOCKED up, Iris, Felicity, Mr. Terrific, and Oliver gathered around and peered down at the Time Courier strapped to Barry's wrist.

"This is it?" Oliver asked. "This little gizmo is going to beat the enemy who cracks open moons and unleashes living weapons?"

"No, it's just going to give us a fair shot at beating him," Barry said. He explained that the Time Courier was a personal temporal teleportation device that could transport the user anywhere and any*when*. "I'll set it for the End of Time and . . ."

He made a magician's *poof!* gesture.

"I'm not on board with this," Iris said. "I get that the Big Bad is using Reverse-Flash to power some kind of machine that's causing all of these . . . crossovers to happen in the present. But you can't just show up at the End of Time without any kind of reconnaissance. You could be running right into a trap. Say . . ."

Iris gnawed at her lower lip for a moment, thinking. "You've got the Time Courier, right? Why not go back to Earth 38, jump forward a few days, and grab Supergirl from when she's healed?"

Flash shook his head. "Too risky. There's still a lot of antimatter contamination over on Earth 38, and that could interfere with the Time Courier. And before you ask, we can't go grab her from the past, either—if something horrible happened to her, it would create a time paradox." Barry hooked a thumb over his left shoulder, where Superman stood with his arms crossed over his chest. "Besides, have you met my secret weapon? More powerful than a locomotive. I think between the two of us, we can handle whatever's lurking at the End of Time."

"Between the *three* of us," Green Arrow said, stepping over to join them. "I'm coming with you."

Barry opened his mouth to protest, but Superman put a hand on his shoulder to stop him. "Don't be so hasty, Flash. Green Arrow's a lateral thinker and an accomplished strategist. On my own Earth, I have a good friend who's the same, and while he may be only human, his skill set and perspective make him a force to be reckoned with. I get the same feeling from Green Arrow."

"How is it that you say something like *only human*, but you do it in such a way that I don't take offense at it?" Oliver asked in a tone of true wonderment.

Taken aback, Superman knitted his brows together in concern and apology. "You took no offense because I *meant* no offense. Some of my very best friends are only human, Green Arrow."

"You know, you can call me Oliver if you like."

“The names we assign ourselves are important and powerful,” Superman said. “It’s a measure of respect to use them.”

Green Arrow shook his head. “You have an answer for everything, don’t you?”

“I wish I did. I don’t know who or what is waiting for us at the End of Time. But I know this: We’ll encounter it and defeat it *together*.”

Everyone in the room went silent as the Man of Steel’s words and emotions washed over them.

“Oliver,” Felicity said into the solemn moment, “I love you dearly, but if you don’t come back, am I allowed to marry *him*?”

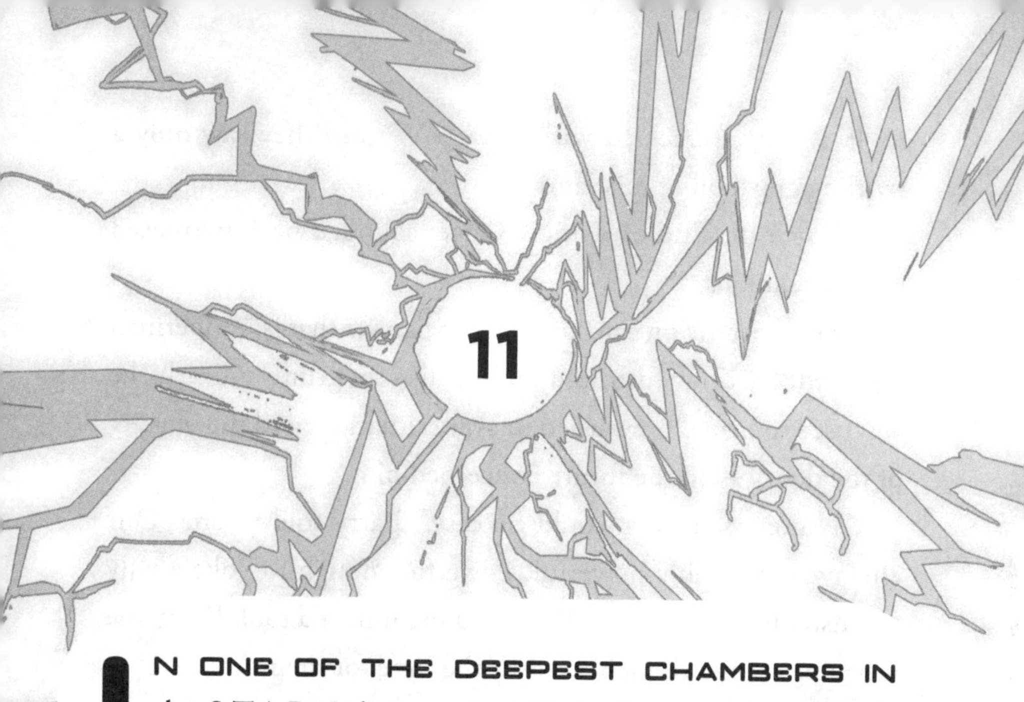

11

IN ONE OF THE DEEPEST CHAMBERS IN the S.T.A.R. Labs complex, Flash, Superman, and Green Arrow prepared for their jump to the final moments of the universe. They did not know what might happen when using the Time Courier to move so far into the future, so they isolated themselves in a room four stories belowground, surrounded by steel and concrete walls.

Barry adjusted the Time Courier, following the instructions Ava Sharpe had given him. "According to her," he said, "there's nothing at the End of Time except for what's left of the headquarters of an organization called the Time Masters."

"Maybe one of them is our enemy," Oliver speculated. "Or maybe they'll have some sort of records or information that will lead us in the right direction."

Superman nodded. "Good thinking. Let's go, Flash."

Barry triggered the Time Courier. A rectangle of light fizzled into existence, opening neatly like a window through the air itself. Its edges crackled with energy. Within, they saw only a swirling gray boil of mist and fog.

"Is *that* the End of Time?" Oliver sounded both perplexed and incredulous.

"My super-vision can't penetrate whatever that is," Superman reported, his brow furrowed and his lips set grimly. Clearly, he was used to being forewarned in every situation, and the opacity of the doorway to the future concerned him.

"No one said this would be easy," Barry told them. "Our enemy is incredibly powerful. Powerful enough to yoke a wily speedster like the Reverse-Flash and use him as a tool. If anyone is having second thoughts, now's the time for them."

Green Arrow snorted. "I've never backed away from a fight."

Superman said nothing. He simply smiled and stepped into the gap in reality carved by the Time Courier.

Barry didn't even give himself time to blink; he dashed in on the Man of Steel's heels.

The last time Barry had traveled to the future, he'd been on the Cosmic Treadmill; his jaunt from the thirtieth century to the sixty-fourth century had been as casual and as simple as a jog along the banks of the Gardner River on a lazy weekend afternoon.

The time before that, he'd run on his own power from the present to the thirtieth century, an arduous, punishing race against time itself that had depleted his speed, sucked out his very life force, and left him almost dead.

He wasn't sure what to expect when using the Time Courier, but Ava Sharpe had described it as being "as easy as falling down the stairs," so he didn't anticipate any problems.

The mist enveloped him.

And then his entire body seized, as though flooded with electricity. Somewhere nearby he heard a familiar voice—Oliver's—doing something very *un*familiar: screaming. Another voice, bellowing in pain and shock: Superman.

Superman was being hurt.

Barry himself had begun vibrating his body into a phase state as soon as the first tingles of pain wriggled along his extremities. Even while intangible, the agony was exquisite, racing along his nerves, exploding in his brain.

And then everything was black.

And then he was falling.

12

BEFORE OPENING HIS EYES, BARRY felt a pain throbbing along his left side. He hissed in a breath, testing his ribs, which seemed uninjured. A massive bruise, then, along his left flank.

He opened his eyes. He lay on a substance that was both yielding and solid at the same time. Levering up on his elbows, he glanced left and right. Superman lay crumpled next to him, his cape tipped over his head. And there was Oliver, likewise unconscious, sprawled out.

Vibrating to phase must have borne the brunt of the impact, he thought. *Whatever the heck it was we impacted with in the first place.*

He looked up and gasped. He *knew* this place. Or at least something like it.

The architecture—buildings without right angles or windows, hovering structures suspended in midair by antigravity—was vintage thirtieth century. He'd been "here" before, when he'd encountered the Tornado Twins on his way to the sixty-fourth century. Dawn and Don were their names. They'd possessed speed almost equal to his own, and they were the ones who'd revealed the Cosmic Treadmill to him and sent him on his way to the farther future.

Dawn and Don. He thought of them often. They'd been a help to him and he'd felt a connection to them, but there hadn't been enough time to explore it.

He stood up and turned in a slow circle, gazing up at the floating vehicles drifting in synchronous pathways overhead. What were the odds he'd end up back in the same century as before? Why hadn't the Time Courier taken them to the End of Time?

He checked his wrist, expecting the borrowed gadget to spit sparks, its surface cracked and permanently damaged. But the Time Courier was intact, in perfect working order.

Why didn't we get to the End of Time? Why here and now?

With a groan, Superman rolled over and—as Barry watched in amazement—floated into a standing position without any of the typical human confusion of balance and adjusting limbs. "I haven't felt something that powerful since I faced off against the Galactic Golem," he said mildly. "Are you all right?"

"I'm OK," Barry said, "but Oliver might—"

"Just some bruising and contusions," Superman said, glancing up and down Green Arrow's unconscious form. "And he has a bone spur on his left clavicle that he might want to look into at some point in the next few years. But otherwise, he's in remarkable physical condition."

"Thanks," Oliver mumbled, rolling over. "I need to tell you both that I think the End of Time sucks."

Barry laughed and reached down to help Oliver to his feet. "We're not at the End of Time." He explained to both of them what era they'd arrived in, though he admitted he couldn't explain why.

"Wait, did you say the thirtieth century?" Superman asked.

"Yeah, that's—"

A loud siren sounded a burst for a moment, startling them. Barry looked over his shoulder. A floating metallic disk hovered a few feet above their heads. A railing ran around part of the disk, and a woman held it with one hand while using the other to point a weapon of some sort at the three of them. She wore a two-tone skintight outfit that was gray with a wide, deep blue stripe down the center, as well as a shiny white helmet with green goggles.

"[illegible]" the woman said in a language Barry had heard before. It was Interlac. He dearly missed the telepathic earplug that had allowed him to understand it. "[illegible] [illegible]."

Oliver stiffened and went for his bow. "I don't care what year we're in," he snapped. "No one points a weapon at me."

Superman drifted between Green Arrow's bow and the woman hovering above them all. "It's not a weapon," he said, and spread his hands out in a show of peace. “It’s a chronometric scanner.” Then, to the woman, “[illegible].”

Barry did a double take at the sound of flawless Interlac coming from Superman’s mouth.

“Superman speaks Future,” Oliver said as the Man of Steel conversed with the floating woman. And then, muttered under his breath: “Of *course* he speaks Future.”

Superman turned back to Oliver and Barry and smiled broadly. “Gentlemen, this is Science Police Officer Cusimano. She was scrambled here because our entry into the thirty-first century caused a spike in tachyon emissions, so she had to investigate.”

“Wait, thirty-first century?” Barry asked. “Not the thirtieth?”

“Yes. And we’re fortunate. I have . . . friends here.”

The three of them followed Science Police Officer Cusimano down a broad boulevard to a plaza created by its intersection with another wide road. *Road* might have been a misnomer, Barry thought. In the future, vehicles seemed mostly confined to the skies; the ground was for pedestrians and a surfeit of robots in all different shapes, colors, and configurations. Barry tried not to gawk at some of the citizens casually ambling along the pathway—in addition to average humans, there was a mind-boggling assortment of alien beings. He saw eyes on protracted stalks, wavering antennae, hands with too many fingers, arms with too many hands. Insectoid carapaces and sluglike tails dragged behind.

"Are you seeing this?" he whispered to Oliver.

Oliver rolled his eyes with a forbearing expression. "Don't be a rube, Barry."

"A problem with aliens, gentlemen?" Superman asked.

"Some of my best friends are aliens," Barry retorted. "I'm just not accustomed to seeing so many, so open."

"By the thirty-first century, Earth has become a hub of interstellar commerce and politics," Superman told them. "The population is something like 22 percent extraterrestrial."

Barry and Oliver exchanged a quizzical look. "You seem to know an awful lot about the future," Oliver said.

Superman nodded. "I used to travel to the future often when I was a boy. I joined the . . . Ah! Here!"

The plaza opened up before them. Hovering twenty feet above them was a silvery structure. As with all the buildings, it had no square corners or windows of any sort. It was just a polished, gleaming construct, seemingly molded out of a single block of pliable alloy. It had the vague shape of a chair missing its seat, with a relatively narrow "back" topped with a saucerlike piece, then two long "arms" stretching out from either side.

"This is it," Superman said. "The headquarters of the Legion of Super-Heroes."

"Wait a second," Barry said. This made no sense. Kara had told him about the Legion—a veritable army of teenage superheroes from the far-flung future. Her onetime boyfriend,

Mon-El, had been a member of the group, and her friend Brainiac 5 was as well, "on loan" to the past.

But that was on Earth 38.

"We're in the future of Earth 1," Barry pointed out. "How can the Legion be here?"

Superman opened his mouth to answer, then closed it, musing for a few seconds before shrugging with one shoulder, his expression placid and unconcerned. "Good question. Let's go figure that out."

After thanking Officer Cusimano for the escort, they stepped into the massive shadow cast by the building, striding under its enormous bulk. Oliver and Barry gazed upward at the underside of the building. They were only a tiny bit concerned that it might come crashing down on them.

"Perfectly safe," Superman assured them.

A moment later, a cylinder of yellow light descended from the bottom of the building, levitating the three of them up and into a door that irised open in the floor. Once inside, they hung in space for a moment as the door closed, then were gently deposited on the floor.

Barry was somewhat familiar with the architecture from his previous visit to the future, but the reality of it still stunned him. It could best be described as *in-your-face minimalism*, with blank walls in garish hues. The vestibule into which they'd been levitated was a bright blue color, with seams visible along the walls. Barry knew that those seemingly dull, blank walls could actually turn transparent to provide a sight line to the outside, as well as project holograms anywhere in the room.

"This is the future." Oliver put his hands on his hips and turned a slow circle, scrutinizing the decor. "Cleaner than I imagined."

"It's been a thousand years of progress," Superman reminded him. "A lot has changed. People are much more refined and—"

"Holy crap!" a voice called.

Along with Superman and Green Arrow, Barry spun at the sound of the voice and was shocked to see a familiar figure standing there. A short, dark-haired man in his twenties, wearing typical twenty-first-century garb—striped dress shirt, loose sweater-vest, jeans—regarded the three of them with a surprised expression on his face.

"Winn?" Barry exclaimed. "Winn Schott?"

Winn Schott was a twenty-first-century type like the three heroes, a denizen of Earth 38 and one of Supergirl's very best friends. He was a genius-level hacker and engineer who'd helped the DEO face off against any number of threats.

"Superman!" Winn exclaimed. "Flash! Green Arrow! Wow!"

Tucking a very slender tablet under one arm, he ran to them, pumping Superman's hand in excitement, embracing Barry . . .

"No hugs," Oliver told him.

"I wasn't even gonna try," Winn assured him. "Do you fist-bump, sir?" He held up his fist questioningly.

Oliver sighed and dapped Winn's offered knuckles, which made Winn cackle in glee. "I fist-bumped Green Arrow. This is definitely going on my blog."

"Blogs are still a thing in the thirty-first century?" Barry asked.

"Not so much. But I'm trying to make them cool again. Along with Katy Perry music, the sartorial splendor that is the sweater-vest, and the films of David Lynch." He leaned in and whispered conspiratorially from one side of his mouth. "It's slow going, guys. The future is *very* resistant to change."

"Winn, how are you even *here*?" Barry asked.

"I swapped places with Brainiac 5," he explained. "There's this killer virus that affects artificial intelligences here, so they asked me to—"

"No, I know that part," Barry interrupted. "But you went into the future on Earth 38. And we've just traveled to the future of Earth 1."

Winn seemed taken aback. "Really? I suspect time travel shenanigans. Let's conference in an expert." Before anyone could stop him, he whipped the tablet out from under his arm and spoke to it. "Get me Rond Vidar."

An instant later, a hologram appeared in the center of the room—a lanky young man with black hair and skintight gray-and-white coveralls under a yellow jacket. The hologram was so perfect that it seemed less a hologram and more as though the man had simply spontaneously appeared there. Oliver actually reached out and brushed against it with the tips of his fingers to be sure—they passed right through the man's shoulder.

"Rond!" Winn cried. "Buddy! Pal! I have a favor to ask of you!"

Rond Vidar pinched the bridge of his nose with the expression of a man who has been asked too many favors. "For the last time, Toy Boy, I will *not* adjust the Time Viewer so that you can watch the fourth season of *Twin Peaks*. Stop asking."

"Toy Boy?" Barry laughed.

"That's not my name!" Winn howled.

"It does make sense," Superman said. "Your father was Toy Man, so . . ."

"Stop it!" Winn exclaimed. "I don't want a code name. Especially *Toy Boy*. Anyway," he said, turning back to Rond, "look—we have guests from the far-flung past!" He made a *ta-da* gesture at the threesome.

Vidar's eyes tracked them quickly. "Good to see you again, Superboy. It's been a while."

Superman opened his mouth to speak, but Barry beat him

to the punch. "See, this is the problem! Winn is here and you know Superman, but isn't this Earth 1? How is it possible for two different Earths to share a future?"

"I don't think they do," Superman said. "I think when we traveled into the future, we somehow crossed over to Earth 38. You may have done the same when you traveled alone into the future, Flash."

"But why?" Oliver asked. "Look, I don't know much about quantum physics and time travel, but I know this: When you shoot an arrow, it follows a path. It doesn't suddenly veer off for no reason. Something has to redirect it. If Barry ran straight into the future from Earth 1, why and how would he end up on Earth 38?"

"Pretty easy way to figure this out," Winn said cheerfully. "Rond, are we on Earth 1 or Earth 38?"

Hesitating slightly, Vidar said, "This is actually considered Earth ∂. There's a whole new nomenclature for describing the Multiverse that arose in the mid-twenty-first century."

Which meant after Barry's time.

"There was a crisis of some sort," Vidar went on. "Historical records from so long ago are spotty and incomplete, but we know that the universes had been previously isolated and separate, for the most part. Then they experienced a . . . a . . ."

"Crossover effect," Barry supplied.

"Yes. Timelines became entangled. There's a whole theory of hyperstrings that indicates that it may be possible for two separate universes to share common timelines."

Oliver shook his head. "Wait. Are you telling us that two completely different Earths could have the *same* future?"

Vidar shrugged as though this absolute impossibility bothered him not one whit. "All of the universes of the Multiverse are quantum-entangled to some degree. There are doppelgängers across the Multiverse. Similarities in history and in structure and in the very laws of physics. If matter and energy can cross over, why not time?"

Superman nodded slowly. "The greater the interaction between universes, the more they become entangled. To the point that they begin to share time itself. This all makes sense now."

Oliver nudged Barry with his elbow. "I see they have a strange definition for *makes sense* in this century," he whispered.

The time travel physics of it all were over Barry's head, too, but he could grasp the basics of it. Would it really matter to him if, for example, it turned out that the tenth century was slightly different from what history books claimed? For Vidar to worry about which twenty-first century preceded his own was like Barry stressing over details of the Middle Ages.

"Maybe we can discuss the physics another time. Right now, we need your help," Barry said. "We're looking for—"

"Oh!" Winn shouted. "Oh! I know why you're here! You came for the Legends!"

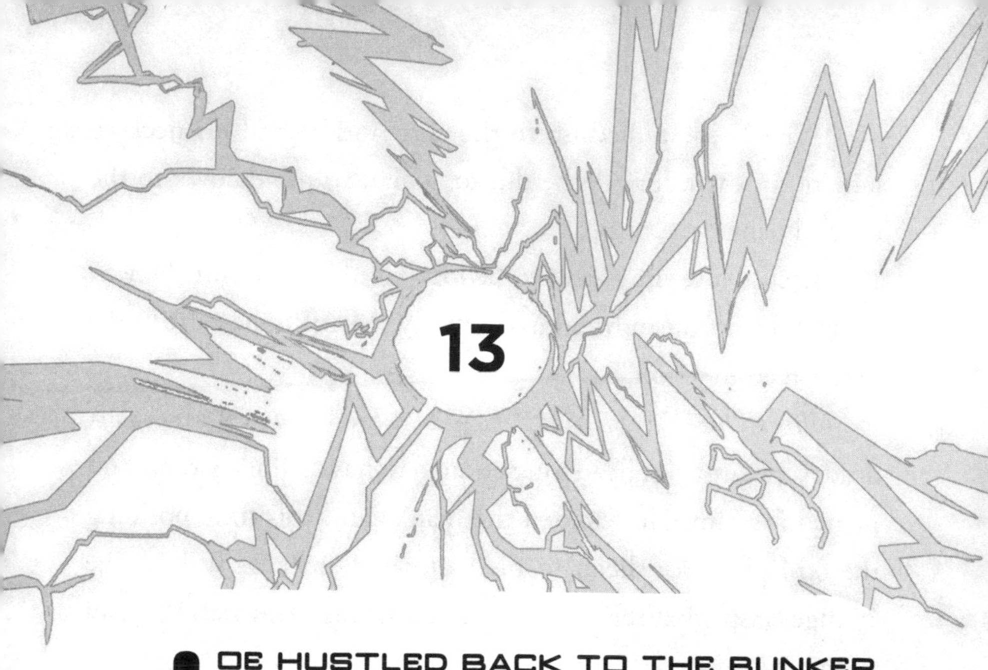

13

JOE HUSTLED BACK TO THE BUNKER as quickly as possible, the bee rattling and buzzing in the plastic cup on the passenger seat next to him as he drove. Out of an abundance of caution, he'd borrowed some tape at the bodega and fastened the lid on, then covered the straw hole. He could think of murderers he'd taken less care with transporting.

"Joe, do you read me?" Dig's voice came through loud and clear on Joe's earbud. "Like you suggested, Lyla repurposed an A.R.G.U.S. satellite to scan for bees and, uh, we have a problem."

Joe figured there was a pretty good joke about *finding a bug in the system* just waiting to be made, but Dig's tone told him that now wasn't the time for it.

"It seems there's a massive swarm of bees gathering over Star City. And it's growing."

"What?" Joe pulled up to the curb and craned his neck to look out his window. As he did so, a man stumbled over to the car and bent over to speak.

"Excuse me, sir, I seem to be lost. Could you point the way to the Oliver Queen Memorial Library? My qPhone can't find a broad-fi connection."

Oliver Queen Memorial . . . As best Joe knew, Oliver wasn't dead. Certainly not dead long enough to have a library built and named for him. He scanned the man again, this time noticing the odd plasticky sheen to his pants and shirt, as well as the strange clasps that served in place of buttons. And wait . . . had he said *qPhone*?

Sure enough, the man brandished a perfectly round gadget with a glowing screen.

"You're from an alternate Earth, aren't you?" Joe asked. "You fall through a big blue swirly thing?"

The man considered. "I *did* notice some sort of strange fog around me on my morning commute. What are you saying happened?"

Joe passed a hand over his face. "Sir, I'm gonna ask you to wait right here. I'm going to call the local police and get you to a shelter. We're in the middle of two or three crises right now."

As Dig had indicated, a fuzzy black cloud had gathered overhead. It wasn't all that big, but it was certainly big enough to notice even from the ground. A few passersby on the sidewalks had taken note and stopped to gaze upward and snap a photo or two.

“We think Ambush Bug’s massing his swarm for his attack,” said Dig. “Remember how Bert said the bees could construct more of themselves?”

Staring up, Joe imagined the bees pollinating one another, so to speak, creating more and more bees, which would create even more bees . . . Until there were millions of them, enough to descend on Star City and sting everyone in the city within seconds.

Some of the victims would just be annoyed and given a jolt of pain. Probably most of them. But some of them, like Ambush Bug himself, would have an allergic reaction to the synthetic apitoxin. People would go mad, like the Bug.

And many would die.

Barry, he thought as he dialed SCPD on his cell for the accidental universe-hopped Flash, *you and your pals better figure this out fast.*

“I’m inbound with a bee sample,” Joe told Dig. “We’re gonna figure this out.”

Overhead, the swarm of bees massed and bunched, a buzzing black cloud threatening to rain pain and death.

Joe slammed a foot down on the gas pedal and wished he had a siren to blare.

14

WINN LED THEM THROUGH A SERIES of identical corridors, all of them shining like highly polished silver. A large globe the size of an overinflated basketball zipped down the corridor. It was made of shiny metal, with a section cut away to reveal a transparent screen on which yellow waveforms undulated against an orange background.

"Breep!" the globe announced. "Mr. Schott, may I assist you?"

"Hey, Computo," Winn said. "I need to get into the infirmary."

The waveforms danced for an instant. "I have been authorized to permit—*breep!*—access to the infirmary to you. Please enter. And have a nice day!"

The Legion's medical bay was so pristine and empty that Barry thought he'd been led into the wrong area of the headquarters. Long and narrow, it had the same curved, metallic walls he'd seen elsewhere in the building. Against one wall, something that looked very much like a cloud bobbed gently in the air, a downy cocoon. Holograms drifted nearby, showing what appeared to be MRI results, vital statistics, and more. Barry made out a human figure within the cloud.

"Her name's Zari Tomaz," Winn said soberly. "We don't know . . ." He trailed off.

Barry gazed down at her. Bruises along her jawline and temple seemed almost healed, but Zari lay far too still, her eyelids not even flicking in the way that betrayed REM sleep.

"I don't understand. They don't have her on an IV drip. Or a—"

"She's fine," Winn said quickly. "I mean, not *fine* fine, but, you know, fine. They don't use things like IVs here in the future. They have some kind of microscopic robot—they call it an *Imskian surgimech*—that crawls through her bloodstream. It keeps her cells fed and also breaks up blood clots and prevents bedsores. It's kinda amazing and . . ." He realized Barry was glaring at his enthusiasm for the tech. "And I wish it wasn't necessary."

Before anyone else could speak, the door behind them hushed open. Turning, Barry blinked at a welcome, familiar sight.

"Sara!" Oliver exclaimed.

"And me!" proclaimed Ray Palmer, holding out his arms.

Sara Lance—the White Canary, leader of the Legends of Tomorrow—ran to them and threw her arms around Oliver. Ray stood, turning from side to side, arms still outthrust, eager for a clutch. "No hugs for Ray? Really?"

"Drop it, Haircut," Mick Rory said as he elbowed his way into the room.

Ray targeted Superman and strode over, offering a handshake. "Hi! Ray Palmer, shrinking scientist extraordinaire. Love the costume. I'm a big fan of the whole red-and-blue color scheme."

The Man of Steel accepted the handshake. "These are the time travelers you were telling me about?" he asked Barry. "The ones from the Time Bureau?"

"Some of them," Barry said, stepping away from Zari. "Ray, what happened to the others?"

Ray and Mick shared a cloudy look. "We need to talk."

Meanwhile, Oliver and Sara had finally broken their clinch. "Oliver! What are you doing here?"

"I was about to ask you the same thing," Green Arrow replied. Stoic to the last, even Oliver Queen couldn't maintain his grim facade in the face of discovering Sara was alive. He held her tightly again. "We were all so worried."

"Especially Ava Sharpe," Barry put in.

"How did you know to come to this time period?" she asked.

"We didn't."

Between the three of them—with some assistance from Winn—they explained the crisis in the twenty-first century, Barry's acquiring the Time Courier from Ava, and their slamming into some sort of barrier in the time stream.

At the mention of Ava, Sara became pensive. "I . . . She must be so . . . I've been gone so long . . ."

"It's only been a few days for us." Oliver put an arm around her. She shook it off.

"No time for that," she said, clenching her fists and tilting her jaw up. "Sounds like we've got a serious Big Bad to deal with."

In clipped, economical phrasing, she explained how she and the others had ended up in the thirty-first century.

"That burst of energy you experienced must have been our enemy reaching back to crack open the moon in the antiverse," Barry mused. "From the temporal zone, you can access most of the Multiverse, so it would be the easiest way to cross the vibrational barrier."

"Let's conference in an expert!" Winn exclaimed, and before anyone could stop him, once again there was a hologram of Rond Vidar standing among them.

"Winn!" Rond shouted. "I'm in the middle of very delicate—"

"Forgive us, Mr. Vidar," Barry said quickly, "but we're out of our depth here. And we think you may be able to help save, well, *everything*. Including your century."

Rond sighed and pinched the bridge of his nose. "Of course. Of course. I'm sorry. I've just been trying to figure out a certain problem for weeks now. I haven't been sleeping much, and the Kathoonian stimshots are wearing off. Catch me up."

Between Superman, Barry, and Sara—with Winn occasionally chiming in—they managed to bring Vidar up to speed.

"It sounds as though you collided with the Iron Curtain of Time," Vidar said. The high-resolution hologram did an all-too-effective job of conveying his shock. "That's precisely what

I've been spending so many sleepless nights trying to puzzle out. You're very lucky to have survived the experience."

Iron Curtain? Barry mused. He knew that in the mid-twentieth century, there'd been an "Iron Curtain" that stretched between the borders of those countries controlled by the Soviet Union and those of the free West. There was no *literal* curtain made of iron—it was just a political metaphor to describe the way the Communist Soviets contained information and emigration from their side of the border, restricting the flow of news and people from East to West. This *Iron Curtain of Time* sounded like a similar metaphor.

"The Iron Curtain of Time?" Oliver's voice was skeptical. "That's not a thing. That can't be a thing."

Vidar shrugged noncommittally. "Technically, you're right, Green Lantern."

"Green *Arrow*."

"Right. Sorry. I get my history confused. In any event, the Iron Curtain of Time is not, in a very real sense, a *thing*. It has no physical, corporeal characteristics. It is a temporal barrier athwart the time stream itself. We believe it to be constructed by a being from far in the future, a being called the Time Trapper."

"You can't build a wall across Time," Barry protested. "It's not just impossible—it's nonsensical."

"And he did not," Vidar agreed. "The Iron Curtain is just a convenient metaphor to explain that now it is impossible to travel past the year 3102. What we refer to as an *Iron Curtain* is in reality a series of interlocking tachyonic breakwaters, a subatomic bombardment of superluminal particles that travel back and forth in time so quickly and precisely that they prevent passage."

"I understood that it's a metaphor," Oliver admitted, "and not much else."

"This Iron Curtain thing makes no sense," Sara complained. "The Legends have been to the End of Time before. There's nothing there except a place called Vanishing Point, where the old Time Masters had their headquarters." She paused. "They're not, uh, an issue any longer."

"Vanishing Point is at the End of Time, where your specific universe collapses under its own weight and coldness," Vidar told her. "Your foe—*our* foe—is at the End of *All* Time. Where every universe has its terminus."

Barry felt a chill. Not merely the end of the world, or the end of the universe. Not even just the End of Time, as J'Onn had seen. It was the end of *every* universe.

That was where their foe lived. And they had no way to get there.

"Rond," Superman said, "you've been studying the Iron Curtain, right?"

"Yes. As soon as it appeared on our scanners at the Time Institute, my colleague Circadia Senius and I immediately sent probes to analyze it. None of them came back. We've had to make do with remote viewing."

"The Curtain blockades the year 3102 and beyond. In theory," Superman said, "could we travel to the year 3101 . . ."

"And just *wait*!" Oliver snapped his fingers. "The Curtain stops time travelers, but it won't stop people just *living*, right?"

Rond shrugged. For the first time, the hologram fuzzed ever so slightly. "We considered this. Once you passed the point at which the Curtain exists, you'd still need to time-travel to the End of All Time. But the enemy is capable of moving the Curtain at will, it seems. He would just reerect the barrier elsewhen, and you'd be right back where you started." He pursed his lips, pondering. "Quite literally. And eventually, the enemy's strikes throughout the timeline and Multiverse will corrode the barriers between eras and universes. The crossover effect will reduce the Multiverse to a single moment of entropy, destroying it entirely."

Oliver threw his hands in the air.

"Great news," Barry muttered.

"I refuse to believe that we can't find a way to fight this enemy," Superman said. "I've yet to encounter the foe who doesn't have a weakness."

"Do we think this guy can reach through the Curtain from his side?" Sara speculated. "Can that help us somehow? Can we lure him out?"

"He's using Reverse-Flash to power some sort of machinery on the other side of the Curtain," Barry said. "With all of that vibrational energy at his disposal, he doesn't *need* to come through the Curtain. He can just reach back and do things like release Anti-Matter Man from his prison and have *him* do his dirty work."

"Vibrational energy . . ." Winn mused. "Rond, you said the Iron Curtain was . . . Hey, Computo, play it back."

The words floated from the air, a dead-on replication of Rond's previous statement: "*What we refer to as an* Iron Curtain *is in reality a series of interlocking tachyonic breakwaters, a subatomic bombardment of superluminal particles that travel back and forth in time so quickly and precisely that they prevent passage."*

"Clear as mud," Sara pronounced.

"No, no, wait!" Winn said excitedly. He used his tablet to project some graphs and images into the air. Despite himself, Barry found his curiosity piqued and meandered over to watch.

"The breakwaters are actually moving at varying vibrational rates. That's how they can block time travelers in the first place."

"Time travel is all about vibrations," Superman murmured.

Barry knew this was true. The Cosmic Treadmill had allowed him to sync up his vibrations with the sixty-fourth century. Then, when he'd relaxed those vibrations, he returned to his home time.

"Reverse-Flash's vibrational energy powers the machinery that reaches back through time," he said slowly, beginning to perceive the edges of an idea. "If we can generate enough vibrational energy . . . we could possibly penetrate the Curtain."

"You weren't able to break through," Ray pointed out. "So that machine must be amplifying Reverse-Flash's vibrations. We'd need . . ." He surrendered. The numbers, the concepts, they were too massive, too enormous and broad even to contemplate.

"Are there any members of the Legion with vibration powers?" Barry asked. "Or who could amplify my own?"

Winn tapped his chin as he thought.

And thought.

And thought.

And—

"Any day now," Oliver said testily.

"Sorry!" Winn yelped. "Look, there's a *lot* of Legionnaires, OK? It takes a minute."

"There's no one," Superman said. "As I said—I used to be a member, when I was younger. I know the team well. No Legionnaire can amplify your powers or produce the necessary vibrations on their own. It's up to us."

"You'd need more than a *thousand* Flashes," Winn said very unhelpfully, "with a whole mess of vibrational energy . . ."

And then Green Arrow started laughing.

Bemused, Superman looked over at the Emerald Archer. "Would you share with the rest of us?" he asked. "We could all use a good laugh right about now."

Oliver Queen wiped his eyes and gazed around the room at the geniuses and superheroes staring at him as though he'd lost his mind. "Sorry. It's just funny because . . . I've figured it out."

Flash's jaw dropped. The hologram of Rond Vidar inclined its head skeptically.

"No, seriously," Oliver promised. "I've got it all worked out. I know how to get through the Iron Curtain of Time."

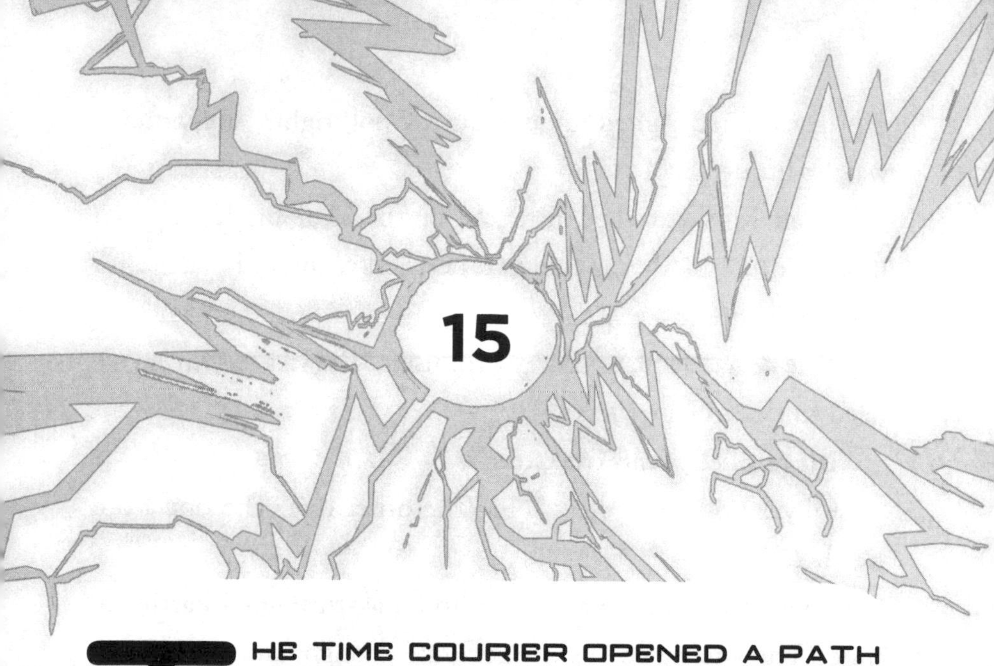

15

THE TIME COURIER OPENED A PATH into the S.T.A.R. Labs Cortex. Barry stepped through with Oliver and Superman, right into Iris's waiting arms.

"Hey!" he said in surprise. "You were standing in the right place!"

They hugged and he gave her a long kiss.

"Did you get there? To the End of Time?" Iris's eyes shined with hope.

"No," he told her. "But don't worry. We have a plan." His eyes flicked to Oliver. "Sort of."

"And we brought friends," Oliver said, gesturing to the portal opened by the Time Courier.

White Canary and Heat Wave stepped through into the twenty-first century. The Atom followed them in a new, sleek version of his costume. "Hey, everyone!" he said. "Check it out! They put me together with some Imskian tailors in the thirty-first century and redesigned my costume. Cool, right?" He struck a weight-lifting pose.

Mick Rory smacked him on the back of his head, then inhaled deeply. "Ah, car exhaust, beef jerky, and old plastic. It's good to be home."

"We *do* have a plan," Barry promised. "Thanks to Oliver. We need to talk to James Jesse."

Iris recoiled. "The Trickster?"

Oliver grinned at her. "No. The other one. The one from Earth 27."

"We need vibrational energy to break through a barrier in time," Barry told her. "I can't generate enough, and Wally's still somewhere in the sixties." They had no idea where Wally had chosen to take his vacation from the Legends, so they couldn't just go get him, unfortunately.

"So we're going to use the speedsters from Earth 27," Ray interjected. He laughed out loud, surprising Iris, Mr. Terrific, Caitlin, and Felicity. But Superman only smiled in response, and Oliver and Sara both cracked modest grins.

Mick pawed through a bag of fries someone had left on a counter.

"We're going to build a gigantic treadmill," Barry said, "and put ten thousand speedsters on it and have them run us through the Iron Curtain of Time!"

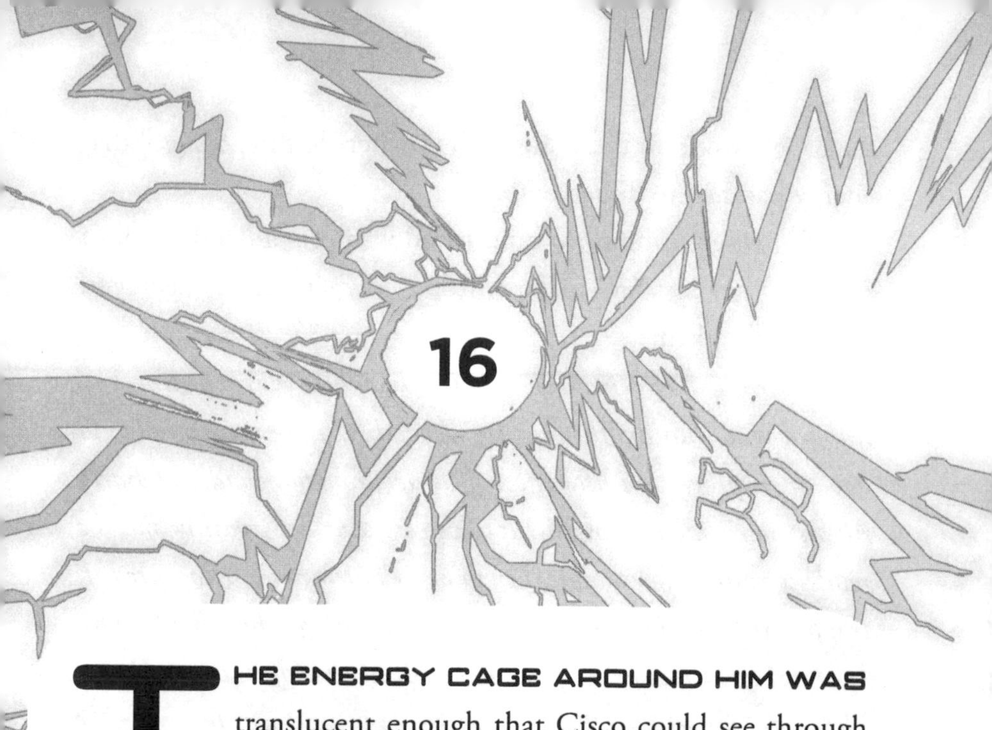

16

THE ENERGY CAGE AROUND HIM WAS translucent enough that Cisco could see through it. Surrounding him was a flat, dead plain, pockmarked here and there by crumbling boulders and shallow pits. Above, the sky was speckled with hard black circles surrounded by dim halos of light. They were dead stars, Cisco realized, throwing off the last vestiges of their heat and light as their nuclear fuel waned, the atoms at their cores finally fusing to cold, dead iron.

"Like you, I can perceive the other reality. I was born when Flashpoint was reversed. The ripple effect of the time stream's damage warped the very fabric of space-time, pushed along on a wave until it crashed on the shores of the very End of Time itself."

Cisco thought it made sense—he tried to imagine the time stream as a heavy length of rope anchored at the End of Time. When TV Barry caused and then reversed Flashpoint, it was as though he'd given the rope a jerk. That jerk had rippled along the rope until it hit the wall. With nowhere left to go, all of that energy had had to do *something.*

"So, when a mommy time paradox meets a daddy wall of entropy, they kiss and make a little . . . whatever the heck you are?" Cisco asked.

"I am the Time Trapper. For I have taken your timeline and trapped it within another reality altogether. Your timeline should have merely been an aftereffect of a decision not made, of Barry Allen's potential to not *disrupt history. But by creating me, he made it possible for your reality to be so much more. I captured it, trapped it, and exploited its existence, spinning what should have been a single timeline into an entire Multiverse of its own, a near-identical twin of the other Multiverse. And thus was born . . . the Megaverse!"*

Fuming, Cisco said, "So, in other words, the TV Barry Allen screwed up, messed with history, then *re*-messed with history, and we're the ones who get punished for it? Not cool."

He'd heard enough. He had the power to escape from this cell, and now that he had gathered some crucial intelligence on his foe, he was going to use that power.

Furrowing his brow, Cisco focused on the space just beyond the energy field. All around him—through him—the vibrational frequencies of the universe sang in unison. He plucked at the strings of reality and a breach opened before him—

And then the breach closed on its own, and he heard himself say, "So, in other words, the TV Barry Allen screwed up, messed with history, then *re*-messed with history, and we're the ones who get punished for it? Not cool."

He decided to breach out of the prison. Focusing, he opened a breach—

And it closed by itself. To his astonishment he was speaking again. ". . . messed with history, then *re*-messed with history, and we're the ones who get punished for it? Not cool."

What was happening to him? Somehow he was reliving the same few seconds over and over again. Opening the breach, watching it close, jumping back a few seconds to do it all over again.

"I have been waiting for you to exploit your powers," the Time Trapper said, standing motionless. *"Now that you have done so, I am able to manipulate your personal temporality. Your vibrational frequency was closed to me until you projected it into the fabric of the universe. Now it is mine to control. And so I have trapped you in the same fifteen seconds, where you will use your breaching abilities over and over again, allowing me to tap into that power and use it to enhance my speedster-driven machinery. Due to your ability to perceive alternate timelines, I suspect you are able to experience and recall these fifteen seconds each time."* For the first time, the Time Trapper moved, raising one purple-cloaked arm to gesture non-committally with his right hand. *"I surmise that this will drive you irretrievably insane in short order."*

Cisco yearned to protest, to scream, to holler. But he had no control over his body or anything tangible at all. He was cut loose from time, tethered to himself, but helpless, able only to observe as the universe in his very specific area rewound itself.

He could say nothing to the Time Trapper. Nothing save, "So, in other words, the TV Barry Allen screwed up, messed with history, then *re*-messed with history, and we're the ones who get punished for it? Not cool."

And then open a breach.

And watch it close.

And then do it again.

And again.

And again.

17

JOE PACED IMPATIENTLY AS BERT Larvan—the brother of the Bug-Eyed Bandit—perched on a stool in the Bunker and peered through a microscope at the bee Joe had recovered from the bodega. Dinah, Dig, and Rene had not been sanguine about allowing a civilian (and one related to a super villain, to boot) into the Green Arrow's hidden lair, but Joe had prevailed. They needed someone to examine the bee and reverse-engineer its signal ASAP, and with all the usual geniuses out of town, Bert Larvan was their best bet.

"The swarm is 20 percent bigger, according to this thing," Wild Dog said, gesturing somewhat laconically at one of the computer displays. "How big's it gotta get before we get serious and call in the people with powers?"

Dinah snorted in offense. But Joe took Rene's point. Dinah's Canary Cry was a great power, sure, but basically useless against a swarm of bees located thousands of feet straight up. They needed a Flash or a Vibe or an Atom or someone who could get up into the air and deactivate the swarm.

None of those folks were available to them. They had Bert Larvan.

"Anything, Bert?" Joe asked, ending his pacing right behind Larvan. "Anything at all?"

"Detective West," Bert said testily, not even bothering to look up from the microscope, "you can have me do this job *properly* or you can have me do it not at all. Which do you prefer?"

Grinding his teeth together, Joe stepped away a few paces. Holding his tongue was not his forte, but Larvan was doing them—and the world—a big favor. He'd put aside his animosity toward the police in order to figure out how to help stop the swarm and capture Ambush Bug. That bought him a little consideration for his . . . *prickly* personality.

"I say we find one of those jetpack things," Wild Dog said nonchalantly, "and fly up there with a flamethrower and *BWOOOOOSHHHH!*" He mimed spraying fire indiscriminately in a wide arc.

"Great idea," Dig deadpanned. "I'll get right on it."

"Hundreds of thousands of melted, flaming, sizzling little bees dropping out of the sky," Dinah added. "That's not a problem."

Rene shrugged. "I don't see anyone else coming up with anything."

Bert Larvan cleared his throat loudly and significantly. The message was clear: *Everyone shut up. I'm working.*

Joe huddled the four of them together at Rene's seat near the console. "Look," he said, his voice low, "we've got Bert and that's about all we can count on right now."

Rene chuckled mirthlessly. "You really think we can count on him? He hates the cops for arresting his sister."

"If there's one thing that drives him," Joe pointed out, "it's that love for his sister. He can't stand that Ambush Bug is using her bees for his own purposes. If nothing else, we can trust Bert to help stop the Bug."

Rene shrugged.

Dig folded his arms over his chest. "When you've got one option, it's automatically your best option," he told Rene.

"Whatever." Wild Dog leaned back in his chair and pretended to check the computer again.

Dinah pulled Joe aside. "Cop to cop, Joe: You trust him?"

Joe quirked his lips. "I don't know for sure. I've seen informants suddenly lose their nerve, undercover agents go bad . . ." He winced as he said it—Dinah's own boyfriend had been an undercover cop in Central City and eventually turned into the murdering Vigilante. "Sorry."

"Don't be." She brushed it off. "Ancient history." Her eyes flicked to Larvan's workbench. "Let's just keep an eye on this guy, OK?"

"Hello, my beauty . . ."

Bert Larvan squinted into the microscope as he gently peeled back the artificial exoskeletal material constituting the shell of the bee Joe West had retrieved from the bodega. It was a near-perfect replica of *Megachile pluto*, the largest of the Indonesian resin bees, once thought extinct. Brie, his technological genius sister, had developed the nanocircuitry and the synthetic aeronautics algorithms that made the bees possible. Bert had been at her side—sometimes literally, sometimes virtually—explaining the physics and anatomy of biological bees. She had incorporated his knowledge, using her genius and his to synthesize something never before seen—an artificial replica of life so perfect that it was indistinguishable from the real thing. Except for the improvements.

Probing gently with the point of a scalpel that had been honed to mere microns, he located the slight catch on the underside of the bee that opened its sealed inner compartment. Within lay the metaphorical heart of the mechanical "bug."

Bert grinned to himself.

For you, Brie, he thought.

18

AT THE END OF ALL THAT EVER WAS and ever could be, the Time Trapper stood motionless before a holographic control panel that spun, twisted, and flashed on its own.

Here at the End of All Time, reality teetered on the precipice of outright ablation. The machinery at the Time Trapper's disposal had been defunct and ruined millennia ago, and so the Time Trapper had reached back through history, summoning each component, stealing each tiny circuit, each diode, each power source from a moment when it would not be missed, then assembled the pieces together into the necessary machinery.

He—

(And the Time Trapper was not truly a *he*, just as the hours and minutes have no gender. Yet the first human the Time Trapper encountered—the captive speedster racing powerful circles to energize certain machinery—was male, and so the Time Trapper had chosen to think of itself as *he*.)

—had painstakingly connected the components, developing the circuitry and computerization that would bring his plan to fruition.

He took no pride in his work. The machinery was merely a means to an end. The machinery was a doorway to his machinations, to his glory.

With the self-designation of *he* and the completion of the machinery, something new tickled at the Time Trapper's consciousness: an awareness of himself *as* himself. As a discrete, independent being.

With this realization came the emotion of satisfaction. The Time Trapper's first experience with emotion.

Along with satisfaction came a new sensation: doubt.

There was a chance, the Time Trapper realized, an infinitesimal chance that he could fail. That his plan could come to naught. He realized this dispassionately, without self-recrimination or mortification.

And for the first time in his existence, the Time Trapper experienced . . . anger.

Those arrayed against him had no right to challenge him! He was the Time Trapper! The essence of all reality! The natural end point of All That Was! The short-lived specks of dust from the past had no claim to his victory!

And yet they rose up. And there was a chance—small but real—that they could prevail.

He thought. For the first time in his existence, he *pondered*. If he were defeated, what would that mean? Would he care any longer, if he were destroyed?

He decided it did not matter. Even if his enemies vanquished him, he still craved revenge.

Another new sensation to join the anger: a hollow yearning for vengeance. And since there was no one else to avenge him, he would need to avenge himself.

He pondered how best to achieve this goal. How best to assure his post-defeat victory. He would need an agent in the deep past to do his bidding.

As he had with his machinery, the Time Trapper reached out into history, stretching his temporal grasp. He found pieces here and there, the wretched discards of the long ago, bits of circuitry, forsaken and unmissed. Dragging them forward through time, he watched as they assembled themselves at his invisible will, forming a simulacrum of life, a robotic core clothed in synthetic flesh, imbued with staggering power.

His *hypothetica dominium*. Master of molecules. His retroactive, posthumous agent of revenge.

With a powerful burst of energy, the Time Trapper hurled his creation back through history, to where his foes would never find it. Should all reality not fall to the Time Trapper's plans, the agent would activate.

And enact brutal revenge.

The Time Trapper laughed a mirthless laugh.

"*Even if they find a way to defeat me, they will lose.*"

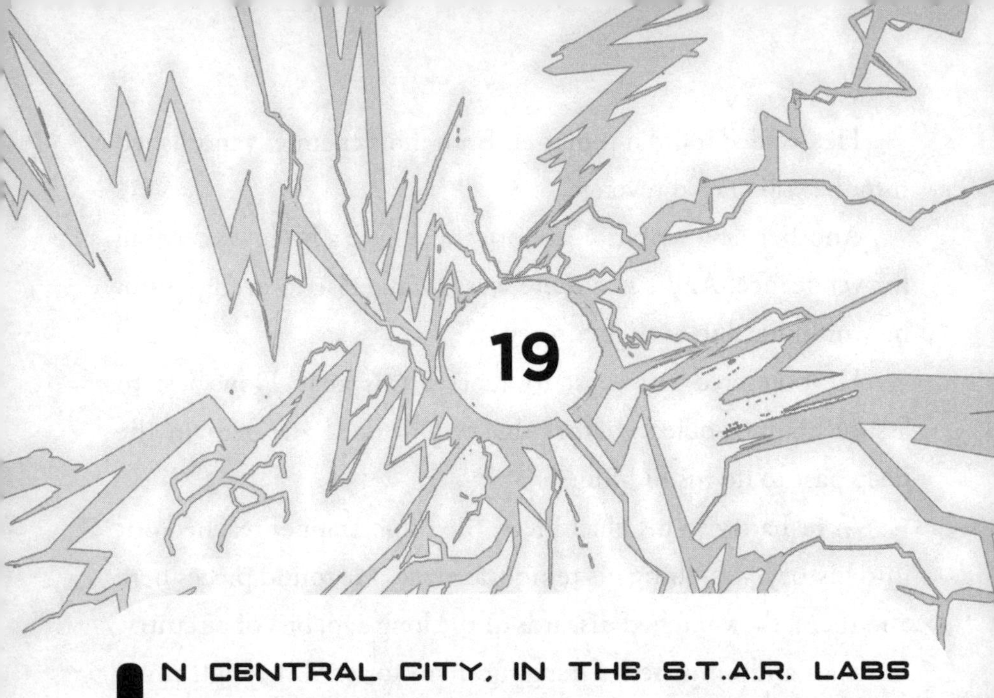

19

IN CENTRAL CITY, IN THE S.T.A.R. LABS Cortex, Mr. Terrific ran a hand through his hair and blew out an overwhelmed breath. He was still reeling from what Barry had described to him just now.

"Can you do it?" Barry asked. "Can you build the treadmill we need?"

"Wow. Uh. Wow. Yeah, it's possible. I mean, throw enough time, money, and tech at something and almost anything is possible. But it's gonna take a *long* time to design and build this thing."

"We don't have a long time, Curtis," Oliver said with gruff earnestness. "The Multiversal crossovers are . . . are . . ." He trailed off and looked to Barry for the science of it.

"The crossovers are weakening the vibrational differences between universes," Barry explained. "Eventually, all universes will occupy the same space in the same moment. And when that happens . . ."

Mr. Terrific gulped. "The entirety of reality will go bye-bye. Got it. No pressure or anything."

"There are ten thousand speedsters at your disposal," said James Jesse. They'd contacted him at the makeshift refugee housing nearby and told him about their plan, explaining the stakes. As the nominal leader of the Earth 27 refugees, he'd pledged their help. "Building it will be a snap. We just need the design and some guidance."

Mr. Terrific nodded solemnly. "Got it. But just the *design* of it. And it *has* to work, perfectly. Or we might not get a second chance. Look, guys, I could *really* use another genius or two."

"Happy to help," Ray said, raising his hand. "But you're right—the more the merrier."

Iris sighed heavily.

"What?" Barry asked, putting an arm around her.

"I know where we can get one more genius."

In the Pipeline, Barry, Oliver, and Superman approached the cluster of cells that held the Crime Syndicate of America. Power Ring had managed to pluck himself off the floor long enough to collapse on the bunk, where he lay facedown, groaning in his sleep. Superwoman had curled into a corner and was fastidiously braiding her hair, as though to show her jailers that their prison did not bother her. Johnny Quick was doing push-ups.

Ultraman slammed both fists against the unbreakable glass, his face contorted in rage and outright shock. "You! You there! I'll kill you! I'll *especially* kill *you*." Barry and Oliver looked from Ultraman to Superman and back again, then to each other.

"They hardly even look alike," Barry said.

"Anger and hate come through to the surface," Oliver commented.

"I'm gonna kick your butt into the Phantom Zone!" Ultraman screamed. "I'm gonna rip your heart out and throw it from here back to Krypton!"

Superman coolly regarded his evil Earth 27 duplicate. "Calm down," he said without heat or anger. "You're not going anywhere, and the sooner you realize that, the better it will be for you."

Much to everyone's shock, Ultraman went silent, his face pressed against the glass in an uneven oval of drool and breath fog. Regarding Superman with narrowed eyes, he slumped, rocked back on his heels, and trudged over to his bunk, where he sat facing the wall.

"Some people just need practical advice," Superman said as Barry and Oliver gaped at him.

The cell at the end of the corridor held Owlman. He stood behind the center of the glass door, hands clasped behind his back, leering at them as they closed in on him.

"They always come to me for help," he said, smirking. "Bruce Wayne always figures it out."

It was less than ideal, asking Owlman to pitch in on the treadmill project. Barry would have much preferred to breach to Earth 38 and get Brainiac 5 to help out. But Brainy had his hands full detoxifying Earth 38's atmosphere and repairing the massive infrastructure damage caused by Anti-Matter Man. For the same reason, Lena Luthor couldn't make the trip to Earth 1, either.

Which left them with an evil version of Bruce Wayne.

"We can use your help," Barry admitted. "In return, you'll get significant consideration when it comes time to decide your future."

Owlman craned his neck to and fro, taking in the entirety of his cell. "You mean there's a possibility of a life outside this thing? How nice."

"You'll have to go to trial for your crimes—"

"Trial?" He cut Oliver off. "What trial? How can any Earth 1 court claim jurisdiction over crimes committed in another universe?" A pause. "*Allegedly* committed, that is."

"We have plenty of witnesses from Earth 27," Barry pointed out.

"Still. Find a court that will claim jurisdiction. We may blaze some new trails in the field of Multiversal jurisprudence, Flash." He laughed. "It's a moot point. I'll help. Of course I'll help."

"Really?" Oliver asked.

"I need a Multiverse to live in, too," Owlman pointed out.

"Then let's get to work," Barry said, and he thumbed the switch that opened Owlman's cell.

Mr. Terrific and the Atom projected their early, rough schematics for the treadmill on the big monitor at the center of the Cortex. Owlman stood below it and stared up, hands behind his back, occasionally grunting.

“Seems workable,” he said somewhat grudgingly. “What are we standing around for?”

While Mr. Terrific and Ray worked with Owlman to finish the design of the treadmill, Barry and Iris slipped away into a side corridor. They held each other at arm’s length for a moment . . . and then Barry breathed out a sigh of relief and leaned back against the wall.

“I am . . . so tired!” he said.

Iris laughed and hugged him tight. “Me, too. Someone should invent a super-caffeine. Maybe HR is out there doing it.”

“In the future, they have something called Kathoonian stim-shots,” Barry told her. “I don’t what they are or what they do, but don’t they sound great?”

“Can we have a minute?” she asked, cheek pressed to his chest. “Can we have just a minute for us, before it all goes crisis-y again?”

He held her close. “I think we can have more than a minute. It’ll take a little while for Curtis, Ray, and Owlman to finish the schematics, even with Superman’s help. And then the treadmill itself . . . even with ten thousand speedsters working on it, it’s not going to be built in an hour.” He kissed her forehead. “Let’s get some sleep. Been a while since we snuggled.”

Iris sighed into him and let him lead her into one of the S.T.A.R. Labs rooms they’d retrofitted into a bedroom.

20

THE NEXT MORNING, SARA AND MICK took a car out to the eastern edge of Central City, opposite the side of town where the Gem City Bridge connected to Keystone. Here, past the highway that encircled the town, Central City gave way to a plain that stretched to the horizon. Dust, scrub, and weeds held dominion.

"That's a big treadmill," Mick said with something close to awe in his voice. Heat Wave did not impress easily, nor reveal it. But Sara knew him well enough to tell—behind that stone-dead expression, Mick was gobsmacked.

It *was* a big treadmill. Huge. Gargantuan.

The framework was made of polished molybdenum steel that measured more than four hundred feet long and a hundred feet across. The belt shone blackly in the morning sun, oiled and sleek on rollers the diameter of telephone poles. Grip bars rose up at regular intervals along the front, with arms along two sides for further stabilization. The back of the thing was open.

A series of stout tethers hung from the rails. Sara imagined how it would work—speedsters in the front and at the sides holding on to the bars for purchase, with the ones in the middle tied together to keep upright. Altogether, the treadmill was an acre in size, sprawling over the flat land outside Central City like an alien mother ship.

"It's like a piece of exercise equipment from God's gym," Sara said.

"Couldn't they just have built ten thousand normal-sized treadmills?" Mick said. He produced a bottle of beer from his jacket and took a pull.

"Wouldn't work." A new voice made Mick jump. Sara didn't. She was League of Assassins trained and had heard Mr. Terrific coming up behind them ten seconds ago.

"We need the vibrational energy from the speedsters to be perfectly in sync," Mr. Terrific went on. He had stripped off his Fair Play jacket and tied it around his waist, wearing only a grease-smudged, sweat-stained T-shirt. In one hand, he held a torque wrench. His eyes gazed out from tired hollows. "If we tried to link together thousands of treadmills, we'd introduce subtle errors in the frequencies. So . . ."

He gestured to the massive treadmill.

"There is no way in the world," Mick pronounced, "this is gonna work."

"It'll work." This time, Sara startled. She'd sensed Owlman's approach only at the last possible instant. She wasn't used to anyone getting the jump on her.

The villainous Bruce Wayne, unlike Mr. Terrific, wore a healthy, wide-awake expression, his eyes bright and his cheeks flushed with satisfaction. "This thing is going to produce so much energy that you'll blast right through the Iron Curtain of Time."

"And then what?" Mick asked gruffly. Sara snickered. She knew that tone in Mick's voice. He wasn't worried or concerned or afraid. He didn't even really want to know what would happen next. In his endearingly nihilistic way, he was merely pointing out that getting through the Iron Curtain of Time was only step one in a plan that had a lot of blank spaces yet to be filled in.

"And then it's up to you guys," Mr. Terrific said, taking Mick very seriously. "We can't predict who or what you'll encounter at the End of All Time. It's possible this is a one-way trip; there may be no way back through the Curtain."

"Until we defeat the foe," Superman said, gently gliding down from above them. "Then the Curtain goes away and we can come back."

"Until." Sara clenched her jaw and beheld the enormity of the treadmill. "Your optimism is . . ."

"Encouraging?" Superman asked, standing arms akimbo.

"Misplaced," Owlman jibed in a gravelly voice.

"Touching," Mr. Terrific chimed in.

"I was going for *not entirely realistic*," Sara admitted. She planted her fists on her hips, realized she was mimicking Superman's stance, and let them drop to her sides. "We'll be lucky to come out of this at all. Heck, we're lucky to get *into* it in the first place."

Mick snorted. "Not sure *lucky* is the word I'd use."

Barry woke next to Iris. He allowed himself three entire seconds to gaze down at her, drinking her in. The slope of her shoulder as it emerged from the tangle of blankets. The curve of her chin, the line of her cheekbone. Her coal-black hair spilling over her face; the whisper of her eyelashes.

Three seconds was a long, long time to the Flash. He inhaled her. He absorbed her. Every breath took days to anticipate and enjoy.

Iris, I'm not going to stop running until I know you're safe. I swear it.

Slipping out of bed silently so as not to wake her, he made his way to the Cortex. Caitlin reclined in one of the chairs at the central workstation, a steaming mug of coffee held before her. Barry paused at the entrance. Since the moment Anti-Matter Man had ripped his way through to Earth 1 (had it been only a few days ago? It felt like centuries), the Cortex had been a chaotic bustle of activity, a beehive swarmed by drones under the command of a mad queen. Now it was quiet, unoccupied save for Caitlin.

"Any more of that coffee?" Barry asked.

Caitlin startled and almost spilled hot coffee on herself. "Barry!"

He apologized for alarming her, then went to retrieve his

own coffee when she pointed to a percolator plugged in next to one of the transparent dry-erase boards. The aroma from the mug was delightful, but when he sipped, the brew disappointed.

"The coffee quality has really gone downhill around here ever since HR went walkabout," he commented, settling into a seat next to her.

"Tell me about it." Her voice was rueful. "If there was one thing that guy knew how to do, it was make an amazing cup of coffee."

"To HR," he proposed, raising his mug. They clinked cups, then drank in silence for a bit.

"It's coming along, I see." He gestured to the main screen, which showed satellite footage of the massive treadmill. The Earth 27 speedsters, working in shifts and following meticulous plans, had constructed the thing literally overnight and were putting the finishing touches on it now.

"Tell me something, Barry," Caitlin said, studiously not looking over at him. "Is this going to work?"

"The treadmill? The science is as sound as anything else we've ever—"

"I don't mean the treadmill, specifically. I mean *any* of it." Staring down into her coffee. "You're headed to the End of All Time without a plan or any sort of intel. Just the name *the Time Trapper* and a handful of superheroes with hope and a prayer. How in the world is this supposed to work?"

"We have the best strategic thinker in the world," Barry told her, thinking of Oliver. "And a Kryptonian. Right there, I feel like 90 percent of all problems get solved. But you know how it is on Team Flash, Caitlin: We improvise. It's what we do."

"'No plan survives first contact with the enemy,'" she said. It was an old Army saying she'd picked up from a med school buddy who'd served.

"Pretty much," he agreed, and then cracked a broad grin. "Don't worry, Caitlin. It's all going to work out. You know how I know?"

"How?"

"Because it always has. How's Madame Xanadu holding up?"

Caitlin drank some of her coffee. "She's mending. Her mind is . . . flighty. I don't think she'll ever truly recover from losing her Earth 27 doppelgänger. It's like there's a piece missing, and she'll be fine, but then occasionally she runs into that missing spot . . . and she just seems so *lost.*"

It made sense. Barry remembered losing his first tooth as a child. It hadn't hurt all that bad—when it got really loose, Dad had suggested chewing gum, and sure enough, the tooth popped right out—and for the most part he never really thought about it. But at least once a day, he would try to bite into something or he would run his tongue along his teeth . . . and the gap surprised him every single time. That must be what it felt like for Madame Xanadu, though without the knowledge that the hole would be filled by a new tooth in due course. She would miss that tooth forever.

Standing, he put a hand on Caitlin's shoulder. "Please take care of her, OK? She's important to me, and when I get back from the End of All Time, my first order of business is to make sure she's settled somewhere and as happy and as healthy as possible."

Caitlin smiled up at him. "You'd make a good doctor, Barry Allen."

"Never as good as you," he told her.

Just then, White Canary and Heat Wave marched into the Cortex. *Marched* was the wrong word—Sara padded in on tiger's feet; Mick stomped in as though crushing scorpions in his path.

"We're going with you, Twinkle Toes," Mick announced. Coming in behind them, Ray struck what he believed to be a confident, tough pose and nodded in solidarity.

"I'm sorry?" Caught off guard, Barry stalled by sipping from his coffee mug.

"What Mick is trying to get across in his usual subtle way," Sara said, "is that we want to join you and Oliver and Superman when you go to the future."

Barry and Caitlin glanced at each other, communicating volumes in a split second. Caitlin, whose back was to the two Legends, pursed her lips and widened her eyes in an expression of *No. Freakin'. Way!* Facing them, Barry tried to be more politic.

"Guys, I really appreciate that, but we don't even know if there's a *there* where we're headed. You don't have any powers—"

"Neither does Oliver."

"Yeah," Mick agreed, and essayed a very clumsy, very insulting mime of firing an arrow. "You gonna trust your back to some Robin Hood wannabe?"

“Look, I don’t—”

“No, *you* look.” Sara advanced and jabbed a finger at him. “We lost team members to this enemy. Zari may never wake up. And the others—Nate, Charlie, Mona, John—we don’t know where or when they ended up. No one has more at stake here than us. We’re the last three standing Legends, the only ones left from the original team, and there is no way in *hell* we’re letting you take the fight to the enemy without us at your side. We deserve it. We’ve earned it.”

Barry flicked his gaze to Mick, who crossed his arms over his chest. “Too many words,” he intoned. “We’re going. Not up for debate.”

“You can science up some gear for us,” Sara pointed out. “I know the Legion gave you guys some tech to survive in space. We’ll take that, plus any sort of weapons you guys can put together. You do this stuff all the time.”

“Usually Cisco puts together custom equipment for us. We don’t have any . . .” A thought occurred to Barry. “Have you ever used a lariat before?”

Sara regarded him quizzically. “The League of Assassins trained me in all sorts of weaponry. Including, yeah, ropes. Why?”

Barry grinned.

Along with Superman and Oliver, Barry convened a meeting with Sara, Mick, and Owlman in the Safe Lab, where Cisco conducted experiments on the worst, most unknowable forms of metals and alloys, disassembled and puzzled out the inner workings of the most wicked weapons from the evilest villains, and fabricated his own dangerous tech. The room was lined with lead, steel, and two feet of concrete. It could be isolated from the rest of S.T.A.R. Labs in an instant, its ventilation cut off at the flick of a switch. It was, as Cisco had once said, a panic room in reverse—you ran *from* here when things went wrong.

On a workbench were two Danger Boxes, forged of a rare metal called promethium that was resistant to most ammunition and energy weapons. Barry and Cisco locked up the ultra-hazardous in them. Cisco called the things that went into the Danger Boxes *Bad Toys*.

Without preamble, Barry opened the first one. Its door clicked open, revealing the first Bad Toy: Superwoman's lasso.

"We need some super-gear for our friends," Barry said to Owlman. "White Canary is an expert in all forms of combat and weaponry. Is there any reason you can think of why she shouldn't be able to use this?"

Owlman stroked his jaw, considering. "You could wield the lasso. There's nothing dangerous to a practiced user. It's technological and comprehensible. Simple mental control through physical contact."

"In other words," Sara said, "I can make it do stuff as long as I'm touching it."

"Why can't eggheads ever just spit it out?" Mick growled.

Sara picked up the lasso. At the touch of her flesh, it seemed to come alive, illuminating in a steady golden glow along its length. She expected it to feel warm, but instead her hands chilled, as though the thing were leeching her heat to power itself.

"Can you use it?" Oliver asked.

Sara grinned. She tried a quick twirl and the lasso obeyed, requiring only the slightest of muscle movements on her part. Then, with a thought, she cracked it like a whip, snapping a beaker off a nearby shelf, sending it hurtling against a wall, where it shattered into a million pieces.

"I'd say I'm sorry," she said, "but I'm finding it really hard to be."

Flash shrugged. "We can get more beakers." He turned to Owlman. "What about the ring?"

For the first time ever, Owlman held up his hands in a defensive posture, stepping back from the second Danger Box. "No. Not the ring. Look, I'm fearless, but that thing scares even *me*. Have you seen what it did to Power Ring?"

Sara and Oliver had already wandered off to test Sara's new toy. Mick leaned against a table, idly picking between his teeth with a scalpel he'd found lying around. So Barry pulled Superman back a couple of feet.

"What do you think?" he whispered to the Man of Steel. "Is he just trying to scare us off from using the ring?"

Superman folded his arms over his chest. "I listened in on his heartbeat and scanned his adrenals with my microscopic vision while he was talking. He's telling the truth. The ring genuinely frightens him."

Barry pondered. Power Ring was a wreck of a human being, a strung-out waste quivering with withdrawal symptoms. The ring took a toll, for sure, but it was *so* powerful . . . ! He recollected

Power Ring blasting chunks out of buildings, lifting multiton air-conditioning units and hurling them with ease . . .

"The ring is the most dangerous artifact I've ever encountered," Owlman spoke up, snagging the Flash's and Superman's attention. "I mean, I've played with the Orb of Ra. I tried to work out how to use something called a Gamma Gong. But the ring . . ." He shivered.

"What, exactly, do you know about it?" Barry asked. "Other than what it did to Power Ring?"

Owlman shook his head. "You're going to get someone killed. Which is fine by me, but not until we've saved the world so that I can keep living."

With a long, confident stride, Superman approached Owlman. "Bruce," he said, his tone gentle but strong, his expression open and sincere. "Bruce, if you know something, tell us. Trust us to do the smart thing."

Owlman flinched. "It is *so* weird looking at you and seeing *him* . . ." He shook his head. "Anyway . . . OK. Here's what I know: The ring requires willpower. And fear. My theory is that it's somewhat alive, in its own way. It . . . it gloms on to someone who's afraid, someone with a weak will. And it gives that person enormous power. But it's not a symbiotic relationship—it's parasitic. The whole time, the ring is eating your will, your sense of self, filling the gaps with power so that you don't notice. And when you take the ring away . . ." He gestured vaguely in the direction of the Pipeline, where they all knew Power Ring lay crumpled in his cell, drooling and quivering.

Superman arched an eyebrow at Barry. “It’s a risk. But I’ll wear it. I can resist it. Corral its power.”

With a frown, Barry said, “I don’t see how we can risk it. If the ring itself is evil . . .”

“Give it to me,” said a new voice.

They both turned to Mick Rory, still leaning casually against the table, focused grimly on a bit of food under his left bicuspid.

“Right,” Barry said, with much less sarcasm than the moment called for.

“No, really. I’ll use it.” Heat Wave cracked his neck, then stabbed the scalpel into the table behind him. “I’m already a bad guy. We got a lot in common, me and this ring. I can make it work for me.”

“Mick . . .”

Heat Wave sneered just the slightest bit. “I know how to be real persuasive, Twinkle Toes. Plus, this Time Trapper jerk left Zari in a coma. I ain’t about to let anything get in the way of some good old-fashioned revenge.”

Barry flicked his attention to Superman. “What do you think?”

Superman gazed at Mick for a long moment. “I say we let him do it.”

Mick grinned like he’d just been given his first book of matches.

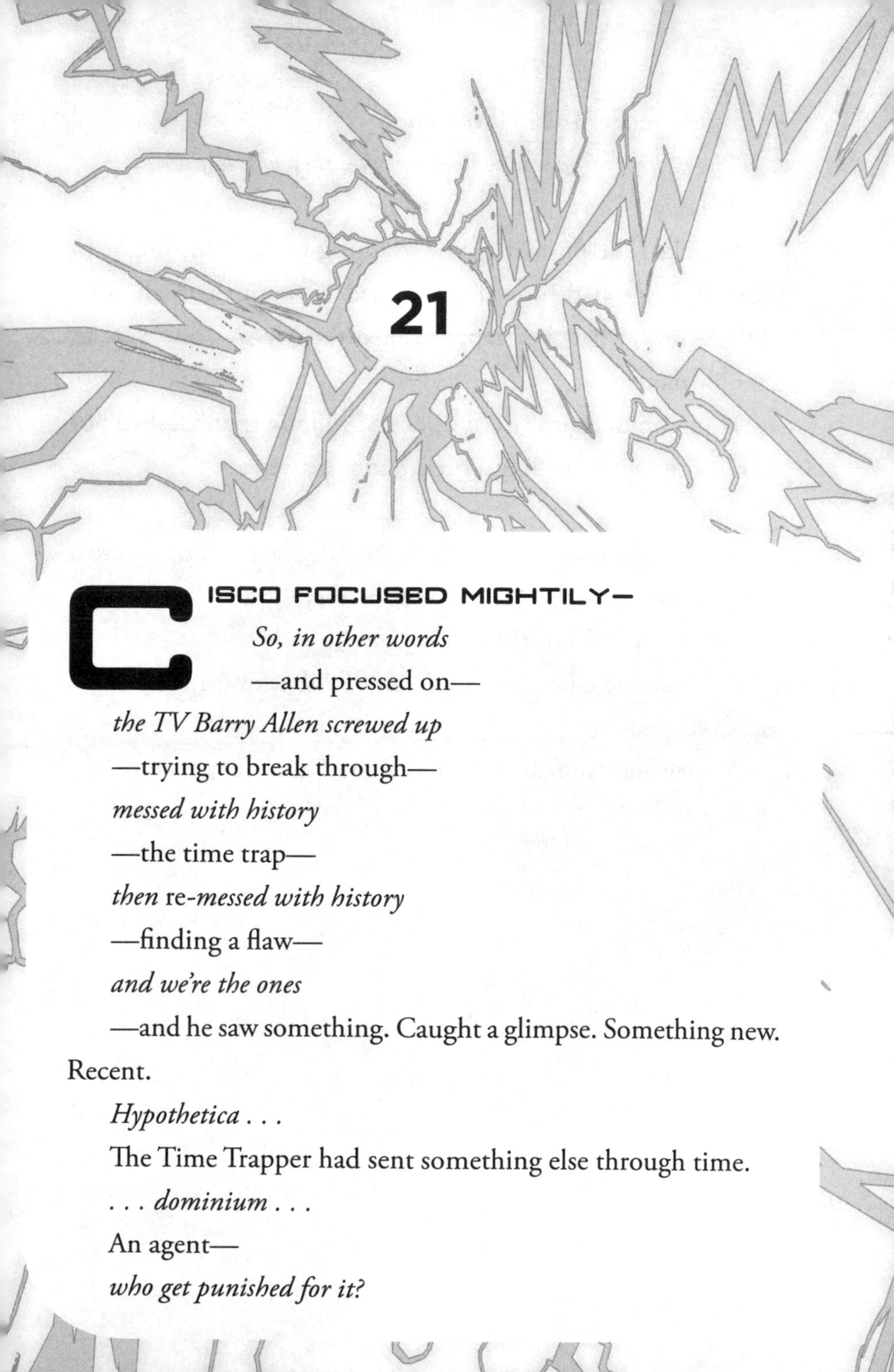

21

CISCO FOCUSED MIGHTILY—

So, in other words

—and pressed on—

the TV Barry Allen screwed up

—trying to break through—

messed with history

—the time trap—

then re-*messed with history*

—finding a flaw—

and we're the ones

—and he saw something. Caught a glimpse. Something new. Recent.

Hypothetica . . .

The Time Trapper had sent something else through time.

. . . dominium . . .

An agent—

who get punished for it?

—of revenge. To kill loved ones.

"Even if they find a way to defeat me, they will lose."

Not cool.

Panicked, he pushed again, straining with all his might to break free. He had to escape. He had to warn them all. Two Multiverses—what the Trapper called the Megaverse—were in horrible danger.

He summoned every last ounce of willpower and lashed out with his thoughts, willing a breach into existence.

And—

"So, in other words, the TV Barry Allen screwed up, messed with history, then *re*-messed with history, and we're the ones who get punished for it? Not cool."

Noooooooo! Cisco screamed, and fell backward fifteen seconds yet again.

Somewhere, somehow, he heard the Time Trapper laughing.

22

A NEW DAY IN STAR CITY, BUT THE same old stress and danger. Spartan and Black Canary dashed down Weisinger Street, dodging around stopped cars and fighting their way through a crowd fleeing in the opposite direction. Ever since Ambush Bug had begun his so-called Reign of Error, these sorts of mass panics were more and more common. But this time the A.R.G.U.S. satellite link indicated no teleporting in the area. As far as the remnants of Team Arrow could determine, the Bug was in hiding as his swarm massed for its attack.

So what could be causing this stampede?

They broke through the crowd into a traffic intersection. Two cars had crashed into each other, both abandoned by now. Crumpled in the intersection, they resembled a child's set of toys played with too aggressively. Chunks of blacktop littered the area, and Dig caught a glimpse of a familiar blue, coruscating energy field as it collapsed in on itself. A breach.

Near the cars, amid the scattering of blacktop, stood a woman in an ankle-length black leather duster over a charcoal gray suit of body armor. Her left eye glowed, replaced by a cybernetic part that whirred and clicked every time she shifted her glance. Around her neck, she wore a burnished-bronze choker with a bright red light that pulsed with a life of its own.

Other than the fact that the left side of her head was shaved smooth down to the scalp and her wearing of the various bionic accoutrements, she was a dead ringer for Dinah.

"I am the Dark Canary!" the woman shouted. "Scourge of Earth 32! Bow down before me!"

"Oh, come on!" Dinah complained. She had joined Dig on this mission and now stood absolutely flummoxed at the presence of her doppelgänger.

Dig drew his weapon and leveled it at Dark Canary. "Hey! Wrong Earth, lady! Hands up!"

"I got this," Dinah said with confidence. She took a step closer to the so-called Dark Canary.

But her double's attention remained focused on Dig. Dark Canary's lip curled as she took him in. "John Stewart. On my Earth, I turned your bones to jelly with the power of my Scream-Song. Then, I could not pause to enjoy it." She licked her lips. "Here, I shall."

Dig didn't like the sound of that—so he squeezed off three shots in rapid succession.

Dark Canary did not so much as flinch. She opened her mouth wide, and the pulsing red light on her choker shifted to a bright blue as she sang out. The note was high and sustained, a single unit of sound that seemed to stretch forever. The air between them vibrated and shook, wavering with its disrupted frequencies. The bullets—every single one of them—hit that wall of sound and *spang!*ed off in different directions, leaving Dark Canary unharmed.

"You, uh, you can't do that, right?" Dig asked.

Dinah snorted and let loose with her Canary Cry. At the same time, Dark Canary narrowed the opening of her lips. The choker shifted to a dull yellow, and suddenly Dig felt a blast of something collide with his chest, lifting him off the ground and hurling him against one of the wrecked cars. He felt like spaghetti thrown against the wall; he was done.

"You pathetic poseur," Dark Canary said, her smile knowing and humorless as she addressed Dinah. "Your sad little song has no effect on me. I am immune to your scream."

Dinah leaned into it, blasting out with her Cry until her throat was raw, but sure enough, Dark Canary merely stood there, unaffected.

And then Dark Canary pursed her lips almost to a whistle's diameter, her voice deepening as she did so. The choker's light went green as she aimed herself at the ground. A massive tremor shook the road beneath their feet, and as Dig watched, the street seemed to unzip itself in an unerringly straight line, opening up and launching clods of pavement into the air from Dark Canary to Dinah.

Dinah threw her hands up in self-defense, jumping back, but Dark Canary's ScreamSong continued and the exploding street followed Dinah wherever she stumbled.

Struggling to stand, Dig felt bent and twisted metal from the car biting into him, catching on his body armor. At least one rib was broken, poking into places it didn't belong. If he moved too much, he might puncture a lung.

Meanwhile, Dinah's luck ran out and a fusillade of flying pavement pummeled her to the ground.

Dark Canary stood triumphant, arms akimbo. "And now, for my next trick . . ." she said.

Dig didn't want to see it.

Joe approached Bert with near-silent steps. The entomologist had been bent over the microscope, his work evident only in the minutest twitches of his hands, for hours now. Sure, Bert needed time and quiet, but this was getting ridiculous. The swarm over Star City was now twice the size it had been when they'd first begun tracking it. Something on the order of two hundred thousand bees. And growing.

"Bert, I'm sorry, but I need to know if you've made any progress." Rene's idea of flying up there with a flamethrower was ridiculous, but Joe was beginning to think that maybe someone at Star City PD could fly a helicopter through the storm or something. *Anything* to break up the swarm, impede its growth, throw a monkey wrench into Ambush Bug's plans.

He expected another prissy rebuke from Bert Larvan, but instead, the man simply sat up straight, groaning as his back unkinked from his hours of work. He set aside his scalpel and rubbed his eyes. "I'm pleased to report progress, Detective. Observe."

With that, he extended one hand out, palm open. As Joe watched, the bee on the microscope's stage roused itself and buzzed a direct path to Bert's hand, where it landed and remained still.

"I've managed to disconnect this bee from Ambush Bug's *hive network*, for lack of a better term. It no longer obeys his commands and can no longer serve as a teleportation end point." He smiled a smug, knowing smile.

"Great," Rene said somewhat acidly. "Now all we need to do is capture two hundred thousand *other* bees and let you spend a few hours with each of them, and this'll all be wrapped up."

Larvan snickered. "Do you really think me that idiotic? This bee can send its new firmware patch to others wirelessly within a certain range."

"Wait," Joe said. "You mean if we can get this one near the swarm, it can reprogram them for us?"

Larvan nodded. "Precisely. In fact, there were four bees within range already. Witness . . ."

He held up his other hand. As they watched, four new bees buzzed as a cluster into the Bunker and separately alighted on Larvan's hands. He had three bees in one hand, two in the other.

Something cold tiptoed up Joe's spine. "Bert? What, exactly, is going on here?"

Larvan grinned. "I am simply offering proof of concept, Detective West."

Rene and Joe exchanged a glance. Years of instinct and experience communicated between them just as wirelessly as Bert's signal to the bees.

"How are you controlling them?" Rene asked. Exactly the question Joe wanted answered.

"I'm using an old implant of Brie's. I had it in my briefcase when you brought me here." He tapped his ear. "It looks like a hearing aid, doesn't it?"

Then he dropped his hands to his sides. The bees remained hovering in midair, then began orbiting him as though he were their personal sun. Their little bodies whizzed and buzzed in the air.

"Don't even think of drawing your weapons," Bert told them, still grinning. "You don't stand a chance against the new Bug-Eyed Bandit."

23

ON-SITE AT THE TREADMILL, CURTIS yawned. He couldn't remember the last time he'd slept. He'd been pounding energy drinks and chewing caffeinated gum in order to stay awake, but it was worth it—the treadmill was finished. A part of him wished they had time for a test run, but . . . How did you test powering a run to the future through an impenetrable Iron Curtain of Time? Especially without alerting the enemy?

He scratched the back of his head as he stared down at the control pad they'd wired up to the treadmill. Something seemed off. He caught the attention of Bruce Wayne's evil doppelgänger from Earth 27, who crouched nearby, wrenching a couple of bolts tighter. "Owlman? Why is there this accelerator circuit patched into the frequency modulator?"

Owlman answered without missing a beat: "Redundancy. Clearly, on this Earth, you expect everything to work perfectly the first time. In my experience, that's rarely the case."

Curtis blinked a few times. It didn't make much sense, but he was both too tired and too eager to stop to question it. "Atomic batteries to power; turbines to speed," he said. "Let's fire this sucker up."

Standing in a corner of the Safe Lab with Sara Lance, Mick held the ring with his thumb and forefinger. It ached and pulsed like a rotten tooth, shooting arcs of pain up his fingers and down along his arm. This was *not*, he knew, going to feel good.

"Are you sure you want to do this?" Sara asked. "I can feel that thing's evil from where I'm standing, and I'm not even touching it."

Mick had never been one for planning things out or thinking things through. He was more your basic *charge ahead and see what happens* sort of crook. The ring looked too big for his ring finger, so he slid it onto the middle finger of his right hand, where it caught for a moment on his knuckle, then kept going. Almost as though it wanted to be there.

Pain.

Pain raced up his arm.

Slender, brachiated green tendrils crawled from the ring, puncturing his flesh, then emerging, only to re-puncture it again as they slithered up his arm, like a series of threads being sewn into his skin. He gritted his teeth and groaned into the agony, fighting it.

"Mick?" Sara said. "Mick, take it off. It's OK; take it off!"

Shaking his head, sweat streaming down his face, he leaned into the anguish, accepting it. It was like holding his hand over a flame, something he'd done innumerable times since childhood, when he'd first discovered his love of fire. The flame could roast his flesh, but he never moved his hand. It was a point of pride. It was a measure of strength.

If flames couldn't cow him, some junky piece of jewelry from another Earth wouldn't knock him to his knees, either. He permitted himself a grudging, groaning wordless cry of distress, then clenched his fist.

There was a voice in his head. *VOLTHOOM!* it said. Demanding his subservience. Offering him everything he'd ever wanted. *VOLTHOOM!* A world consumed by fire. Endless heaps of treasure—gemstones sparkling like waves in sunshine, cold gold coins feigning fire, stacks and stacks of cash . . . *VOLTHOOM!*

mick I am yours you are mine we are together let me in let me in let me in and the world is yours I promise you don't fight me don't resist me I am everything I can give you everything mick mick it's within your grasp just let me in let me in let me in

"There's only one of us in charge here," Mick grunted, wiping sweat from out of his eyes with his free hand. "And it's *me*!"

With a final cry, he raised his right hand above his head. The ring glowed. The tendrils dissipated and a sheath of verdant light enveloped him. The voice in his head quieted to a whisper, like a ringing in his ears—ever present, but possible to ignore.

"Are you all right?" Sara asked. He could tell she wanted to touch him, to put a calming hand on his shoulder, but the green energy coruscating around him warned her off.

"Never been better," he snarled. He lowered his clenched fist to eye level, glaring at the ring perched there. "Lemme tell you something, Captain: I don't know what this thing is or where it comes from, but no matter how bright it gets or how dark it gets, nothing bad is getting past me as long as I'm wearing it."

Sara nodded. "Good enough for me. Let's go."

The Earth 27 speedsters lined up single file outside Central City, ten thousand strong, ready to take their places on the treadmill.

Felicity had taken a break from her duties helping Joe West's team in Star City, long enough to work up an algorithm that determined the optimal placement for speedsters on the acre-sized treadmill belt Curtis had cobbled together with the guy who looked creepily like Bruce Wayne. And a *creepy* Bruce Wayne, to boot. The real Bruce Wayne was handsome and sort of playfully useless in that way some rich men projected. This guy was good-looking, too . . . but his pulchritude only barely concealed a seething, squirming rage and a brute confidence that gave her the heebie-jeebies. The faster she could see the back of him, the better.

The treadmill was practically the size of a football field, with a series of internal railings so that the speedsters could stand in rows, one behind the other. The faster speedsters would be at the front, accelerating, with the slower ones toward the back, using their speed to keep up and generate the necessary vibrational energies.

She and Curtis guided the speedsters into position with the help of James Jesse, who knew or was known to many of them. Some of them, she knew, could only reach subsonic speeds. Others could hit Mach 2 or 3. It wasn't, though, so much about the speed as about the unique vibrations speedsters produced when they ran. Those vibrations would need to be channeled through the special shock absorbers Curtis had constructed under the treadmill belt. They would be converted into a frequency waveform and funneled into a heavy-duty cable that Superman had buried between the treadmill and S.T.A.R. Labs.

It shouldn't work at all, she knew. It was the very maddest sort of the mad science, the kind of thing that would make Cisco Ramon throw his hands up in the air and stomp out of the room in search of Cheetos and Mountain Dew to soothe his offended ego.

But it *had* to work. They had no other options.

"Are we ready?" she asked James.

The Not-Trickster, positioned near the control pad mounted to the side of the treadmill, gave her a thumbs-up.

Felicity scouted a hundred feet down the side of the treadmill, where Mr. Terrific stood at another control pad. She waved for his attention, then fired the thumbs-up down to him.

He nodded. In sync, they both put their hands to their control pads' touch surfaces and rotated clockwise. The pads' screens went from yellow to green, and a whistling, whining sound filled the air.

"OK, SPEEDSTERS!" It was Curtis's voice, projected and amplified so that everyone within a mile could hear it clearly. "GET READY TO USE YOUR SPEED MANTRA! WE BEGIN RUNNING IN 5 . . ."

Felicity checked power levels.

"4 . . ."

She double-checked the conduit connectors. They were solid.

"3 . . ."

A murmuring began on the treadmill: *3X2(9YZ)4A.* Over and over again, spoken by ten thousand tongues: *3X2(9YZ)4A.*

"2 . . ."

The hair on the back of Felicity's neck stood on end. The air had become supercharged with static electricity, like the moment before a lightning strike. She smelled the scent of ozone.

"1 . . . RUN!" Curtis cried.

And twenty thousand feet began to run.

24

IN THE SIXTY-FOURTH CENTURY, CITIZEN Hefa of the Quantum Police made her standard patrol of the planet Earth, checking her quark-fed macrolemetry for any subatomic deviations or disruptions.

There were none. Earth was atomically stable and temporally fit. As usual.

She spent a moment double-checking the data feed from the Prison Spire, where the techno-magicians who had bedeviled two centuries were imprisoned in sleep-stasis. Aliskaiszisamis, Bisebbseidseibseobsebdseidseiseboose, Prupesuptoupchupanupgeoup, and Voikitlakit all still slept. And the man once known as Abhararakadhararbarakh—Abra Kadabra—was now harmless, metamorphosed into an ancient plaything called a *puppet* when his own "magic" was turned against him by the Flash.

Citizen Hefa smiled. The Flash. He had saved two eras from the depredations of the techno-magicians and in doing so had solidified his reputation as one of the greatest heroes of all time. She thought of him often.

And then he was *there*.

The Flash stood directly before her, reaching out to her. His costume, torn in places, hung off him; his body had gone almost skeletal, his face drawn, eyes sunken.

“ϟ !” she exclaimed, forgetting in her shock to revert to ancient English.

“Hefa!” he cried out. “I don’t know if . . . Help . . . Tell them . . . Iris . . .”

And then he was gone.

Citizen Hefa tapped her helmet and quickly scanned the immediate area down to the quark level. There were small perturbations in the strange and charm quark flavors, but nothing that could explain what she’d just seen.

Her helmet’s advanced temporal tech recorded everything around her and could reproduce it as a high-fidelity three-dimensional hologram. She replayed the last few moments to reexperience the Flash’s appearance and disappearance and look for clues.

But when she watched the recording, there was nothing there. Nothing at all.

It was as though he’d never been there.

25

BARRY AND IRIS STOOD JUST OUTside the entrance to the circular collider tunnel under S.T.A.R. Labs. Lights flashed overhead and a siren bell sang out, echoing down the halls.

"That's the signal," Barry told her. "The speedsters are charging up the equipment and sending their vibrations to us."

"Come back to me," Iris said, brushing her lips against his. "Again."

"And again and again and again," he promised, returning her kiss.

Inside the collider tunnel, it was time for what Owlman had called *chronal extraction and insertion*.

Green Arrow, White Canary, the Atom, and Heat Wave waited in the Time Sphere that Eobard Thawne had originally built to attempt to return to the twenty-fifth century. He'd failed, and the vessel had been stored in the Starchives for years.

It could, they hoped, provide protection for the human members of the strike team as they were thrust through Time itself.

Working with Superman, Barry had rewired portions of the S.T.A.R. Labs power grid to redirect the massive power influx to the collider tunnel. The speedsters running on the treadmill had their vibrational energy transmitted to the tunnel, where Barry would use it to propel himself and his team through the Iron Curtain of Time.

In theory.

It was *all* merely *in theory*.

He bounced on his toes, waiting for word from the Cortex that they were a go. Behind him, Mick Rory's face loomed through the plastisteel dome of the Time Sphere. His bald head, awash in sweat, reflected and distorted light from the emergency bulbs set along the tunnel walls. Ever since putting the glowing green ring on his finger, he'd been terser than usual, his eyes bloodshot and rigid with focus.

"What made you decide we should let Mick take the ring?" Barry asked Superman. "You stared at him . . . Were you analyzing his DNA to see how susceptible he'd be to temptation?"

Superman's smile was broad and honest. "I wasn't using any superpowers at all, Flash. What you saw was a reporter sizing up a source. And deciding to trust him."

Barry's jaw dropped. Was he really going to trust a super villain with the most powerful weapon in the universe, all based on a reporter's instincts?

Well, yeah. Look who you married, Allen. You've been trusting a reporter's instincts for a long, long time.

“Let’s do this,” Barry said, and took up a runner’s pose.

Superman effortlessly lifted the Time Sphere over his head. “Hold on,” he warned the occupants. “This may get bumpy.”

“Stop yapping,” Heat Wave said, “and get moving. I got a deadline for my next book, and my editor doesn’t take excuses.”

Sure, Barry figured. That was as good a reason as any to save the world.

“Energy wave incoming!” Iris’s voice echoed loudly throughout the collider tunnel, amplified by a series of loudspeakers. “Lights are red across the board! You’ve got one shot at this before all the circuity melts down! Run, Barry! Run!”

You don’t have to tell me twice, he thought.

And ran.

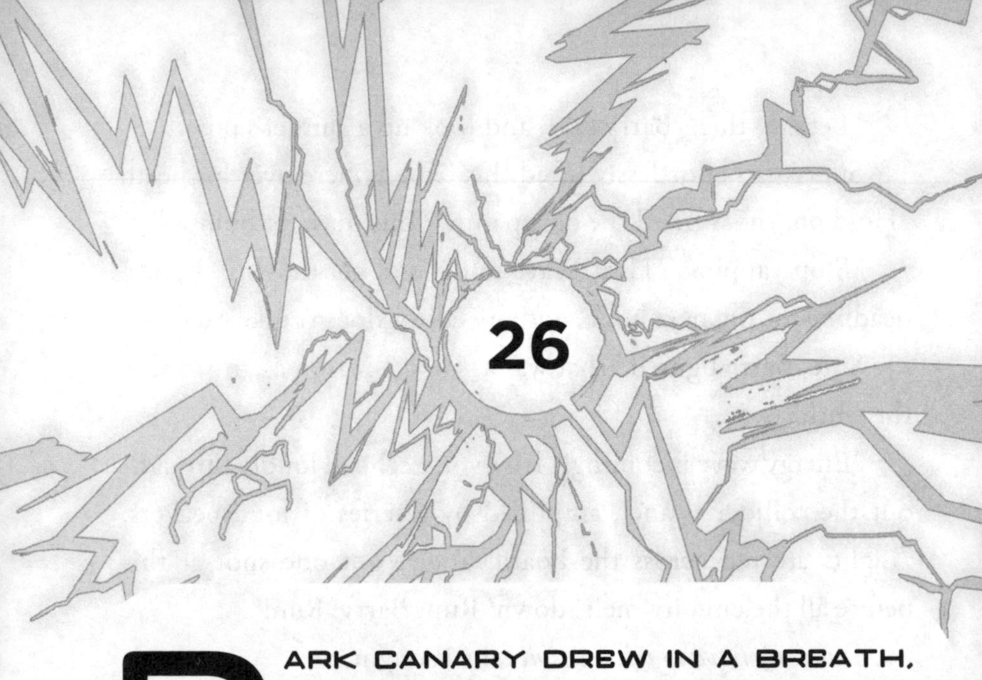

26

DARK CANARY DREW IN A BREATH, and the light on her choker went a deep black. Dig didn't want to imagine what this particular iteration of her sonic powers would do to him, but the comment about turning someone's bones to jelly rang in his memory like a strident church bell.

Despite the pain from his ribs, he lurched up, scrambling to unholster his emergency backup weapon. Maybe if she was using the intense black version of her power, she couldn't also deflect bullets like she'd done before. He could possibly save Dinah and the rest of the city.

At the cost of his own life.

Which . . . was less than ideal. He had a wife and a child he loved. He had dreams for his future.

But John Diggle had always been willing to sacrifice himself for the greater good. That drive had taken him to the military, to A.R.G.U.S., to serve as Oliver Queen's bodyguard . . . and then to take on the mantle of Spartan when Oliver's superhero lifestyle demanded some backup.

He had never imagined himself dying on the street under a threatening cloud of robot bees while fighting an alternate-reality version of one of his best friends, but then again, who ever got to pick their death?

"Hey, you!" he shouted, drawing her attention from Dinah. "I bet Earth 32 is glad to see you gone!"

She swiveled to regard him, her expression unchanged save for a slight narrowing of the eyes. She knew he was baiting her, but couldn't help herself.

"I've killed men for less," she told him.

"Well, get ready to kill me for more." He opened fire.

The recoil set his ribs on fire and he jerked to one side, firing wide and missing her. Still, she had to dodge, losing her balance for a few moments. That gave him just enough time to race to Dinah's side. She was groggy but awake, her face speckled with droplets of blood from flying pavement.

"I should have called in sick today, Dig."

"You and me both, Dinah. C'mon." Groaning in pain as his ribs flared, he helped Dinah to her feet. Only a few feet away was one of the wrecked cars, a possible refuge for a few moments.

"You hear that?" Dinah asked, her voice alive with panic.

Dig tried to answer, but the world was filled with a shrieking, high-pitched tone that swallowed all other sound. He clapped his hands over his ears and dropped to the ground atop Dinah just as the sound intensified. Every bone in his body shivered.

The car he'd thought to use for cover . . . *melted.*

He'd never seen its like before. The steel and glass of the car vibrated for a moment, then began to run like molten wax, oozing sluggishly until it formed a liquefied mass of color and glimmering melted glass before them.

"Oh, this is not good," Dig mumbled.

Dark Canary smirked and inhaled deeply. The choker flashed its black light.

Pop!

"Never hit a lady!" Ambush Bug shouted, and decked Dark Canary with a sweet right hook. She spun around on one heel, knocked off-kilter by the force of the blow.

"Never, ever!" Ambush Bug said. "Oh, wait. Oh, darn." He struck a pose, forefinger to his chin, thinking. "I always thought

that was specifically referring to *nobility*, so you couldn't hit, like, Kate Middleton. But maybe it's supposed to mean *all*—"

"Ambush Bug!" Dig couldn't believe he was warning off the lunatic who'd started all this nonsense, but Dark Canary's choker was heating up and her expression as she glared at the Bug was *not* friendly.

Pop! Pop!

Ambush Bug appeared behind Dark Canary and tripped her. Her sonic blast went awry, blowing a hole in the ground before her. Hot tar fountained up into the air.

Dig and Dinah helped each other to their feet, each using the other as a fulcrum to lever up. "You ready, Dig?"

Dig's ribs hurt too much to answer, so he just nodded, and the two of them charged forward while Dark Canary was distracted.

Together they tackled her to the ground. Dig leaned hard on her cheek with an elbow, pressing her to one side so that her sonic scream would be misdirected if she tried to use it. Meanwhile, Dinah slapped a set of S.T.A.R. Labs meta-dampening manacles on her wrists.

The choker light dimmed, then dulled, then went out entirely.

It hurt to draw in a deep breath, but Dig did it anyway. He deserved it.

A few feet away, Ambush Bug applauded. "Well done, brave members of the Fightin' Arrows!"

Dinah rose on shaky feet. She cleared her throat and puckered her lips, ready to scream her Canary Cry. "Don't move."

Ambush Bug chuckled. "Look! Nothing in my hands!" He raised empty hands, palms out.

"Why did you save us?" Dig asked.

"How else were you going to get out of this? You were totally outclassed. I'll be going now."

"Wait!" Dig shouted.

"One twenty-five!" Ambush Bug shouted back and *pop!*'d away, just as Dinah let loose and hit nothing but empty air.

27

BARRY HAD TIME-TRAVELED BEFORE. More than once, and via more than one method. He'd used his own speed, magnified by Kid Flash's speed, and he'd also used the futuristic Cosmic Treadmill. Each time, he'd experienced the thrill of the run, the pound of his feet, the stretch and burn of his sinews as he raced through the time stream.

But this was the first time running with the vibrational frequencies and energetic waveform of ten thousand speedsters at his back. He did not so much run as find himself propelled forward, churning his legs in order to keep his balance and direction stable. It was the difference between swimming in a pool and surfing a tidal wave.

He ran, trying to stay just ahead of the throbbing wave of vibrational energy that the Earth 27 speedsters had generated for him. It buffeted him and pulsated against him from behind, shoving him unrelentingly forward. Nothing could stop him, he knew. With this much power behind him, with such impossible velocity at his disposal, he could run to the End of All Time, tear through the Iron Curtain of Time . . .

At his side, Superman flew at top speed as well, holding the Time Sphere above his head.

"How are you managing to keep up with me?" Barry asked. *For that matter, how am I managing to speak in the time stream?* Some things, he decided, were better off unexplored.

It was a good and valid question, though—other than the occasional speedster, Barry had never encountered anyone who could keep up with him.

"I'm pretty fast myself," Superman said with a grin. "But truthfully, I'm drafting off your speed and using the vibrational wave behind us to push me ahead and pace you."

Barry nodded. As with the time he'd run to the thirtieth century, the time stream appeared to him as a wildly wavering tunnel of rigidly set-off concentric circles in rainbow colors. Also as with that time, he imagined that the numbers of the years whipped by him as he ran: 2058, 2199, 2207 . . .

Faster than before. Everything was faster than before. He had entered into that rarefied aerie of reality where rules no longer applied, where the speed of light was just a good idea, not a law. He'd transcended mere corporality and mortality. He *was* speed.

3010

3581

Wait. Had they already gone through the Iron Curtain of Time? Rond Vidar told them it was in the year 3102.

Maybe this will be easier than we thought . . .

He kept running.

4983

5879

Millennia crushed beneath his feet. Every stride a thousand years or more. Sweat beaded under his cowl, dripped down into his eyes, wicked away into the heat-chill of the time stream, where friction burned but had no time to scald. To Barry's horror, he stumbled, his right foot coming down at an odd angle. For a nanosecond, he thought the universe blurred into place around him and he caught a glimpse of the Spires of the sixty-fourth century.

"You can do it, Flash," Superman encouraged alongside him. "Kara told me you're the bravest man she ever met. She believes in you, and so do I."

Reinvigorated, Barry slapped one foot down after another. They were well into the 9000s now, then the ten-thousandth century. The techno-magical era of Abra Kadabra was long behind them.

One hundred centuries down. Hundreds of millions to go.

He kept running.

28

SO, IN OTHER WORDS, THE TV BARRY Allen screwed up, messed with history, then *re*-messed with history, and we're the ones who get punished for it? Not cool."

Cisco was tired of hearing himself say it over and over again. He had managed to press forward a little bit before—though he didn't know what *before* really meant when he kept reliving the same seconds. He had to try again.

This time, he tried reaching out differently. Not forward toward the Trapper, but to the side, for his own TV doppelgänger. The Time Trapper had said that TV Cisco had regained his powers. Maybe there was a way . . .

And then he saw it.

He saw the Crisis.

At the same time he was struggling through his own Crisis, the TV Multiverse was suffering its own. But the TV crew's

Crisis had led them the other way, chasing a villain to the Dawn of Time, not the End.

"Ah, you see it, do you?" the Time Trapper interrupted. *"They have re-created their Multiverse from the beginning. They've merged universes that once were separate. This has destabilized their time-line, though they do not realize it. Making it ripe for the taking."*

Wait, what? Cisco's mind spun. This wasn't even about the Multiverse he called home? The Time Trapper was trying to take over the *TV* Multiverse all along?

"And now, back to your torment . . ."

"So, in other words," Cisco said, "the TV Barry Allen . . ."

29

MR. TERRIFIC BLEW OUT A RELIEVED breath that he'd been holding in. According to all the data on the screen before him, everything had worked to perfection. The treadmill had done exactly what it was supposed to do, and the strike team had absorbed and channeled the energy. The Earth 27 speedsters were already headed back to their temporary refugee digs, their jobs done.

Now he just had to wait.

He mentally fist-bumped himself in congratulations, then turned to Owlman, who'd walked over from his own control pad. "Nice work. We're done!"

Owlman craned his neck from side to side. "Well, you're done," he told Mr. Terrific, and then casually punched Curtis into unconsciousness with a single precision blow to the jaw.

He cracked his knuckles and began tapping at the control pad.

30

JOE AND RENE BOTH REACHED FOR their guns in the same moment, a reflex born of necessity and honed over years of training and time on the streets.

Before they could even take aim, Larvan gestured and his bees shot forth, covering the distance between him and the two cops in a hot second. Joe's wrist burned at multiple stings, and he couldn't keep his fingers closed—his gun clattered to the floor, as did Rene's.

"Bert!" Joe cried. "Think this through! A couple of beestings aren't gonna stop us. I'm about two seconds away from picking up my gun—"

"Ever been stung on the eye, Detective?" Larvan's lips jerked into a twisted smile. "Oh, you'll recover. Eventually. After a week or so of blindness."

Joe had been halfway into a crouch, reaching for his gun. Two of the bees hovered just a few inches from his face. Waiting.

Patient. It was wholly unnerving to see them like this. He was used to bees fleeing if he moved too fast, but these were quite willing to outwait him.

"Uh, Joe?" Rene's voice had risen to a note of panic Joe had never heard before. "Is this when I'm supposed to mention that I'm allergic to beestings?"

Joe groaned. Off to his side, Rene was staring at his own wrist, which had swollen like a baseball.

"Let me get medical attention for him, Bert! For God's sake!" He didn't know *how* allergic Rene was. A massive anaphylactic reaction could occur at any minute and close off Wild Dog's breathing passage. Or he could be fine for hours.

"Did you really think I would help you with nothing to gain for myself or for Brie?" Larvan sneered. "I only inveigled my way into your clique so that I could gain access to Ambush Bug's bees for my own purposes."

"To get revenge on the world for what it did to your precious sister, right?" Joe sighed wearily. "I've seen this movie before, Bert."

Joe figured he might be able to bat away one of the bees before the other one stung his eye. Could he recover the gun, aim one-eyed, and fire before another bee could get to his good eye?

Yeah. Yeah, he thought he could.

The idea of being stung in the eyeball did *not* fill him with joy, but he couldn't see another way out of the predicament. He figured he'd let his left eye get stung—he fired his gun right-handed and would need to sight down the barrel with his right eye.

I can't believe these are the kinds of things I have to think about. Man, I'm actually starting to miss the days when Gorilla Grodd would kidnap me for a while.

"Think carefully, Detective." Larvan gestured and the bees quickly crossed paths, switching eyes. "I am in complete control of the situation. Your life and the life of Wild Dog are in my hands."

Yeah, definitely feeling nostalgic for ol' Banana-breath. At least he didn't try to monologue me to death.

Without so much as a word, Joe slapped out with one hand, knocking a bee aside, sending it spiraling off against a wall. At the same time, he lunged for the gun, squeezing both eyes shut, hoping that the thin flesh of his eyelids would provide some protection from the sting.

The sting never came.

He felt the cold steel of the pistol's handle, closed his fingers around it. Momentum carried him bodily to the floor and he rolled once, thinking, *This used to be easier*, knowing that he'd need a day in a hot tub and a ton of ice packs for his back to feel normal again. He popped open his eyes, somewhat amazed that both of them still functioned, took aim—

Bert Larvan was already on the floor, struggling with Dig, who had a headlock on the putative Bug-Eyed Bandit II.

"His ear!" Joe yelled. "In his ear!"

The bees buzzed around them, zeroing in on Dig. Spartan's body armor would protect most of him, but Larvan could still direct them up under his helmet and to his eyes or ears. They had to remove the control bud from Larvan's ear.

But they had a weapon that Larvan couldn't take away.

Dinah opened her mouth to let loose with her Canary Cry—but at that very instant, a bee darted between her lips. Dinah's eyes bulged out in shock and pain as the bee zipped out of her mouth.

"I ung!" she cried in pain, clapping her hands to her mouth. "I ung!" *My tongue! My tongue!* The bee had stung her tongue, and right now the thought of using her power was furthest from her mind. Her mouth and throat clogged as the bee's apitoxin swelled her tongue to three times its normal size.

Dig had Larvan pinned down, but the bees were getting closer, now buzzing around his head, looking for a way under the face shield as Dig jerked his head back and forth, evading them.

Joe scrabbled along the floor on all fours, releasing the gun. His knees protested with blunt, hard claps of pain down each leg, but he forced himself along until he was a body length from Larvan. Then he launched himself at the Bug-Eyed Bandit, landing with a painful thud, the air propelled from him as his belly hit the floor.

Still, he was close enough to reach out and grab Larvan by the ear, which he did, twisting it until Larvan cried out in pain. The little bud lay nestled in the ear canal. Joe's fingers were too thick and too clumsy to reach in there, so he kept twisting and pulling at Larvan's ear. He suddenly remembered a time when Barry—age ten, maybe—had come down with a terrible ear infection. Joe had had to put drops in Barry's ear and then tug at Barry's earlobe to get the medicine to travel down into the ear canal properly. Barry hated the sensation and fought him every time.

Absurdly, it felt the same now, tugging and twisting at Larvan's ear. The major difference was that he didn't really care how Larvan felt about it. He would rip the ear right off Larvan's head, if that's what it took.

Finally, the earbud fell out. Joe croaked out a bark of triumph, and Dig slapped away the last bee, now rudderless and buzzing randomly through the air. Together, he and Joe wrestled Larvan into submission and slapped cuffs on him.

Wild Dog, meanwhile, had managed to scrabble over to one of the workbenches, where he grabbed his messenger bag and dragged it down onto the floor. Gasping for breath, he rummaged inside, produced an EpiPen, and jabbed it into his thigh. A moment later, he inhaled a huge gulp of air, then shot Joe a thumbs-up.

"Man, we can't leave you guys alone for five minutes, can we?" Dig asked.

Joe rose from the floor, dusting himself off, then helped Dinah to her feet. "Thanks for the concern, Dig. How do you feel?" he asked Dinah.

She shrugged and pointed to her throat. She could still breathe, but talking was going to be difficult for a while.

Just then, Joe noticed another presence in the room. Handcuffed to Oliver's salmon ladder was a woman who looked suspiciously like Dinah, with meta-dampening manacles clamped on her wrists.

He sighed. "Care to introduce us to your friend?"

Dig gestured vaguely at the woman. "Meet the so-called Dark Canary. Claims to be the Seamstress of—"

"The Screamstress!" Dark Canary interjected with truly aggrieved pique.

"Right. That. Of the Royal Northwest Collective," Dig finished wearily. "It's an Earth 32 thing, apparently."

"This is not good," Joe said. He gestured to the main monitor. On the screen, the swarm was bigger than ever. Time was running out. "We have to make something happen. Fast. And we just lost our expert."

With a diffident grunt, Joe turned back to the screen. Ambush Bug's swarm would soon hit a critical mass, and the bees would descend.

"We need to put out an alert. Can A.R.G.U.S. get us access to the Emergency Broadcast Signal?"

Dig nodded slowly. "What are you thinking?"

Worrying at his lower lip, Joe took the question very seriously. What *was* he thinking? He would get exactly one shot at this. "I'm talking every TV, cell phone, and computer in Star City lighting up, telling people to get indoors, preferably somewhere without windows or outside access. Seal up cracks. People with bee allergies need to have their EpiPens and meds at hand."

"Won't that cause a panic, hoss?" Now that he was juiced up with epinephrine, Rene bounced on his toes, ready for action, as though he'd never been stung.

"Probably," Joe conceded. "But so will that swarm descending on the city. This way we reduce the number of targets for the bees."

"That's not sustainable in the long term," Dig pointed out.

"No, but it buys us some time. And right now, time is the most precious resource we can hoard."

He looked around the Bunker. Rene nodded. Dig did, too. Dinah shrugged and mimed something that seemed to mean, *OK by me*.

"I am the Screamstress Dinah of the Royal Northwest Collective!" Dark Canary howled, utterly unbidden. "First of her name, and Dark Canary, Warbler of Horrors, Wielder of the ScreamSong!"

No one spoke for a moment. Shackled on the floor, Bert Larvan giggled into the silence.

"We've heard from the peanut gallery," Dig said. "I think the ayes have it. I'll call Lyla and get going on that message."

31

THE TIME TRAPPER SENSED THE press of tachyons and neutrinos as a phalanx of time travelers neared his realm. The Flash and his compatriots. They smashed through the time stream with all the finesse of a cannonball through a waterfall.

They were coming for him. From the deepest past, his enemies forded the time stream, breaching the Iron Curtain of Time with their makeshift vibrational bludgeon. Brute force arrayed against the Time Trapper's elegant plan and contingencies.

And now he experienced another emotion for the first time. This one was . . . joy.

Soon it would all come to fruition. The Multiverse would end, as it was fated to do, and the Time Trapper's plans would culminate in, at last, victory.

And then . . .

And then the Time Trapper would rule the remainder of the Megaverse.

Yes, joy!

Cisco Ramon was his. The final piece of the infinite puzzle.

First had been a speedster's energies, to power the machinery that released Anti-Matter Man. Which led to the weakening of the vibrational barriers between universes, in order to swap matter and energy from one dimension to another.

Then, Cisco Ramon's power to see into the other half of the Megaverse.

Soon.

For a being as powerful as the Time Trapper, his limitations chafed. He could reach through history but not travel there himself. He could summon beings from the long-ago past but not visit them in their own eras. As much as he trapped those who dared rise up against him, he, too, was trapped. Trapped at the End of All Time. Ensnared in the never-ending moment of the finality of all reality. Locked out of the universes, he now trapped them in turn. All to meet his final goal.

Without so much as a flinch, the Time Trapper made a careful adjustment to his machinery. All around him, the dead stars hummed their last radio waves into the void. Scattered hydrogen atoms converged. Everything was coming to an end.

But for the Time Trapper, the end would be the beginning.

32

SUPERMAN," BARRY SAID, AND CAME to realize that his words, his voice, somehow slipped between moments. He looked over to his left. The Man of Steel still flew beside him, still held the Time Sphere in his hands. His expression was one of intense concentration, grim determination.

Did you feel that? he wanted to ask Superman. There'd been some sort of . . . jostle. A judder. The kaleidoscopic tunnel of the time stream around them had shaken, almost imperceptibly.

"My super-vision caught a glimpse of something outside the time stream," Superman said, as though he'd plucked the question from Barry's mind. "We just passed the year 200,650. There was some kind of quantum event . . . I couldn't really make it out."

And then in the next instant he said, "I don't think so." Perfectly conversationally.

The really weird thing, though, was that Barry had been about to ask: *Do you think it had something to do with us?* And Superman had answered as though—

In the next instant, Barry was shocked to hear himself say out loud, "Do you think it had something to do with us?"

He was asking questions after getting the answers. Causality had been flip-flopped, spun around on its axis, tossed in a blender. Effect no longer necessarily followed cause. They'd been in the time stream so long that time itself was losing its grip on them.

"I think the Time Trapper moved it farther into the future!" Superman shouted suddenly.

"Did we already go through the Iron Curtain of Time?" Barry asked. "Is it really this easy?"

Answered before asked.

"Yeah, it's disorienting," Barry told him.

"I think I see the Iron Curtain somewhere around the year two million. Is this . . . is this causality spiral giving you a headache?"

Barry tried to ignore the temporal discrepancies. He just kept running.

The Iron Curtain of Time loomed before them. Causality was beginning to take shape again as the "quantum event" from the year 200,650 faded into deep history. They were more than two million years in the future now, and the barrier athwart the time stream did, indeed, seem like a curtain—a grayish, rippling wall that stretched to infinity in every direction.

"This is it!" Superman yelled.

Yeah, with only billions more years to go once we get through it, Barry thought.

Still, getting through the Iron Curtain was the important part, he knew. The rest of it was just, well . . . running.

The Curtain loomed before them. Barry's heart froze and his blood turned to ice at the sight of it, so infinitely massive, so powerful and adamantine. The *Waverider* couldn't get through this thing—could he?

At his back, the vibrational pattern initially generated by ten thousand speedsters urged him forward. All that power, following them from the distant past into the far-flung future.

Yes. Yes, he could do it. More, he *would* do it.

Now.

Barry slowed ever so slightly, allowing himself to drop back into the tidal swell of the Earth 27 speedsters. The wavefront of the vibrational pattern relaxed against him for a moment, then rebounded, impelling him forward at even greater speed. It occurred to him suddenly that James Jesse and the rest of the Earth 27 refugees had been dead for thousands of millennia, but their hope and goodwill still extended into the future, propelling him onward.

The Iron Curtain of Time rose before him. Barry sprinted ahead, not slowing for an instant as the Curtain loomed higher and higher, larger and larger.

If they'd miscalculated, he knew, he would be destroyed beyond even death, his body shredded at the subatomic level and scattered throughout Time.

"I'm going through!" Barry shouted to Superman. "Hang back half a second so you can pull up if it doesn't work!"

"Not a chance!" Superman yelled back. "We go through together. Our chances are better if we all hit at once."

Barry wanted to argue the point, but there was no time left in which to do so. At a speed that was incalculable and undefinable even for the Flash, they hit the Iron Curtain of Time.

Barry had assumed that the Iron Curtain of Time would slow them down, the same way that the simple friction of a paper screen would slow down someone jumping through it, albeit minutely.

But he'd been reckoning based on the physics of the real world, where friction mattered. Here in the time stream, friction didn't exist—it was a construct of three dimensions, not four.

Bursting through the Iron Curtain of Time, he found himself moving *faster*, not slower. Beside him, Superman's face lit up with pleasant surprise. They bridged dozens of millennia with every step forward, their momentum increasing their velocity until millions of years blurred by with each eyeblink.

Superman's expression of joy suddenly sobered. "There's nothing, Flash," Superman said, his voice strangled with awe. "I'm using my powers to perceive the physical world outside the time stream . . . We've gone so far into the future that the stars are dying. Worlds are frozen, tumbling through a darkening void . . ."

Barry nodded grimly. He had known, deep down, that traveling to the end of the universe meant going to a time when everyone and everything were dead. *Had been* dead for a long, long time. Iris—his heart clenched like a desperate, angry fist—had been dead for billions of years; by now, all that was left of her was random carbon atoms fusing to iron in the depths of the swollen sun, its convective zone having expanded to where the planet Earth had once been.

But I can go back. We can get Cisco and defeat Thawne and win the day and go back.

That thought and that thought alone propelled him farther, faster.

"I see something," Superman said. "I see the end! There's nothing beyond!"

Barry slowed his body's vibrations, matching them to the surrounding physical universe. In a matter of instants, the rushing bands of rainbows around him subsided, dimming, then going translucent, then finally vanishing altogether.

He stood on a rocky outcropping that drifted in a black void. There should have been stars overhead, but there were none, merely spots that seemed a little less black than the surrounding emptiness. Asteroids of various shapes and sizes floated nearby in the abyss, suspended like eroding ornaments on a dead Christmas tree.

Barry stretched out his arms and felt a slight tug, like a tight-fitting jacket. The Legion of Super-Heroes had provided the team with a technology called a "transsuit," which was a "polymeric transparent body encasement." It worked similarly to the ring in which Barry stored his Flash costume—when exposed to a harsh environment, a tiny capsule sewn into the user's clothing expanded into a nearly invisible sheath of special polymers that surrounded the entire body. It filtered oxygen from the surrounding environment, and in a vacuum it could even break down the wearer's exhaled carbon dioxide, ejecting the carbon into space and recirculating the oxygen. They all had them, even Superman, who didn't need one but could use its tech to communicate in a spatial vacuum. The transsuit was invisible and almost undetectable, save for the slight pull when he moved his limbs to their extreme limits.

"What *is* this place?" Ray asked in a hushed voice. The Atom, White Canary, Heat Wave, and Green Arrow had emerged from the Time Sphere and stood nearby on the dead soil.

"The end of everything," Superman replied in a reverent tone. "This is the last outpost of reality, the final moments of existence before the entire Multiverse . . . dies."

"Everything looks almost . . . bluish," Sara said, her voice hesitant, as though embarrassed to bring it up.

Barry and Ray exchanged a glance, sharing a moment of science-think. "Blueshift," Barry said in something like awe. "Never thought I'd see it."

The universe—the uni*verses*, really—had been created in a single moment billions of years ago called the Big Bang. Basically, all matter in the universe had been condensed into a space the size of a single atom. At some point, the pressure of all the mass built up and the atom exploded—it made a Big Bang, hence the term—and spewed matter out into the void, creating the universe.

As a result, everything in the universe was always moving away from everything else. This led to something called redshift—the faster and farther one object accelerated away from another, the closer to the red part of the electromagnetic spectrum it would appear to an observer. Since *everything* in the universe was propelled by the force of the Big Bang and moving away from everything else, that meant everything was redshifted.

No longer. They were now experiencing blueshift. Which meant that the universe was collapsing, not expanding.

"Cosmologists were wrong," Superman muttered. "It's closed, not flat."

Barry immediately understood. Cosmologists had basically agreed that the universe was *flat*. By which they didn't mean it was two-dimensional. The term *flat* simply meant that the force of the Big Bang, the amount of dark energy in the universe, and the density parameter combined to craft a universe that would continue expanding into infinity.

But the Multiverse was the agglomeration of all universes. Perhaps that combination of separate physical models yielded not something flat but rather what cosmologists referred to as a *closed universe*, where gravity takes hold and everything contracts into a Big Crunch. All matter would blueshift as it drew toward each other, eventually compressing into the space of a single atom again.

Barry understood now: By opening breaches and shunting matter between universes, the Time Trapper had artificially manipulated the amount of matter and energy in each universe.

Changing the universal densities and causing fifty-four Big Crunches, leading to this, the End of All Time. The Biggest Crunch of all.

And then there would be nothing left. Forever.

"I think this is why we're here," Superman said, pointing.

They all followed his gesture. A spindly rock floated some distance away, but even those without telescopic vision could make out a steely structure of some sort erected on its surface. And standing there was a large figure swaddled in a purple cloak. Yellow and blue light flickered and flashed there. Two other asteroids drifted nearby, each of them with a metallic structure that—even at this distance—seemed corroded. Everything here was corroded, Barry realized. Everything was as old as anything in the universe could possibly be. The ground was dead. The sky was dead.

"That's our enemy," he said. "That's the Time Trapper."

33

BREACH!" CAITLIN YELLED. "BREACH!"

Sure enough, a blue vortex spiraled into existence in the center of the Cortex. No one should have been breaching into S.T.A.R. Labs. Iris immediately snatched up a phase rifle that she kept in a bracket under her workstation console, aiming it at the cloudy blue mass. Meanwhile, Caitlin and Felicity dived for cover behind some chairs.

Iris blew out a controlled breath, then sighted down the barrel of the rifle as a silhouette formed at the center of the breach. It took a step forward.

"Don't shoot! I come in peace!"

"Kara!" Iris threw down the rifle, not wanting to think how close she'd come to zapping her friend with whatever a *phase-centric photonic array* was.

Supergirl hunched up her shoulders, wrinkling her nose in embarrassment. "Sorry. Didn't mean to spook you guys."

Felicity and Caitlin came out of hiding as Iris threw her arms around Supergirl. "I am *so* glad to see you, Kara! We could totally use a Kryptonian right now."

After returning the hug, Supergirl held Iris out at arm's length, her expression one of disappointment. "I don't know how to tell you this, but my powers still aren't back. I came here because Brainy and Lena have things under control back on Earth 38, and I thought you guys might be able to use an extra pair of hands. Even if they aren't superpowered."

"We can *always* use your help, Kara," Caitlin assured her.

"Even if that extra pair of hands can't, you know . . ." Felicity mimed bending something with both hands.

"Powers or not, we're grateful you're here," Iris said. "It's good to see you up and about. Why don't you settle in at Cisco's old station and take a look at—"

Iris glanced at the computer screen, then did a double take and looked again.

"Hey!" she called out. "Why is there a second pulse coming from the speedster treadmill?"

Supergirl grinned nervously. "I don't even understand the question, honestly."

Felicity craned her neck to peer at the screen. "What are you even talking about?"

"Look at the telemetry from the treadmill," Iris insisted, pointing. "It's all wonky."

Felicity snorted derisively. "*Wonky*. I love when you try to be all technical and precise and . . . Hey!" she exclaimed as she skimmed the readout. "That *is* wonky!"

"See?"

Grinding her teeth, Felicity tapped some keys. "It looks like the speedster treadmill has been modified."

"How would that happen?"

"Dunno." Felicity shrugged. "It's wonky."

Iris growled with impatience. "Well, let's figure it out, because anything that messes with the treadmill can't be good news."

The main screen bleeped for attention. Mr. Terrific's image fuzzed into place. He held an ice pack to the back of his head. "Gang, we have a problem, and its name is Owlman."

34

IN THE BUNKER, JOE WATCHED THE FEED from multiple security cameras. The chaos in the streets of Star City in the wake of the A.R.G.U.S. broadcast was not as bad as he'd feared. Yes, people were afraid, even panicking, but several days of Ambush Bug's madness had prepared them for more craziness. In general, people took the warning seriously and the streets emptied quickly, save for a few teenagers and twenty-somethings who just *had* to stick around and shoot selfies and videos.

"Idiots are gonna die trying to one-up each other's Instagram Stories," Joe muttered.

"Nah, they're probably doing it for TikTok," Rene advised. "That's what all the teenagers are on now."

"I'm glad we settled that," Joe said. On the monitor, the swarm was shifting. It was going to happen any moment now. He could feel it in his bones.

"Any last ideas?" he asked the room. "No matter how crazy? Bert? Your last chance to be a hero."

Larvan snorted and pointedly gazed at the floor between his feet.

"That collar thing she wears seems to let her focus her sonic screams for different effects," Dig mused, pointing at Dark Canary. "What if we took it off her and let Dinah use it?"

Dinah *hmpf*ed and made a show of sticking out her tongue. It was grotesquely bulging and dark red.

"Right. Forgot. Sorry." Dig flashed her a smile, then turned and tossed a grossed-out expression at Joe.

On the screen, the swarm bunched . . . massed . . .

And then dived from the air.

It was beginning.

"Buh . . . Flash isn't back from the future yet," Supergirl said, just barely catching herself before blowing Barry's secret identity. On the screen before her, she saw not only Joe West, Dinah, Diggle, and Rene, but also a handcuffed Bert Larvan and a woman who looked like Dinah's cosplaying cyberpunk twin sister. Kara had questions, but Joe's frantic expression obviated them. Code names were the order of the day, and speed was of the essence, especially with Owlman in the wind again.

They had caught her up quickly on what was going on, from the group of heroes headed to the far future to the fracas in Star City. Supergirl ached to fly over to help out, but thus far her powers had only begun to creep back in. Her hearing seemed a little sharper, and she thought when she walked that there was a little extra bounce that *might* be flight coming back. But she was too darn mortal to do much right now.

"The swarm's hitting *now*," Joe told her. "The A.R.G.U.S. satellite estimates over two hundred thousand bees, and there are still people in the streets. Plus, Ambush Bug is teleporting all over the city and causing havoc. We gotta have Flash here—he's fast enough to grab all the bees and stop this. It's the only way."

"Joe, I don't know what to tell you. Flash and Superman and the others ran off to the End of All Time and haven't come back. We don't even know if they'll come back at all, to be honest."

"I've got an entire city about to look like something from a fifties horror movie!" There was real panic in Joe's voice. "We're holding the line, but we need help and we need it now, Kara, or you're looking at a major American city going the way of the dodo!"

She could never be certain what, in that moment, sparked the idea for her. But a notion suddenly smacked into Supergirl's awareness with such force that she actually rocked back a bit in her chair, as though physically struck.

"Joe, hold on." She put his feed on pause and hit the button that connected her to Curtis. Mr. Terrific was still out by the treadmill.

"Curtis! I have a crazy idea!"

"You've come to the right place!" Curtis said cheerfully.

35

SARA SWALLOWED HARD. BARRY'S pronouncement—*That's our enemy. That's the Time Trapper*—echoed deep within her. She took in a deep breath, aware how precious air was and that a tear in the synthetic, invisible transsuit would mean her death.

Oliver sidled up to her. "A long way for two party kids from Starling City, eh?"

His nonchalance buoyed her spirits. Good old Oliver. So deadly serious and so committed, but also so ready to puncture the moment right when it desperately needed puncturing.

"I think I imagined something like this one night when I was drunk on that terrible absinthe you brought back from England," she said casually. "But at least I just woke up with a miserable hangover."

"No waking up from this." It was Mick, standing at her side. His face and bald dome were awash in sweat. He'd brought the ring to heel, but it was taking a toll on him.

A part of her thought, *Is this even worth it?* They were billions—*billions!*—of years in the future. So far from home that the very word *home* had lost all meaning in the distant past. Anti-Matter Man had been defeated on Earth 38. Couldn't they just . . . go back to the present? Snuggle up with their loved ones? By the time this current moment came to pass, they'd all be long, long dead.

But she knew that wasn't an option. The Time Trapper existed at the End of All Time, but his threat stretched back through history and across the Multiverse. They had to beard this particular lion in his den and end his threat. For good.

"I'm starting to feel a little outclassed," Sara admitted. She hefted the golden length of rope she'd been given. "Even with this ace up my sleeve."

Oliver chuckled knowingly and gestured to the Time Trapper, looming in the distance. "You know what? We've faced some seriously Big Bads in our time, and we're still standing."

Sara nodded. It was true. And beyond being a superhero and a trained assassin, she was also the captain of a timeship. It was time to take charge.

"Let's stop staring and get planning," she barked. Everyone startled and turned to her. "We're not gonna kick that guy's butt by glaring at him. We need a strategy."

"And recon," Oliver put in. He pointed out into the void. "I see three separate targets, the only sites visible with any sort of construction."

The spindly rock where the Time Trapper stood they called *Needle* because of its taper. The other two they called *Globe* and *Egg*—one was round, the other oval.

"We need more than names," Sara said. "We need intel."

"Easy enough," Superman said, and glanced in the direction of the Time Trapper. "Wait . . . Wait, something . . ."

"Everything all right?" the Flash asked.

"Something . . ." Superman twisted his head this way and that. "Something's wrong. My super-vision isn't working the way it should."

Barry nodded. "Here, at the end of the universe, physics itself is breaking down. Distance has no meaning. Light doesn't work the way it used to. Your sensory powers—"

"—are useless," Oliver finished.

"Not quite," Superman said. "My vision is still working, just not the way I'm used to. I can still see . . ."

He squinted, peering ahead.

"OK. On Needle, the Time Trapper himself is adjusting some machinery in front of him. But on Globe, I see a massive metallic sphere."

Sara located the rock Superman had mentioned. The sphere he described looked tiny, which told her that it was quite a distance away.

And wait . . . If that one is closer to us, but we can still see the Time Trapper on the outcropping farther away . . .

Oh man. He must be huge.

She didn't want to think about it. Shoved it out of her mind. *The bigger they are, the harder they fall* might be true, might not. No time to worry about it, though.

The sphere Superman had mentioned. That was her focus now.

"That sphere seems to . . ." He paused, thinking. "I don't

know how to describe it. It gives me the same feeling I get when I look at you, Flash. When I perceive the Speed Force energies coursing through your body."

"That's where Thawne is, then," Oliver said confidently.

"The only other object of interest," said Superman, clearly struggling to gaze far overhead, "is on the underside of Egg." He pointed. "It's a smallish boxlike structure, big enough for a person."

"Cisco," Flash said. "It's got to be. If Thawne is on the one asteroid, Cisco must be locked up on the other."

"Now what?" Ray asked.

Oliver glanced over at Sara. He'd always thought of himself as the strategist, but in the years since she'd become captain of the Legends, she'd grown as a tactician and commander. He had his own thoughts about how to proceed, but he didn't want to step on her toes. She had transformed herself into a capable leader and deserved her shot without him running roughshod over her.

"What have you got, Oliver?" she asked, assuaging his fears.

"We don't know what we don't know," he began. "According to the Legion of Super-Heroes, the Time Trapper's been up to something for a while. We have to imagine that he's ready for a lot of eventualities, that he's planned for everything. At the same time, we know he reached back through time and released Anti-Matter Man, then guided Anti-Matter Man from the anti-verse to Earth 27, then Earth 1, then Earth 38. He's not just a planner—he's got major power, too."

"But some of that power comes from Thawne," Barry pointed out.

"Exactly," Oliver agreed. "That's where I was headed. His power isn't infinite. He needs to supplement it. So if we can disrupt it . . ."

"You mean like yank the batteries out?" Mick said.

Oliver shrugged. "Sure, think of it that way. He has Thawne for a reason. He has Cisco for a reason. I say we split up into two teams. Go to Globe and take down Thawne. Liberate Cisco from Egg. Cut off at least some of the Trapper's power so that he's a little more vulnerable."

"Has anyone thought maybe we just go beat the stuffing outta this guy?" Mick asked. As he said it, a large, glowing green boxing glove appeared from his ring. "Like, just hit him until he goes down and then kick him until he stops moving. That's how we did it back in the old neighborhood, and lemme tell you something—it worked on the big guys as well as the little guys."

"Something tells me a frontal assault isn't going to do the trick," Oliver said.

"We're talking about an entity that can erect a barrier in the flow of time itself," Superman said.

"Which is theoretically impossible," Ray added with disturbing good cheer. "We're gonna have to invent a whole new branch of physics to make sense of this. Um, assuming we survive, that is."

"We need two strike teams, then," Sara said. "Thawne is a danger to us. We don't know if he's helping the Time Trapper voluntarily or not, but we have to assume he won't be happy to see us."

"So we send the heavy hitters after Thawne." Oliver skimmed the group. "Superman. Mick, since you've got that ring. And Barry. Sound good?"

Superman nodded in agreement. Mick shrugged. Barry . . .

Barry seemed distracted, gazing off into the empty middle distance. "Barry?" Oliver waved a hand before Barry's face. "Flash? You want to join us?"

The Fastest Man Alive jerked as though tased. "What? Yeah, sorry. I just . . . I felt something. It distracted me."

"Felt something?"

Barry shook his head. "It's nothing. Let's do this."

Holding the Flash in his arms, Superman glided through the vacuum that stretched between the outcropping where they'd arrived and Globe, where Eobard Thawne ran. Barry didn't really like being shuttled over there in the Man of Steel's grasp, like a babe in arms, but he didn't have much of a choice. Mick could fly under his own power, apparently, and had even offered to whip up a glowing green platform for Barry to stand on, but Barry still didn't entirely trust the ring.

He trusted Mick. Mostly. Just not the ring.

Mick wobbled, pitched, and yawed as he got the hang of channeling his willpower through the ring in order to fly. Barry watched him with mild envy and daydreamed briefly about the time he'd had with Brainiac 5's borrowed Legion flight ring. Yes, it had been during a terrifying time of near apocalypse for

Earth 38, but on the other hand . . . he'd been *flying*! It had been amazing. Superspeed was an incredible superpower, but flight was the dream power, the one every person living coveted.

And Heat Wave didn't look like he was enjoying it at all. Whereas Superman gracefully alighted on Globe—hardly disturbing the gritty surface—Mick collided with the ground, clouds of dust billowing up. His knees buckled to absorb the impact, but his center of gravity was too high and he stumbled forward, fell down, and skidded about ten feet on his chest before coming to a stop.

"Graceful," Barry commented.

"Not another word, Twinkle Toes," Mick grumbled as he stood. Between the transsuit and the energy field projected by the ring, he was not only unhurt but also nearly spotless.

"Landings are tricky." Superman patted Mick on the back and flicked away a speck of dirt from Heat Wave's shoulder. "You'll get used to it. First time I flew, I crash-landed behind the barn and darn near took out the wheat thresher. I think I was more worried about Pa's reaction to the crater in the back forty than I was excited that I could fly."

Mick stared in disbelief. "What kind of Day-Glo Norman Rockwell painting did you come from?"

"Guys, I hate to put a damper on all this wonderful male bonding, but . . ." Barry gestured to the sphere, only a couple of dozen yards away from them.

This close, the thing was enormous, easily a hundred meters in diameter. The surface shone here and there with a metallic sheen that glimmered dully in the dying light of the distant, dim stars, but most of it was coated in haphazard overlapping layers of grime and rust. It vibrated subtly, shaking the grains of sand and dirt around them.

"You're tellin' me the Reverse-Flash is in there, just running around in circles?"

"Let's find out for sure," Superman suggested, peering ahead at the sphere. A moment passed and then he frowned. "Nothing. My X-ray vision isn't quite . . . working."

Barry stepped forward. "We don't need to see through it. I can *feel* the speedster frequencies radiating from that thing. Perturbations in the Speed Force. Hyper-accelerated wave-particles. Thawne's in there."

"Uh, Volthoom has something to say." Mick pointed his fist at the sphere, and suddenly a wavering, shimmery green beam of light appeared at the top of it before trembling off into space, headed for the chunk of rock on which stood the Time Trapper. "According to the ring, there are . . . Hang on . . . Say that again?" He grimaced. "No, I ain't making any deals with you. Say it again, you piece of junk jewelry. OK, Volthoom says *rapidly accelerated, hypercharged ionic energy is being beamed off-site.* I guess that's the green line he made there."

Deliberately not asking why or how Mick had decided the ring was a *he*, Barry mused, "So, Thawne produces the energy, and the Time Trapper sucks it all up and uses it to do things like reach back through the Iron Curtain and set Anti-Matter Man free."

"How does he only need one speedster to go through the Curtain, but we needed ten thousand?" Mick asked, his tone annoyed.

Superman shrugged. "Simple: The Time Trapper is so powerful that he just needs the boost of *one* speedster."

Barry shivered. He didn't like the sound of that. "This is probably how he's maintaining the breaches between universes back in our time."

"We can ask once we've cut off his power supply."

With that, the Man of Steel flew forward toward the sphere, leading with his fists. Barry ran after him, his steps gigantic and wobbly in the low gravity of the planetoid. Mick cruised alongside him, already gaining confidence in his flight abilities.

Superman had a head start—he reached the sphere first and slammed into it full tilt with both fists. The sphere shook and rocked backward as Superman ricocheted off it, pinwheeling through space for a moment before regaining his equilibrium and steadying himself in a standing position above the surface. A massive dent formed where he'd struck the sphere as sheets of dirt and rust flaked away, cascaded off the thing's skin, and wafted slowly to the ground.

"That blow should have ripped the thing open," Superman commented. He seemed to be breathing heavily. "I don't get it. What's it made out of?"

"How 'bout we try this?" Mick produced a gigantic green, glowing can opener with the power ring. It hovered in the air before them, both ominous and hilarious.

"Maybe something a little less . . . savage?"

With a shrug, Mick conjured an enormous chain saw, complete with buzzing noise and the *putt-putt* sound of a gasoline engine. "Better?"

"Might as well try," Superman said. "Flash?"

Barry said nothing. There was something very wrong here. He couldn't tell what, exactly, but . . .

"There's still Speed Force energy coming off that thing, but . . . I feel something else, too. Do you guys feel anything? Like . . . like something right behind you? Like static electricity in your hair?"

Superman shook his head, puzzled. Heat Wave shrugged. Barry took a moment to peer around the rock on which they stood. The surface wasn't much larger than a couple of football fields. In the distance—perhaps a mile or two away—hung the icy ball of rock on which the Time Trapper stood, manipulating his odd alien machinery.

"OK," he decided, "maybe I just have the heebie-jeebies. Mick, go ahead and try . . . I don't know. Something. Use your imagination."

Mick's eyes lit up, and suddenly there appeared before them a massive, glowing green acetylene torch, spurting a focused swath of verdant flame. "Oh baby, yeah!" Mick chanted, licking his lips. "Bringing the fire!"

"Still think it was a good idea, giving him the ring?" Barry whispered to Superman.

Superman wrinkled his nose. "Let's just say I'm rethinking some recent decisions."

With a wild yawp, Mick soared into the air and aimed his blowtorch at the sphere. The green flame lengthened and tightened, becoming a hot, focused cutting beam. Sparks sizzled into the non-air as the fire touched the outside of the sphere. If there'd been an atmosphere to carry sound, Barry would have expected to hear the sizzle of melting metal, the roar of flames, the hiss of molten steel as it cooled. But since they were in a near vacuum, he heard nothing but Mick Rory's rapturous cackle as he wielded the blowtorch with the verve of a true pyromaniac.

"Burn, baby, burn!" Mick howled. "C'mon! Hotter! We'll never run out of gas, so keep it up!"

"He *is* doing this for the greater good," Superman commented.

"I'm just wondering how we get him to stop." Barry put his fists on his hips. Mick had sorta-kinda reformed since his thieving days, and according to White Canary, he'd taken to the cause of helping others with at least a grudging sincerity. But that was before Barry put the most powerful weapon in the universe in the palm of his hand.

As the brilliant British historian Lord Acton had once said: "Power tends to corrupt, and absolute power corrupts absolutely."

The sphere split open under Mick's relentless, fiery assault. The blistering hot, red-glowing edges of the incision Mick had made emitted a blurt of yellowish light. Then a chunk of the sphere slid free and crashed soundlessly to the ground, kicking up a cloud of dust and grit. Barry couldn't do anything about it—normally he would just whirlwind his arms to create a windstorm to blow the cloud away, but there was no air here to manipulate.

Superman suddenly pushed Barry to one side. That chunk of the sphere had rolled through the haze of dust and almost smashed into Barry. It struck the Man of Steel a glancing blow—and Superman actually staggered back.

"Are you OK?" Barry asked, rushing to the Man of Steel's side.

"We gotta wait for the dust to settle," Mick said, landing nearby. He grinned in self-satisfaction at his successful landfall. "Can't see anything yet. Hey, what's wrong with the cape guy?"

"I'm not sure . . ." Barry helped Superman steady himself. The Kryptonian hero had a wan and sickly look about him. "Are you OK, Superman? Clark?"

"Yes." He nodded. "But something's wrong. There's . . . The sun . . . Or, suns, actually." He glanced around. "They're all distant. And dying."

Barry wondered where this sudden concern was coming from . . . and then remembered: Most of a Kryptonian's superpowers came from the light of a yellow sun. Flight and superstrength were a function of low gravity, but all the others—the super-senses, the invulnerability, the heat vision—came from yellow solar radiation.

Here at the End of All Time, stars were in short supply, and those that remained were old and dying.

And red.

There were basically two kinds of stars: small ones, like the sun around which Earth orbited, and massive ones. As small ones aged, they became white dwarfs and then eventually cooled into black dwarfs, which emitted no light. The big stars went supernova and became black holes.

But no matter what the size, every star turned red late in its life cycle. Here at the End of All Time, *late* was a way of life.

"I've been draining my reserves since we got here." Superman spoke with an infuriating and almost incomprehensible calm, as though he hadn't just learned that the source of his power no longer existed. "Pretty soon, my cells will have no more yellow solar radiation to draw on. And I'll basically be a human being."

"You're taking this pretty well," Mick commented.

"It's not like getting upset about it will change things," Superman said. "I'll figure out a way around it. I always do. The dust seems to have settled. Let's move on."

36

RAY'S NEW ATOM SUIT WAS PARED down from its original design, but he still had small retrojets in his boots. They had been put there to help him counter crosscurrents when shrunk down and drifting through the air, but right now they acted as nice little boosters to convey his group to Egg, the asteroid bearing Cisco. He held Oliver and Sara by their hands and used the booster rockets to jolt them across the void. Since everyone was essentially weightless, it took almost no effort on his part to drag them along. Still, Sara felt like some kid's kite.

"Not the most dignified travel arrangements I've ever had," Oliver deadpanned.

"Time travel has done wonders for your sense of humor," Sara commented.

Oliver chuckled. "There's no point being grim and gritty when you're stuck at the end of the Multiverse with a quiver of trick arrows strapped to your back."

"True."

Their landing on Egg was undignified, to say the least. Ray had limited experience with this sort of low-gravity flight, while Sara and Oliver had precisely no experience touching down under these sorts of circumstances. The three of them collided on impact with the ground, became entangled, and rolled along for several yards before managing to stop and extricate themselves from one another.

Sara bounced up first, buoyant and light in almost no gravity. She brushed dirt from her pristine White Canary outfit. "No matter what happens next, we all agree that we will never, *ever* talk about what just happened."

"Agreed," Oliver said, rising.

Ray hopped to his feet. "Can I include this anecdote in my memoirs, as long as I agree not to have them published until fifty years after we're all dead?"

"You're writing your memoirs?" Sara asked.

Ray's head bobbed with verve. "Of course I am! The book is tentatively titled *Big Time: How Being Small Taught Me to Feel Huge*."

Oliver glanced at Sara and did a terrible job suppressing an amused smile. She resisted the urge to return the smile—if she did, she knew she'd start laughing and not be able to stop.

"Fine, put it in your autobiography, Ray." She turned on one heel and led them toward the metallic rectangle Superman had described to them.

"It's not an autobiography," Ray argued as they took bounding moon steps toward the structure. "An autobiography is a factual history of your life, from your point of view. A memoir is a time-delimited reminiscence of a specific—"

"We get the point." Oliver, Sara noted, was deliberately hanging back, eyes up, scanning the dead skies. Expecting an attack.

Other than the Time Trapper, though, what was left to attack them? Everything else in the Multiverse was already dead. They were the only living beings in all of Creation.

She shivered at the thought.

The "building" didn't really meet the standards of being a building. It was more like a plinth for which the sculptor had forgotten to create the statue. It was a story and a half high, made of rusting, dull metal. It looked like a pyramid with the top chopped off and covered over.

"OK," said Oliver, catching up to them. "Now, how do we get inside?"

THE DUST HAD MOSTLY MEANDERED to the ground, with only a smattering of it still turning in the near vacuum, twinkling dully in the faint light of the End of All Time and trapped in mid-fall by the weak gravity of the rock. Barry kept a careful eye on Superman as the three of them made their way to the sphere. The Man of Steel seemed no worse for wear, his bearing still upright and powerful. In anyone else, this would have come across as denial. But somehow, in Superman, it seemed both right and rational. As though the *super* part of his *nom de superheroing* came not just from his powers, but from something deeper, something innate.

"How are you feeling?" Barry asked.

"Not bad," Superman said. "I'm not a mere mortal yet, Flash. Don't worry."

The dust cloud parted before them. The sphere hulked over them, one-third of it cleanly sheared off by Mick's power ring–generated blowtorch. The edges of the incision had already cooled in the near vacuum. Barry wondered briefly if the atmosphere inside the sphere had outgassed. It was possible Eobard Thawne was already dead from vacuum exposure.

Good riddance, Barry thought with uncharacteristic savagery. He was not, by nature, bloodthirsty or given to revenge, but Reverse-Flash had murdered his mother. There would be no tears wept at his demise, however it happened.

Mick and Superman glided up to the makeshift opening and peered within. Barry dashed up the side of the sphere—tricky footing, running on a curved surface, but he made it—and teetered on the edge, looking down with them.

"Looks like an environment field snapped into place when Heat Wave breached the hull," Superman said. "I can just barely make out an atmosphere in there."

Barry ran around the edge of the opening for a better vantage point. When Mick sliced off a piece of hemisphere, part of the inside of the sphere had collapsed in on itself. There was debris and wreckage down there, like sediment left in the bottom of a bottle of apple cider vinegar.

Within the sphere, a series of overlapping treadmill belts intersected along the inner wall. What appeared to be antennae jutted out here and there, aimed at the center of the sphere. The tech was eons beyond anything Barry had ever seen before, but the geometry of it all made perfect sense: gathering energy from the center of the sphere, from Thawne's running, then piping it along the antennae and beaming it like Mick's ring had shown them.

Speaking of Thawne . . .

There. He spied a swatch of yellow fabric among the wreckage.

"I have to be sure he's dead," Barry said. He zipped into the sphere, startled momentarily by the brief tickle of the environment shield as he progressed from vacuum to artificial atmosphere.

"Hurry, Flash," said Superman. "My telescopic vision isn't at its best, but it looks like the other team has reached the asteroid with Cisco's prison."

"Yeah, plus now that we've yanked the batteries out of his toys, I'm betting the freak in the purple bathrobe is gonna be looking this way any second."

Mick was right. Wobbling a bit, Barry raced down the concave surface of the inner sphere. He tossed some debris aside to uncover Thawne entirely.

And gasped.

A jumble of emotions slammed into him simultaneously—disappointment, horror, anger, shock, regret. And at the same time, his speed-enhanced mind ran through all the possibilities in an instant, arriving at the only possible conclusion.

"It's a trap!" he yelled.

38

SUPERGIRL FINISHED HER CONVERsation with Mr. Terrific, who assured her he would follow her instructions and get her plan to help Joe in motion. Before she signed off, though, Iris nudged her to one side and leaned in to speak to Curtis.

"Have you figured out exactly what Owlman did to the treadmill yet?" Iris asked, her voice laden with urgency.

Still on-site at the treadmill, Mr. Terrific waffled a hand back and forth. "Hard to say. He lowered the frequency, which boosted the power of the signal. I'm not sure why—the strike team was already in the time stream and theoretically already had the power they needed. The speedsters are already off the treadmill, but this thing stored up a lot of their power, and now Owlman has it pumping through the conduit to S.T.A.R. Labs."

Supergirl was still amazed at the whole *let's build a giant treadmill* plan, but the idea of all that energy flowing to

S.T.A.R. Labs cut through her wonderment and filled her with dread.

Iris shook her head. "Just pull the plug."

"That . . . doesn't sound like a great idea," Kara told her.

Mr. Terrific concurred. "I don't think we should do that. We're talking about a *lot* of energy here, Iris. I don't know for sure what'll happen if we shut it down before we really understand the modifications Owlman made."

Iris summoned Felicity to join her and Kara in their conversation with Curtis. "What do you think?"

Tapping a pen against her top teeth, Felicity considered. "I think Curtis is right. And I think if Owlman is sending all that excess energy here, there must be a reason. He's ordered and pragmatic, not chaotic and crazed like the rest of the Crime Syndicate."

At the words *Crime Syndicate*, Supergirl's spine stiffened. "The Crime Syndicate. His partners."

"What about them?" Felicity asked.

But Iris had already figured out where Supergirl was going with this. "He's using that energy to break them out of the Pipeline!" she exclaimed. "Kara, let's go!"

Together they ran out of the Cortex.

The security system in the Pipeline showed all functions green, meaning that the Crime Syndicate members were still locked up in their cells. Iris paused outside the entrance to their wing of the Pipeline.

"What are you waiting for?" Supergirl asked. "Doesn't green mean *go* on Earth 1, too?"

Iris bit her lower lip. "Just because the readout is green doesn't mean something hasn't happened in there. Owlman might have already sprung them."

Supergirl considered this, frowning, then brightened. "Well, Barry told me they weren't all chummy with one another. Maybe they've already knocked each other out."

"Ha! I wish. They're all on a strange Earth. Better the devil you know, right?"

"Yeah, I guess Owlman would prefer his old frenemies to the uncertainty of gathering allies from Earth 1."

Iris reached out for the lever to open the hatch into the Pipeline, but Supergirl touched her hand.

"You know I'm not going to be super-helpful if there's a bunch of released villains in there, right?" Supergirl said quietly.

Iris shrugged. "I'm hoping they'll see the costume and your sunny confidence and not even try to fight."

Supergirl snorted nervous laughter. "Oh, great. I love this plan."

They stepped into the Pipeline together, and Supergirl proactively struck her most powerful arms-akimbo pose, figuring it might intimidate whichever villains were on the loose.

But the cell doors were still closed. The Eddie Thawne of Earth 27 slept on his cot, while the man named Power Ring lay curled in a fetal position on the floor of his cell. Superwoman idly glanced in Iris's direction and sniffed, then deliberately turned away.

Ultraman stood at the front of his cell, arms crossed impressively over his massive chest. Trying to intimidate them.

"You have no powers," Iris reminded him.

"I don't need powers to make you regret you were ever born," he told her.

Well, all right, then.

Ultraman narrowed his eyes, glaring at Supergirl. "You look familiar. Did I kill you on Earth 27?"

Supergirl ignored him and glanced around the chamber. No sign of Owlman. But that didn't mean he wouldn't be on his way.

"Nothing worth seeing here," she said, deliberately shifting her gaze to Ultraman as she said it. "Let's go somewhere useful."

Iris nodded and double-encrypted the lock to this part of the Pipeline as they left, then shut the blast door. No one would get in there.

But where was Owlman? And what was he up to?

39

DESPITE THE RUSTED APPEARANCE of the structure on Egg, it was still intact and sturdy. Sara, Ray, and Oliver paced its perimeter, probing for weak spots, but found none.

They did locate a slender, nigh-invisible seam that began where the structure met Egg's ground, then ran vertically for about eight feet before taking a sharp left turn, going on for another three feet, then descending. They'd almost missed it under the grime, rust, and dirt that lay on everything. It looked like the seam to a door of some sort, but there was no mechanism to open it, and the seam itself was so narrow that no one could get their fingers in there to prize it open. Sara tried sending her borrowed rope in there, but even the rope was too thick.

Ray shrank down until he disappeared from sight entirely. It was unnerving to watch, Sara realized. A moment later, though, he popped "up" again near the wall.

"I couldn't slip between," he said. "It's sealed up too tight. No matter how small I got, I was too big."

"Stand back." Oliver unslung his bow and aimed an arrow as Ray ducked out of the way. Sara opened her mouth to shout a warning and stop Oliver—he wasn't thinking clearly. An explosive arrow might kill Cisco in there. At the very least, it would almost certainly attract the attention of the Time Trapper, and that was attention they did *not* want directed toward them.

She was too late, though—the bowstring snapped forward and the arrow flew unerringly in the low-gravity environment, hitting the edge of what they believed to be the door. Sara winced in anticipation, but nothing happened.

No sound.

Of course not. There was no air here to carry the sound. She opened her eyes wide, expecting to see curls of smoke, but instead she saw only Oliver's arrow, jutting out of the wall.

"It's not like you don't impress me with your speed and aim," Ray said, stroking his chin as he gazed at the arrow, "but I still have to say that this is really anticlimactic, Oliver."

Sara approached the arrow. It was, she realized, not an explosive arrow. It wasn't a trick arrow at all, in fact. It was just a run-of-the-mill *arrow* arrow, its head wedged quite solidly in the almost-invisible door seam. Its only distinctive characteristic was its lack of feathers at the tail end of the shaft.

"Fletches are to stabilize arrows, in case there's air drag along the bottom," Oliver said, reading her mind. "There's no air here, so I stripped off the fletching. Otherwise there was a chance I could send the arrow spinning head over tail instead of straight."

"I love how you think of everything!" Ray enthused.

"Everything except actually getting into the door," Sara said, jerking a thumb at the arrow. "You didn't exactly blow the door off the place."

"I didn't need to." Oliver hooked his own thumb at Ray.

It took Sara only a moment to catch on, and when she did, she felt like an idiot for missing it the first time. Fortunately, Ray didn't get it, either, so she didn't beat herself up *too* much.

"The arrow widened the seam just a bit," Sara said. "Maybe enough that—"

"Already gone, Captain!" Ray shrank down, vanishing once again.

Cold, timeless moments passed. "You really just sort of take charge, don't you?" Sara asked idly. "No *Hey, guys, I have an idea!* or *What if we try this?*"

"I've been trying not to take over, but at this point," Oliver said, shrugging, "I figure the life of everything that has ever existed or ever will exist is measured in minutes. Don't see the point in slowing things down."

Same old Oliver, Sara thought. *Always figuring it's better to beg forgiveness than ask permission.*

It rankled. But only because she knew she was the same way.

The door slid open silently, showering rust and dust that

floated in the vacuum, spinning and colliding like a miniature asteroid field. Ray beamed at them from inside. "Palmer Locksmithing, at your service!"

Sara nodded to the open door. "You just going to charge in, Green Arrow?"

Oliver grinned. "After you, Captain Lance."

They strode into the structure. Light panels flickered to life overhead, activated by their motion, then—without warning—died, leaving Sara with only an afterimage to process.

The space she'd glimpsed had been no larger than her first apartment, a dingy little studio she'd rented out near the Glades, in the worst possible neighborhood she could tolerate. She'd done it to annoy her father, and it had worked. She shook her head now at her immaturity then. It had taken being shipwrecked, lost at sea, taken in by the League of Assassins, killed, and resurrected for her to grow up . . .

But at least she had.

A shiver ran down her spine. The darkness ahead seemed limitless and pregnant with bad intent. *Ava, I swear I'm coming back to you. I swear it.*

Oliver launched an arrow ahead of them. It hit a far wall and erupted into a reddish light, like a road flare. Shadows leaped and cavorted before them as the flare spat and sparked. But even with the distraction of the shadows, she could tell . . .

"It's empty," Ray complained. "Totally empty."

"Isn't Cisco supposed to be here?" Oliver sounded puzzled.

Ava. Oh, no, Ava. I'm sorry. I'm sorry I was so stupid . . .

"It's a trap," Sara breathed.

"No," said a voice like shards of glass clashing against each other in a spinning vat of hot oil. *"Time is a trap."*

There, behind her as she spun around, was the Time Trapper.

40

ALL I KNOW, J'ONN HAD SAID AFTER his telepathic probe of Anti-Matter Man, *is that whoever or whatever it was, the enemy from the future used a special machine to open the breaches through the Multiverse for Anti-Matter Man. A machine powered by a person. I caught a glimpse of a man within that machine, running in a circle. Moving fast. Like you do, Flash. Only, he was a yellow blur.*

"Hey!" Mick yelled from outside the sphere. "The big guy's gone!"

Moving fast. Like you do, Flash. Only, he was a yellow blur.

Barry's mind raced. A trap, yes. And they'd fallen for it. Divided their forces, sending the weaker members to rescue Cisco, while their strongest members were useless here because . . .

"Wally . . ." he whispered.

There in the heap of debris within the sphere lay not Eobard Thawne but Wally West, Kid Flash.

Barry's adoptive brother. Joe's son. Iris's brother.

He was a yellow blur.

They'd assumed that yellow blur was Thawne, but it had been Wally all along. Abducted from the time stream, no doubt, when he'd gone on "shore leave" from the Legends of Tomorrow in the late 1960s. Dragooned from the Summer of Love to the End of All Time, where he was put to work as a speedster battery to power the Time Trapper's evil machinery and devious schemes.

"Flash!" Superman barked. "There's a situation and we need to—"

"I need a second!" Barry yelled back up. He knelt down by Wally. Kid Flash's costume was torn in places but still relatively intact. Barry disconnected the lightning emblem from the chest piece and exchanged it for his own. Cisco had designed the suits to upload data to the logos; swapping one out allowed the new user to read the data on that "drive."

A pair of lenses dropped down to cover his eyes. According to the readout scrolling at superspeed across them, Wally's vitals were low but stable. He'd been running at top speed for weeks at a time. Barry couldn't figure out how, but somehow his weight and metabolism had remained stable, even as he burned endless amounts of calories.

I bet the Time Trapper did something to his body so that it kept replenishing itself as he ran.

Wally was breathing, shallow but steady.

"We got a situation up here!" Mick cried out.

"And I've got one down here!" Barry yelled back.

Mick peeked over the edge of the sphere, his expression hardening when he saw his former teammate laid out, unconscious. A moment later, a green, floating stretcher, complete with neck brace and restraints, materialized into existence around Wally's limp form.

"Mick!"

"I'm gettin' the hang of this thing. And Volthoom is keepin' his yap shut for once."

As Mick cautiously airlifted Wally out of the sphere, Barry zipped up the curved wall, emerging into the eternal black night at the end of everything. The Time Trapper, ever present over at his own chunk of drifting ground on Needle, had disappeared.

He—it?—was not the towering giant Sara had spied from afar upon their arrival. Instead, he was a human-sized figure in a bedraggled, torn purple robe with a hood that opened only into a series of overlapping shadows. Impossible to see his—again, its?—face. Had it ever been that titanic figure? Had that been an illusion? Could it reduce its size, like Ray?

And why was she thinking such things at a time like this?

"Down!" Oliver shouted, and Sara reflexively ducked out of the way as an arrow whizzed through the space where her head had been. Good old Oliver, counting on her instincts. He'd used her body as a screen, nocking and drawing an arrow when the Time Trapper couldn't see it, firing from behind a blind.

The arrow sailed through the vacuum. Without windage or friction to worry about, it traveled in a straight line, unerringly headed at the black space in the opening of the Time Trapper's hood.

The Time Trapper had no time to dodge. The arrow was already there.

It can't be this easy, can it? she thought from the ground, where she'd flung herself.

And just before the arrow struck its target, it . . . vanished.

The Time Trapper did not so much as flinch.

Oliver swore. He'd already nocked another arrow and sent it sailing through the air. This one, too, disappeared faster than a soap bubble on hot grass.

"You sent them away." She picked herself up off the ground, dusted herself off.

"No. The arrows never existed. All of time is at my command."

Oliver heaved out an annoyed sigh. "Maybe Mick was right."

"Wait." Sara held out an arm. Oliver had been ready to charge the Time Trapper and pummel him with his bow.

But the Trapper had just shown them his power. If he could make Oliver's arrows vanish, he could do the same to them, right? And yet he didn't. He simply stood before them, passive.

Attacking him would get them nothing. But maybe—just maybe—they could talk to him.

"What do you want?" Sara asked. Behind her, she could hear Oliver's breath, fast and hot in his transsuit. Ray stood off to her side, fists clenched, waiting for a command. Or an opening.

The hood of the cloak tilted slightly, but she still could not make out a face. *"Want? Want is for the short-lived. I have all that I need at my disposal. And soon I shall have everything else as well."*

41

THE SHORTEST, QUICKEST PATH from Central City to Star City cut through two major interstates and a couple of minor state expressways. That day, those roads thundered out of nowhere, shaking as though two competing earthquakes had collided just beneath them.

The rollicking, quaking shock waves blasted along Route 70 out of Central, then along the straightest course to U.S. 90 into Star City. Cars and trucks alike pulled to the side of the road as the phenomenon whipped along like a living, pulsating, hurricane-force wind.

It was more than six hundred miles from Central City to Star City. In a car, without rest stops, a driver could make the trip in half a day. Barry Allen could do it in less than a minute.

Led by James Jesse, the ten thousand Earth 27 speedsters made it in under two hours.

• • •

“Picking up major tectonic activity just outside of town,” Dig warned from the Bunker. “It’s either the Big One or . . .”

Out in the field, Joe wore a protective hazmat suit to stave off attacks by the swarm of bees buzzing everywhere. The air was thick and black with them. He didn’t need Dig’s warning from the relative safety of the Bunker, which was hardened against anything short of a nuclear attack. The rumble of the ground vibrating up through his feet told the tale, and he was pretty sure it wasn’t the fabled Big One, the massive earthquake predicted to sever the West Coast from the rest of the country.

No, this “quake” portended something else.

Pop!

“Joe!” Ambush Bug put a hand on Joe’s shoulder. “You’ve changed! Your face is all flat and shiny now. Your skin is saggy.” He plucked at the loose-fitting hazmat suit. “Your diet is all kinds of mucked up. Wheatgrass, Joe! It’s the wonder food of the next millennium!”

“You maniac! You’re going to kill people!”

Ambush Bug shrugged. “Background characters! No-names! NPCs!”

Joe took aim, knowing it was pointless. *Pop!* The Bug was gone.

He turned around. Thundering down Weisinger Street came the beat of twenty thousand superfast feet. Joe grinned. Supergirl couldn’t bring the Kryptonian muscle, but she’d come up with something almost as good: ten thousand speedsters.

He’d make do.

42

IN THE CORTEX, SUPERGIRL PACED BACK and forth, furious at herself.

"It's not your fault you don't have your powers," Iris told her.

"Well, technically . . ." Felicity chimed in, "she made the decision to go all super-flare on Anti-Matter Man, so it *is* her fault. But, uh," she added quickly at a glare from Iris, "it was *totally* the right decision to make."

"If I had my powers, there'd be nowhere on this Earth or any other where Owlman could hide from me," Supergirl fretted. "I feel useless just standing around here."

"Mr. Terrific is on his way back from the treadmill," Iris told her. "Once he gets here, we can use his tech to search the building from top to bottom."

"He might not even be in the building," Felicity put in. "He could be halfway to Opal City by now."

"He's not going to Opal City," Supergirl snapped a little more harshly than usual. Being a mere mortal grated on her nerves. "He sent all that energy *here*. He's got a reason for that. A purpose. And it has to do with something in this building. Which means he's already here. I guarantee it."

Iris pursed her lips and rested her hand near the emergency sanctuary switch. Once pressed, it would lower blast shields over every entrance and exit into and out of S.T.A.R. Labs.

"I can close off the building, cut us off from the outside world entirely . . ."

Supergirl shook her head. "No. That would just alert him, give him a heads-up that we're onto him. I'm going to go find him."

She spun on one heel and headed for the door.

"How are you going to do that?" Iris asked in disbelief.

"Any way it takes," Supergirl said defiantly.

43

"OVER THERE!" SUPERMAN CALLED. "He's with the others!"

The Man of Steel pointed to Egg. Barry, having just emerged from the sphere, cursed himself in terms so vociferous that even Mick blushed.

They hadn't breached the Iron Curtain of Time after all, Barry realized. They'd been lured through it.

They'd walked right into a trap. They'd split their forces poorly, sending their weakest members right into the Time Trapper's grasp.

"And every second that passes, Superman's powers fade more and more," Barry said. "The Time Trapper has us just where he wants us."

"Guys, it's a trap!" Sara's voice crackled over their comms channel. "Cisco isn't—"

And then nothing.

“They’re gone,” Superman said, his voice hollow. “Even my limited telescopic vision would see them, but . . . They’re gone.”

“He killed them? He *killed them*?” Mick’s fist clenched. The ring glowed a green so intense it was hot. Heat Wave’s eyes began to take on a greenish hue that Barry recognized from fighting Power Ring.

“Don’t do it, Mick!” Barry grabbed Mick by both shoulders. “Don’t give in to the ring. Control it; don’t let it control you.”

Sweat beaded on Mick’s forehead and dripped down his cheeks. “But . . . But he says . . . He says he can get revenge. All I have to do is let him . . . let him . . .”

Superman put a calming hand on Mick’s shoulder. “Vengeance is a poor reason to lose yourself, Mr. Rory. I have a good friend who’s spent his entire life proving that. The easiest thing in the world is to find the biggest weapon and lose yourself in it. But there’s another way. A path outside of revenge: justice.”

Hyperventilating, Mick darted his greenish eyes this way and that. His lips curled back; his teeth gnashed. The struggle with Volthoom was etched into every line in his face, the hollows of his cheeks, the rivulets of sweat collecting along his jawline, the crow’s feet around his eyes.

“Take the ring,” Barry said quietly. “Take it away from him.”

“He can beat it,” Superman said confidently. “I believe in him.”

Barry opened his mouth to speak, but at that moment, he heard a soft groan. Wally was waking up. He dashed to his brother’s side.

"Barry . . . ?" Wally's eyes took a moment to focus. "What are you doing here?"

In literally half a second, Barry explained everything that had happened since Wally had gone missing in the 1960s. Only a speedster could keep up with that rapid burst of speech.

"Oh man, just when I thought things were freaky with the Legends . . . Then *this* stuff happens?"

"No one ever said being a superhero would be easy," Barry told him, and grinned.

Wally chuckled softly. "You got any power bars? Maybe a chocolate milkshake?"

Barry produced two soft gumdrops and held them out. "I have a couple of Caitlin Snow specials. They'll have to do."

To keep up with speedster metabolisms, Caitlin had developed the gumdrops, which were gelatins made up of hyper-condensed glucose, proteins, and carbohydrates. They had an absolutely insane calorie count, with each gumdrop being roughly equivalent to a steak dinner with mashed potatoes, gravy, and creamed corn. Unfortunately, they tasted like motor oil sweetened with honey, but in a pinch, there was nothing better, nothing packed with enough energy to top off even a speedster's metabolism.

"Oh, my favorite." Wally grimaced as he took the two gumdrops and put them in his mouth. Chewing, his face contorted into the expression of a man eating a live rat.

Checking over his shoulder, Barry saw that Superman had managed to talk Mick down from his near dive into the evil embrace of Volthoom. Heat Wave still trembled with rage, but his eyes had returned to their normal color.

"Did I hear right?" Wally asked. "Are Sara and Ray dead?"

"And Oliver," Barry said soberly. "We knew there was a risk, but I didn't think . . . I didn't think it would get so bad so soon."

"We need a plan," Wally said. "And we need it now."

"The Time Trapper has left his machinery," Superman pointed out, gesturing across the void to Needle. "We don't know what that gadget does, but if the Trapper was working on it, it can't be any good. I say we strike while he's gone and destroy it."

"Sounds good to me," Barry said.

"We'll need a distraction," Superman said. "The Time Trapper isn't just going to let us—"

"Distraction?" Mick growled. "Consider it done."

"Wait!" Barry yelled. But Mick was already flying off into the night.

"I'll go to the machine," Superman said. "I still have enough power to get there on my own and destroy it."

"And what am I supposed to do?" Barry demanded. "Sit around and twiddle my thumbs?"

"You need to figure out how we're going to defeat the Time Trapper once and for all," Superman told him. "And I know you will." With that, he took off.

Mick soared through space, so focused on his target that he couldn't even take a moment to marvel at what the ring allowed him to do. Volthoom was still screaming at him, still wheedling and insisting, but Mick pushed it away like a bad headache. His back teeth hurt from clenching his jaw so much.

There, just ahead on Egg, he beheld the Time Trapper, standing alone. As soon as Mick came into range, the creep turned, tilting that blank, black, hooded face up, as though out to watch some birds.

"You made a big mistake, pal!" Mick roared. "You pissed me off, and I'm your worst nightmare, a pyromaniac with the biggest flamethrower in the universe!"

And then, indeed, Mick had the biggest flamethrower in the universe. Volthoom complained, but Mick shoved him aside and forced the ring to do his bidding, assembling a massive flamethrower the size of a battleship. The thing glowed green and hung in the void like the world's most twisted, violent Macy's Thanksgiving Day Parade balloon. Mick built it from memory and loaded it with the most volatile mixture of flammable chemicals he could imagine.

"Eat heat!" he screamed.

The fire that blistered forth from the flamethrower was, of course, green, but it still burned hotter than hot. It was as though Mick had unleashed part of a sun on the Time Trapper. The sky lit up green for miles in every direction. Heat—almost absent from a Multiverse where even particles had slowed to a crawl and begun to condense—flared to life once more, one final gasp of life in a near-dead reality.

The heat was vaster and more fervent than anything Mick had ever experienced before. His breath came quick and hard as the flames licked the planetoid, scorching the surface, swallowing the purple hooded figure whole. Mick figured he could die happy now. He'd made the biggest fire the universe had ever seen, a fire to rival the sun itself. He cackled into the void as sweat poured off him. The ring felt like a band of molten lava on his fist, but he didn't care.

The flamethrower ran out of fuel. Mick took in a deep breath and heaved it out. Volthoom was offering more power, but Mick didn't think he needed it. He'd just thrown a planet's worth of hot hell at the Time Trapper.

"That oughtta do it," he whispered to himself.

Below, the vacuum made short work of the green flames flashing and flickering on the surface. Egg had been charred in its entirety, its surface gone black, crumbling and flaking off pieces like a log turned to charcoal.

And in the midst of it, a spot of purple.

The Time Trapper.

Impossibly, still standing.

Barry tended to Wally as best he could, given the lack of medical supplies available. He had a second transsuit with him and had put it on Wally before Mick raised him out of the sphere, and according to their emblem-to-emblem connection, Wally's vitals were improving. No doubt thanks in part to Caitlin's speedster confections, which were doing a good job replacing electrolytes, boosting amino acids, and just generally replenishing Wally.

But those physical aids were only part of the battle. Wally

ricocheted between seeming all right and traumatized. There was no way to know how long he'd been in the Time Trapper's device or exactly what it had been like in there for him. Barry understood Mick's urge for revenge very, very well in that moment. If he could get his hands around the Time Trapper's throat, he would have no compunctions whatsoever about squeezing for what the Trapper had done to his brother.

Speaking of the Time Trapper . . . Barry turned and craned his neck. Mick was a green blur in the distance. An enormous flamethrower—a massive, hulking thing straight from a nightmare—floated nearby, gushing fire onto Egg. Barry thought of a marshmallow left too long over a campfire.

The flamethrower finally ran out of fuel. Barry watched smoke and fire peel away from the planetoid. He half expected the rock to crumble into pieces as he watched.

Instead, something else happened.

Incredibly, the Time Trapper appeared there, growing from a space on the surface of the planetoid to a monumental figure who dwarfed that same planetoid. And then he continued to grow, bigger than Anti-Matter Man. Hundreds of meters tall. Mick was a green speck, a dying emerald ember.

"I am Entropy," said the Time Trapper, his voice the texture of eel flesh and sandpaper. *"The end-death of everything."*

Barry realized he was shaking, ever so slightly. Entropy. The most powerful force in the universe, really. All life and all matter and all energy were the result of *movement* at various levels: molecular, atomic, subatomic, macro-atomic. But motion could not continue forever; motion could not be perpetual. Eventually, the theory went, energy ran out; systems flagged, tired, died.

And now, billions of years in the future, the universe itself was running out of energy and collapsing into itself, ending all space and time.

It was happening on a Multiversal scale, with the various universes of the Multiverse collapsing individually and then into one another. Meeting in a single point of dying energy. A single point of dying energy that had a name now. A name and a will and a plan.

"I am the End of All That Ever Was. My victory is preordained."

Then why are you working so hard for it? Barry wondered suddenly. There was the Iron Curtain of Time. The machinery to

poke through it. Kidnapping Wally so that he could power the machinery that liberated Anti-Matter Man. Opening breaches between universes . . .

If the Time Trapper was the logical, natural end point of reality, then why did he have to scheme and scam and build traps?

"Why are you working so hard for it?" This time Barry said it out loud.

"You . . . you think he's not as powerful as we think?" Wally asked slowly.

"No." Barry stroked his chin, thinking. "I think he's probably *more* powerful than we think. But it's not about power—it's about how it can be used. I think his power is enormous but constrained. I don't think he can leave the End of All Time."

And something else occurred to him: The Time Trapper had

kidnapped Cisco for a reason. And he wouldn't have merely stood by while Mick turned Cisco into a charcoal briquette along with the rest of that planetoid. So that meant . . .

"If Cisco isn't there, then the only other place . . ." Barry's gaze flicked to the central asteroid, Needle, where the Time Trapper had been when they'd arrived. Superman was almost there.

44

AFTER A BRIEF CONVERSATION WITH James Jesse to explain the plan, Joe got out of the way and let the Earth 27 speedsters do their thing. The fastest among them were no more than 10 percent as fast as Barry Allen, but what they lacked in sheer velocity, they made up for in overall numbers. There were ten thousand of them, so each of them only had to grab and crush twenty bees.

Sonic booms reverberated along the concrete and glass canyons of Star City. Shop windows fractured and spiderwebbed. Joe winced. Barry knew how to vibrate his body so that he didn't create sonic backlash, but the Earth 27 speedsters were still new to their powers. Oh well—a little property damage was better than dead bodies in the streets.

He tried to watch the action, but it was just a series of overlapping, vibrating blurs, a moving, shifting kaleidoscope of flashing colors and bursts of light. The sight nauseated him, so he turned away. The space around him began to unclot as the speedsters plucked bees from the air and crushed them underfoot.

"Get out here for crowd control and to hunt the Bug!" Joe ordered Dig. He knew that in mere moments, Diggle, Dinah, and Rene would be out of the Bunker and out on the streets. The speedsters could handle the bees, but Joe wanted to be the one to bring down Ambush Bug. He'd been mocked and made a fool of too much.

As the swarm thinned under the aegis of the speedsters, Joe checked the complicated gee-whiz science gadget strapped to his wrist. They still had the satellite tracking data that could track the Bug as he teleported. According to that telemetry, the Bug had just teleported nearby.

He rounded a corner. Ambush Bug was *pop!*ing from bee to bee as a speedster fruitlessly zipped around in an ever-tightening circle, trying to get his hands on the Bug. Teleportation was still faster than superspeed, though, and the speedster was clearly flagging. Ambush Bug teleported right over the speedster, dropped onto his shoulders, bearing them both down to the ground, then teleported across the street, then back again to kick the speedster while he was still down.

"Ambush Bug! Freeze!" Joe leveled his weapon.

"Joe West! Thaw!"

Pop!

Joe struggled as the Bug, who'd teleported to his side, grabbed his gun.

Pop!

Joe winced as the gun was torn from his grip. Ambush Bug was gone, returning an instant later without the gun.

"Where'd you leave my gun?"

"Rooftop," Ambush Bug explained, then frowned. "I seem to have a *lot* fewer places to go right now. Say, Joe, are you up to something nefarious?"

The speedsters were doing their jobs—eliminating the bees and reducing Ambush Bug's possible teleportation targets.

Pop!

And Ambush Bug was behind Joe, who spun around to confront him. "Give it up. With every second that passes, we're winnowing down your escape routes."

"Winnowing? Did you say *winnowing*? You never hear *winnow* anymore these days. It's a good word. Why don't people use it more often?"

And then Ambush Bug waved goodbye, took a step to the left—

Nothing.

"Hey!" the Bug complained. "*Nothing*? Really? C'mon, this is a moment of existential crisis* for me and all I get is *nothing*?"

He took another step—

"I get it already!" he shouted. "I take another step, try to teleport, and it doesn't work! I got it the *first* time. Don't make me look like an idiot, Lyga. I'm crazy, not stupid."

Joe advanced on Ambush Bug. "You're under arrest."

---

* Ooh, I said *crisis*! Red skies! And look—a footnote! Cool!

Ambush Bug looked up. "I seem to be under the sky. *Under the Tuscan Sun. Underworld Unleashed.* (Hi, Mark!) Don't mind me—I'm just free-associating because there's nothing else to do."

Joe sighed in deep relief and strode over to the Bug.

"Oh man, there's some space before the bottom of the page. Is this the end of the chapter?"

"It's the end of your story," Joe said, and happily punched Ambush Bug into unconsciousness with a single blow to the jaw.

45

SUPERMAN LANDED ON NEEDLE'S surface, suddenly grateful for the Legion transsuit he'd worn for its communication abilities. He'd lost his powers before, been under red suns before—he knew the signs and the portents. The first one was this: cold. The sensation of cold. It was unfamiliar to him, but when it came, he knew what it meant. It meant that his powers were fading. His invulnerability was going away. He needed to breathe now.

Just like a person.

It'll be OK, Clark, he told himself. *You've been powerless before, and you've always made it through.*

Behind him, the Time Trapper loomed enormous and impossible. He hoped Heat Wave and the Flash could hold him off, or at least distract him. There was too much to do here and now.

The Time Trapper's machinery was enormous—a massive, metallic Gordian knot of impossible-to-follow cables, tubes, and conduits. Energy crackled around it, black spots vibrating and sloughing away, bleeding off into infinity. He knew the fundamentals of Kryptonian technology, so much more advanced than Earth's, but this technology was as beyond him as a cell phone was beyond a caveman.

He didn't really need to understand it, though. He just had to destroy it.

He'd been accused in the past of thinking with his fists. His best friend often chided him for relying too much on his powers, not using his head enough. It wasn't really a fair criticism, Superman thought. He relied on his powers so much because the foes who came his way tended to have abilities that matched or outstripped his own. But when the time came for outthinking an enemy, he was more than capable of doing so.

And he might have to do it now. His strength flagged. His invulnerability, which would protect him from harm as he smashed the machinery, was almost gone. A chill enveloped him. *This is what Lois complains about on cold nights*, he thought. And he imagined her, wrapped in a sweater, feet tucked under her as she sat on the sofa, pounding at her laptop, writing yet another exposé. Making the world a better place, one story at a time.

Asking him how to spell *misanthrope.* Her spelling was awful, and she didn't trust the computer's spell-check.

I'm coming back to you, Lois, he thought. *I swear it.*

He stared at the machine, willing his X-ray vision to work one more time. To show him some weakness he could exploit.

Instead, it showed him Cisco Ramon.

Shocked, he turned around. The Time Trapper had grown even more, now bigger than most skyscrapers. He raised his arms, laughing into the void. How could they hear him, with no atmosphere?

And why was Superman even worrying about such things?

He figured he had one chance to get Cisco out of this contraption. He knew what he needed to do, and he also knew how risky it was. If it didn't work, he would be rendered powerless.

Then again, even if it *did* work, he would still be rendered powerless.

Super Flare. It was his last chance. He had a little heat vision, a little flight . . . In short, he had all his powers, but at drastically reduced potency. No single power—strength, freeze breath, whatever—had enough juice behind it to break into the machine and liberate Cisco.

But if he combined all of them, compiled the last dregs of yellow sunlight in his cells, it might make a Super Flare strong enough to crack open the prison.

Even if it didn't, he'd be left powerless.

Lois always likes to say that the man *in* Superman *is the important part. Let's find out if she's right.*

He put his hands far apart on the skin of the machine. He focused as hard as he could, channeling all the yellow solar radiation stored in his cells.

With a scream of pain, he allowed the power to explode out of him. His eyes erupted with yellow bursts of energy, sizzling along the surface of the machine. The metallic layer began to bubble and warp, softening beneath his fingers.

For the first time in a long time, he felt heat. His own heat. His fingers burned.

No time for regrets or for pain, Smallville. Lois's voice in his head. *This looks like a job for Superman.*

Crying out in anguish, he sank his fingers into the melting metal. It would cool and re-harden rapidly in the cold vacuum of space, so he had to move quickly. With the last of his strength, he clawed the metal apart, opening a gap in the machine's exterior. His breath came too fast, his heart pounding as he strained mightily.

Something electrical within the machine cracked and sparked. Superman staggered back, his fingers throbbing with pain.

From the smoky darkness of the gap he'd made, a figure appeared, then reached out, probing tentatively.

"So, in other words," a voice said, "the TV Barry Allen screwed up, messed with history, then *re*-messed with history, and we're the ones who get punished for it? Not cool."

The hand hung there.

"So, in other words . . ."

Superman grabbed the hand and pulled. Cisco Ramon stumbled out of the machine.

". . . messed with history," Cisco said, dazed, "then *re*-messed . . ."

He suddenly shook all over, then blinked rapidly, as though disbelieving the evidence of his own eyes.

"Whoa! I never thought . . . I never thought I'd get out of there!" He blinked some more. "Wait a sec—you're dressed like . . . Please tell me that *S* on your chest stands for *Supergirl's pal.*"

Superman struggled to catch his breath. "Actually . . . stands for . . . *hope.*"

"Well, I '*S*' there's a plan, because the Time Trapper is the biggest of the Big Bads." He looked up into the sky, where the Trapper loomed like God's older, angrier cousin. "Oh man. I didn't know he could *grow*. Why do all the really powerful bad guys have to do that? Is it like an intimidation thing?"

Superman shrugged and put a hand on Cisco's shoulder to steady himself. "Maybe they're compensating for the smallness of their souls."

"Could be. Well, go get 'im, Man of Steel!" Cisco jabbed a finger at the sky, now filling quickly with the form of the still-growing Time Trapper.

"Wish I could. But I used up my power to rescue you."

Cisco tapped his foot on the ground, his nervous energy stirring up clouds of dust. "Usually I'd tell you you made a bad decision, but since it was me, I'm going to hold off. C'mon."

He gestured and a breach opened. Cisco helped Superman step through.

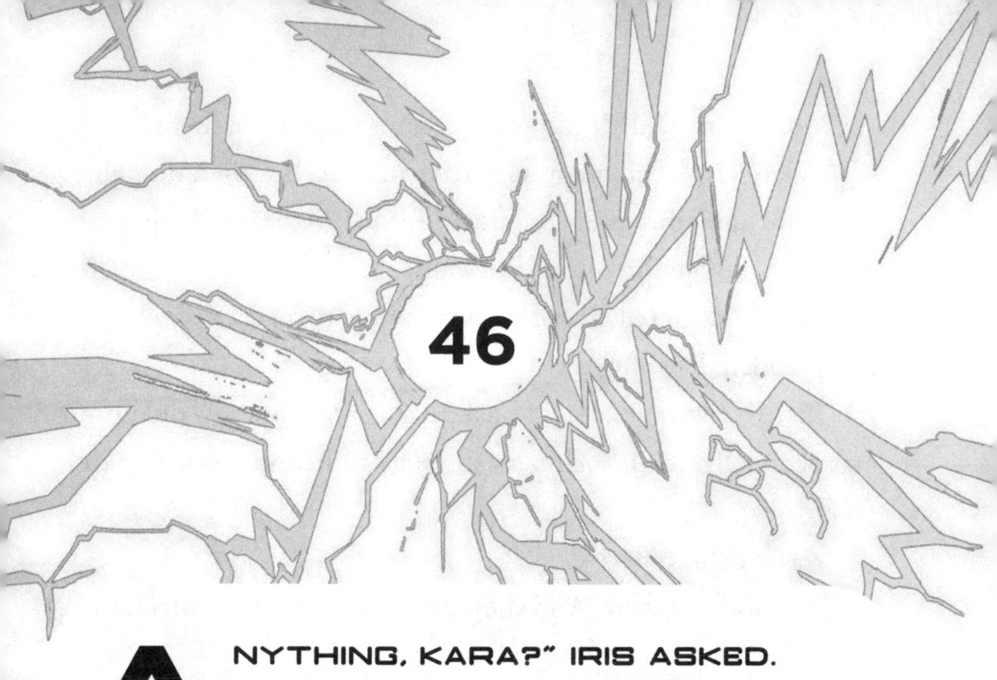

46

"ANYTHING, KARA?" IRIS ASKED.

Supergirl sighed and touched the comms bud in her ear. She was two floors down and halfway across the building from the Cortex, in a dark and silent corridor. "Nothing new in the last two minutes, which was the last time you asked."

With the tiniest fraction of her powers returning, Supergirl felt pretty confident in her search for Owlman, but she knew Iris worried about her friend putting herself in harm's way. Especially when that could mean standing between a menace like Owlman and whatever his ultimate target happened to be.

But Supergirl couldn't just stand by and do nothing while a threat potentially stalked her friends. Her X-ray vision was wobbly and her super-hearing wasn't the greatest right now, but her senses were still sharper than any of the humans at S.T.A.R. Labs. In one more day, she'd be all powered up again. Right now, she'd make do with what she had.

"Sorry," Iris said. "I'll stay off comms so you can focus."

Supergirl opened her mouth to thank Iris, but then thought she heard something. She couldn't be sure. A breath? A heart-beat? Just a mouse in one of the walls?

Impossible to tell. She stopped moving, turned a slow circle, ears prickled, listening . . .

There it was again. A . . . hush? A shush? Wow, how did normal people live with such a small range of hearing available to them?

Was it behind her?

No. Nothing there. And she'd just come from that direction. She would have . . .

Oh man, she thought, realizing, *I can't believe I fell for the oldest trick in the* . . .

She ducked to one side just in time as Owlman pounced from where he'd been lurking above her. He landed on the floor in near silence, making not a sound.

"Heard you coming a mile away," Supergirl bluffed. "Super-hearing."

"Ultra-hearing," said Owlman, then sniffed. "Hh. I'm familiar with it." He looked her up and down. "There's something about you, though . . . Something about the way you stand . . ."

Supergirl tightened her lips and struck her most powerful and threatening pose, the one she used to face down fellow Kryptonians, Daxamites . . .

Owlman grinned. "I've spent years watching him. Studying him." She knew who he meant—Ultraman. Kal's evil doppelgänger. "He has a way of standing . . . Like he could take off at any moment. But you . . . You . . . Gravity got you down?"

He *knew*.

Supergirl went on the offensive, hoping to take advantage of the element of surprise. With any luck, he wouldn't expect Non-Supergirl to attack, and that would give her a second to—

KRAK!

Her head seemed to explode with pain as he backhanded her with a solid, well-placed blow to her temple.

She shoved the pain aside and lashed out with a spin kick that Alex had taught her. It caught him off guard, and she enjoyed the momentary expression of shocked pain that flitted across his face.

"More to you than the powers," he said, taking a step back. "Nice."

Then, with a snarl, he leaped at her. She dodged to the side and let fly with a punch that should have flattened him, but he brought up his arm at the last second to block it. Supergirl used her cape, twirling it to distract him, then tried a front kick at his chest.

Owlman grabbed her ankle in midair. She was slower than she thought.

"Nice try," he grunted, and swung her to one side, smashing her against the wall.

That wall was the last thing she saw before crumpling into unconsciousness.

• • •

Mr. Terrific returned to S.T.A.R. Labs just as Iris's worry about Kara devolved into absolute panic. She hadn't responded to comms hails in several minutes, and now Iris was beyond worried. Curtis immediately sent a coterie of T-spheres through the corridors, each of them equipped with infrared and ultraviolet sensors, as well as radar and heightened noise detection. "Don't worry," he told Iris with confidence. "My little buddies are on the job. They'll find Kara, and if Owlman's in the building, you can bet they'll find him, too."

Nibbling at her left thumbnail, Iris hoped he was right. Barry and the others had left hours ago, and while she understood that the vagaries of time travel made it imprecise if not impossible to predict when they should return, Kara's radio silence—combined with the idea that Owlman had mucked with the speedster treadmill—made her more nervous than usual.

"This dude is like the Batman of his world, right?" Felicity asked. "Do you think that means that *our* Bruce Wayne—"

"Not a chance," Iris said absently. "Earth 27 is a funhouse mirror version of ours, remember? Our Bruce Wayne is a rich playboy. Theirs is a badass. Opposites."

"Right," Felicity said. "But what if the effete-fop thing is an *act*? What if our Bruce Wayne is a *secret* badass?"

Iris threw her hands up in the air. "Sure, sure! And the president is a shape-shifting alien, and the guy on the ten o'clock news on WGBS is really a superhero and—"

"Ladies!" Mr. Terrific interrupted. "I have a ping!" He consulted the control module for his T-spheres. "Sphere 10-9-HG has picked something up. I knew it would be 10-9-HG," he said happily. "I love that little guy."

"Curtis!" Felicity snapped.

"Oh, right. Anyway, picking up an extra heat signature in the medical bay, near Madame Xanadu's room."

Iris smacked herself in the forehead with the palm of her hand. Of course. Owlman had threatened Madame Xanadu once already.

"Caitlin!" she called into the comms channel. "Are you in Medical?"

"Where else would I be?" came the response.

"Are you armed?"

A BREACH SPUN OPEN NEXT TO Barry and Wally. Superman staggered through, looking as though he'd gone fifteen rounds with Muhammad Ali wearing kryptonite gloves. Immediately behind him was none other than Cisco.

Barry whooped and threw his arms around Cisco in a massive bear hug. Superman crouched down next to Kid Flash and checked his vitals.

"I'm glad to see you, too, buddy," Cisco said. "You guys have an escape plan, or am I going to have to Leia this rescue?"

Barry managed to crack a grin. "Let's say we're trying to think on our feet and improvise."

"So . . . situation normal?"

"We've . . . we've already lost some people . . ."

"Situation much, much worse than normal," Wally said.

Cisco sighed. Up in the sky, Mick fired blast after blast of green energy at the Time Trapper, all to no effect.

In quick, clipped sentences, Cisco filled Barry in on everything he'd learned about and from the Time Trapper, finishing with ". . . so there are two entire Multiverses at stake here. And the poor TV schnooks don't even know they're at risk."

Opening his mouth to respond, Barry was distracted by the glowing green object hurtling toward them. As they watched, Mick pinwheeled through the vacuum and crashed nearby. Barry ran to Mick's side. Heat Wave was still breathing, and the green cocoon of energy around him seemed to be doing its best to stitch together his wounds.

In an instant so quick that even Barry missed it, the Time Trapper shrank back down to a human scale and stood before them on the asteroid.

"You. Barry Allen. A gnat from the distant past who has dared travel through my realm."

The voice made his ears hurt. It seemed to vibrate on multiple frequencies at the same time. There was nothing but a black blank within that hood, but it sounded as though there had to be more than one mouth speaking.

"Welcome. To the End."

"It's not over yet!" Barry said with more confidence than he actually felt.

"It has 'been over' for eons. I have already won. All life across the Multiverse has been extinguished, save for those here. And soon, you, too, will be dead."

Barry tilted his chin up. "You seem pretty confident, given that we've already broken your machinery and rescued your two prisoners."

The Time Trapper did not chuckle or even move, but something in his demeanor changed subtly, communicating to Barry that it found this argument amusing.

"And yet in so doing, you have brought to me a second speedster. And a verdant omnithought band! How delicious. The last of them were destroyed eons ago during the Gray Crisis, but you have delivered one to my hands. My gratitude."

"You'll have to take it from me." Mick spoke from behind Barry, slowly sitting up. "And that won't be easy."

As though Mick hadn't spoken at all, the Time Trapper went on. *"In recognition of this service you have done for me, I return your companions to you, time-lost these last moments, trapped within a field of no-time. They are inconsequential. As are you all. For shortly all of existence will cease to be."*

The Time Trapper's cloak billowed, and suddenly Sara, Oliver, and Ray exploded forth from the lightless hollow of the hood, spilling onto the ground like strewn pebbles.

"And now I will rebuild my machinery. Re-yoke Cisco Ramon to my tuning equipment. And with the ring and the power of a brace of speedsters, my will shall become reality!"

"Bite me!" Sara yelled suddenly and lashed out with the glowing golden rope. It snapped and wrapped itself around the Time Trapper, its glow intensifying.

The Trapper's hood inclined as though considering the rope around him.

"All of history is at my disposal. I can push back the Iron Curtain of Time at will and exploit anything I wish. See here, Sara Lance—the League of Assassins, reborn."

And in that instant, a veritable army of ninjas leaped forth from nothingness, taking form as their feet touched the ground. Sara spun around, dodging a throwing star. Oliver nocked an arrow and fired.

"Take the fight to the Trapper!" Barry ordered Mick. "You're the only one who can do it right now." And then he ran off into the thick of the battle.

Sara gaped as Malcolm Merlyn strode toward her, nocking an arrow. She was pretty certain he'd been dead for eons by now and even in her own present hadn't numbered among the living. But that was time travel for you. Temporal relocation, Ava liked to say, meant always getting the chance to say you're sorry . . . and never really saying goodbye.

Ava. Ava. Ava.

The word, the name, became a repeating mantra in her skull as she fought for her life. Somewhere up above, in the sky that was not a sky, Mick was hurling green energy at the Time Trapper. Down here, there was an endless army of ninjas, assassins, and other ne'er-do-wells that she and Oliver and Ray had to contend with.

"Stand down!" Malcolm yelled at her. "I have a bead on your heart."

She believed him. Malcolm's archery skills rivaled Oliver's, and the arrow aimed at her did not so much as tremble.

So she let the rope do the work for her. Standing completely still, she mentally commanded it to slither along the ground, then wrap around Malcolm's ankles. By the time he realized what had happened, she'd already jerked the rope, yanking him off his feet. The arrow went awry.

The next thing Malcolm saw was the White Canary launching herself at him. She landed a punch to his right cheek, then a devastating kick to his jaw. There was a satisfying, bony crunch and Malcolm collapsed to the ground, unconscious.

Nice, Sara thought, commanding the rope to coil itself in her hands.

A new breach opened. Not one of Cisco's—this was one of the Time Trapper's. A gaggle of men and women and alien creatures came forth, wearing garish costumes. Some of them wielded lightning. Some heat. Some grew to enormous size. It was the world's worst cosplay convention, and it was being dumped on their heads.

"The Legion of Super-Villains!" Superman exclaimed from somewhere behind her.

Great. The League of Assassins was bad enough. Now they had to deal with a legion of bad guys with superpowers?

Electricity blistered across the sky, arcing in deadly jagged spikes. Sara hit the dirt, lashing out with her rope. It snaked around the ankles of the guy wielding the lightning. She commanded the rope to tighten, then to jerk him off his feet and spin him in a circle like a lasso wielded by a dogie-seeking cowboy. The magic lasso did as she bade it, with no movement necessary on her part. The lightning wielder yelped and spun around. Blasts of lightning radiated out from him, striking his companions.

That was, by her count, ten down. Infinity to go.

• • •

The asteroid they'd named Globe swarmed with villains. Barry sped through the phalanx of assassins, knocking spears, swords, knives, and throwing stars out of hands. Moving this fast without much gravity was tricky, but fortunately momentum and velocity weren't dependent on gravity. As long as he didn't do something stupid like run right off the planetoid, he was okay.

"I am Lazon!" shrieked a blond guy in a skintight orange costume. "Light-speed killer!" He was as fast as Barry and could fly. This wasn't good.

Barry dodged Lazon's first attack, drawing him away from where Wally and Superman had managed to huddle in the shadows created by the sphere.

Wally was still too weak to run, but he apparently was vibrating while holding Superman's hand, making the Man of Steel phase on and off. Superman was using the phase to punch through weapons and armor, knocking out attackers left and right.

Superman stepped back as Lazon flew by, still ranting about how he was the *slayer of heroes* and *made of living light!*

"You may be as fast as light, Lazon," Superman called, "but you're still as sloppy a flier as you were when we were kids!"

"You'll never escape me!" Lazon crowed as Barry led him on a steeplechase along the dips, crenellations, and outcroppings of the asteroid. "I'm faster than—"

"Faster than light, right, got it," Barry said, and suddenly slammed on the brakes. "But who's trying to escape?"

Unable to dodge in time, Lazon flew face-first into Barry's

fist. His nose crunched satisfyingly, and his entire body flipped head over heels and collided with a slender spine of rock.

"He's just gonna keep conjuring up people from the past to fight us," Barry said, skidding to a halt next to Cisco. "We have to cut him off somehow."

"I have an idea," Cisco said. "But it's gonna take me out of action for a while."

Barry contemplated for a tenth of a second. "Do it." Then he rushed off into the fray. A bald man in a skintight black suit had just hurled a wicked-looking high-tech mace in Oliver's direction. It was too dicey to grab the mace, so Barry shouldered Oliver out of the danger path and kept going, leaping to kick a man with a handlebar mustache who wore an animal skin on his shoulders and wielded a wicked sniper rifle.

Someone shouted, "He's taken down Orion the Hunter!"

Barry figured that was good news and kept going.

Wally pushed himself into a sitting position, leaning on one elbow. The battle was going badly—Teams Flash and Arrow and the Legends had a lot of power on their side, but there were just too many bad guys, with more pouring out of breaches every time he blinked. Aliens and interdimensional wizards and what appeared to be an entire army of cyborgs screaming, "FOR THE KHUNDISH EMPIRE!"

He was feeling stronger, but his speed was exhausted. He didn't have any more to lend to Superman.

"It's OK, Kid Flash." Superman tapped the metallic clasps along his collarbone, jettisoning his cape. He retrieved it from the ground, tore it in half, and wound the fabric around his hands.

"What do you think you're doing?" Wally asked.

"I'm going to help fight," Superman said.

"You don't have any powers, man!"

The Man of Steel shrugged. "Some of my best friends don't have any powers."

Cisco found a spot with a clear line of sight to the Time Trapper, then made sure there was a big boulder at his back. Not that this would stop an attack coming from that direction, he acknowledged sourly. With all the superpowers being thrown around on the battlefield, the boulder was theoretically no better than a paper plate as far as armor went. Still, its solidity against his back made him feel better.

"Here goes nothing," he muttered, and held both arms out, fingers splayed.

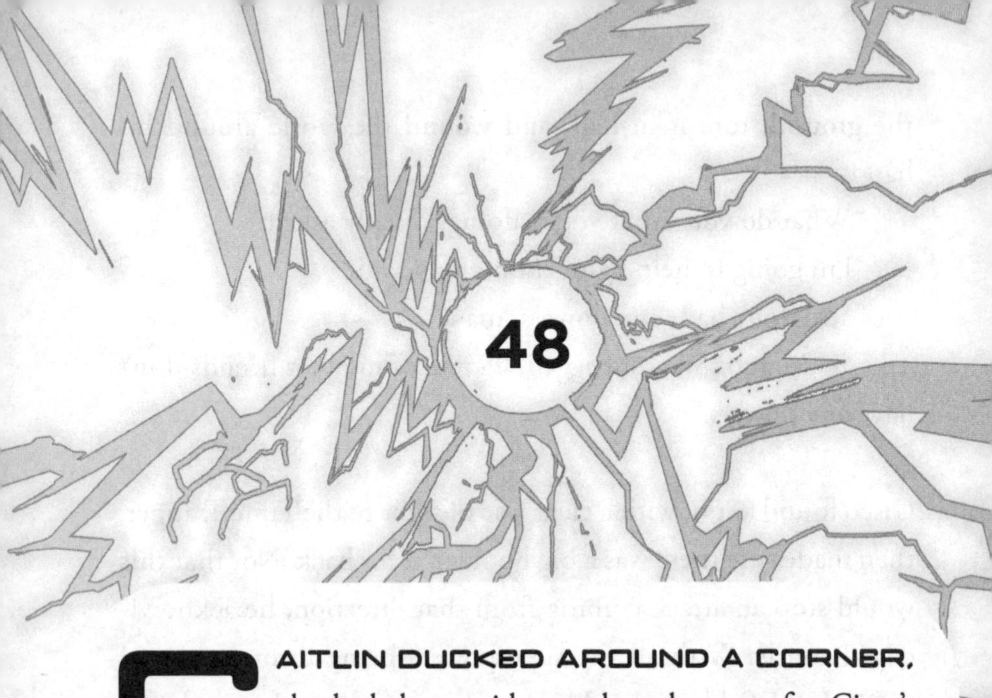

48

CAITLIN DUCKED AROUND A CORNER, checked the corridor, and made a run for Cisco's lab. She was not exactly thrilled to discover that she was the only person on this level, along with a murderous lunatic like Owlman. When she'd interviewed for the position at S.T.A.R. Labs, Harrison Wells had promised her "excitement and stimulation." Then he'd grinned and said, "I promise you this much, Dr. Snow—you'll never be bored here."

Yeah, well, running from super villains hadn't exactly been what she'd had in mind at the time.

In Cisco's lab, she touched her earpiece and whispered, "I'm in the lab. Where's Owlman?"

"Still in Xanadu's room, according to Mr. Terrific."

"Copy."

"Save a piece of him for me." It was Supergirl's voice, filled with uncharacteristic anger. Caitlin spun around, shocked to see the Girl of Steel standing in the doorway.

"I'm writing you a prescription for *stay out of this until your powers are back*," Caitlin told her.

"I'm at low power," Supergirl conceded, "but still more powerful than you are."

Caitlin tilted her head and blinked meaningfully at Supergirl, who blew out an abashed breath.

"I'm sorry. I didn't mean to imply . . . I'm just frustrated."

"I feel you," Caitlin said. "I think we've all hit our limit of crazy and evil and more crazy. Help me find something."

"What are we looking for?" Supergirl asked, scanning the room at the same time. Cisco was a genius, but not much for sharing. He had an organization system for his workshop, but he had never bothered to explain it to anyone.

Caitlin described what she needed and the two of them began pawing through the junk piled everywhere. The workbenches were littered with the detritus of his various experiments—polymer swatches for costume prototypes, wiring and cabling for weapons systems. Nothing intact that they could use, so Supergirl started going through drawers.

She found what they needed in the fourth drawer down on the second workbench. Supergirl held it up with a quizzical expression on her face. Caitlin's grin confirmed she'd hit paydirt.

"Great, hand it over."

"Nope. I'm not letting you—"

Caitlin sighed. "Do you even know how to use it?"

Supergirl's mouth opened in protest, then shut. With an air of resignation, she handed the gadget over to Caitlin.

“Is Owlman still in the room with Xanadu?” Caitlin asked over her comms bud.

“Yes,” came Iris’s voice. “Do you have it?”

“Yep. Kara found it in a drawer, next to paper clips and Post-it notes.”

“Will it work?”

“Who knows?” Caitlin asked rhetorically.

Iris said nothing for a moment. Caitlin and Supergirl sneaked out the door. Down the corridor was the medical bay. “Caitlin, it’s too dangerous. Let Kara do it.”

“She’s right,” Supergirl said with a note of apology in her tone.

They tiptoed down the hallway toward Madame Xanadu’s room. “Nah. We’ll do it together.”

“He could *kill* you,” Supergirl told her.

“Details, details,” Caitlin muttered. She shoved open the door to Madame Xanadu’s room, stepped inside, and took aim. Beside her, Supergirl tensed, ready to leap into action.

“Freeze!” Caitlin shouted, and pulled the trigger on the gun she wielded.

With a casual, cool air, Owlman turned from Madame Xanadu’s bed and crossed his arms over his chest. “You’re supposed to shout *Freeze!* and then give me a chance to surrender before you pull the trigger.”

Nothing had happened when she’d fired, though. Frustrated, Caitlin whacked her palm against the side of the weapon. It had an uncomfortable grip and a big tank strapped to the top of it. It was heavy and hard to aim, and it was making her really angry right then.

"Uh, Caitlin . . . ?" Supergirl muttered out of the corner of her mouth. "*Do* something . . ."

"You don't . . . It was supposed to be a joke . . ." She whacked it again. "It was funny because this is—"

"Do either of you have anything you'd like to say," Owlman asked solicitously, "before I knock you unconscious?"

Caitlin realized the problem. She hadn't disengaged the safety catch on the gun. Mostly because she hadn't known it was there. Cisco usually didn't have time to add such niceties to his gadgets.

"Freeze!" she yelled again.

Owlman rolled his eyes. "I told you . . ."

The gun bucked in her hands this time and a blast of cold air whooshed out. In an instant, the cold gun that Cisco had originally built as a counter to heat-based villains froze the water in the air around Owlman's feet. Patchy blocks of ice formed from his knees down to the floor, anchoring him there.

Caitlin enjoyed the expression of sheer disbelief on Owlman's face as he tried to tug his feet free. She sauntered over to him.

"Now," she said, "do you have anything you'd like to say before *I* knock *you* unconscious?"

He opened his mouth to speak, but she didn't give him a chance; she swung the butt of the cold gun at his jaw and knocked him out.

"I coldcocked him!" Caitlin turned to Supergirl and crowed, then giggled at her own pun. "Cisco would be so proud!"

49

BARRY WATCHED AS THE FIRST breach formed in front of one of the Time Trapper's. A half man, half robot in a half-yellow leotard skipped directly into the second breach—Cisco's—and ended up running into the Time Trapper. He was followed by a green-haired woman with a giant floating eyeball, a man with an ax, another man with what appeared to be a cloudy fishbowl on his head, and a . . .

A *thing*. Barry wasn't sure what it was. It was enormous, built like a huge, hairless gorilla, with no eyes and a transparent dome where a head of hair should have been. Lightning crackled around the visible brain matter.

"Validus." Barry turned to see Superman standing nearby. He had a black eye and a split lip. A trickle of blood wended down from a nasty cut along his hairline. Without powers, he'd fought his way from Wally's safe spot to here. "The Time Trapper has summoned the Fatal Five."

"Fatal Five? The bad guys name their groups now? I can't keep track of all the villains we're facing," Barry said.

"Cisco's smart," Superman said. "This is a good strategy."

Barry nodded, watching as Cisco conjured breaches to match the Time Trapper's. Every enemy who emerged went straight into a new breach and ended up running into the Time Trapper. Most of them were confused and outraged by their time-napping, and they immediately attacked the Trapper. Those who didn't found themselves in another breach, dumped out into empty space.

Even from this distance, Barry could tell the toll this was taking on Cisco.

"We have a little reprieve," Barry said over comms, "but I don't know how long it'll last."

"We need to come up with a plan while the Trapper's distracted," Superman agreed.

"Fall back into the sphere!" Sara yelled over comms, pointing to the cut-open prison where Wally had been running for who knew how long. "We need shelter!"

Oliver sent an explosive arrow into a cluster of super villains and ninjas. Screams buffeted them. "No one give me any grief about lethal force!" he warned. "These folks have all been dead for billions of years."

Yeah, they had a few moments while the Time Trapper dealt with the overlapping series of breaches that Cisco Ramon had summoned. That might be enough time to regroup, but then what?

Still, she did what any good field commander would do: take advantage of the moment and call a retreat. And also called in air support.

"Mick! See if you can help take some heat off Cisco!"

"Someone say *heat*?" Mick asked, dipping low in the sky. It was truly terrifying how quickly he'd taken to the power ring. She worried about how they would take it back from him when this was all over.

Mick created a giant green baseball bat and smashed the Time Trapper in the head. He followed this up with a Gatling gun the size of a small moon, pumping round after round of glowing green ammo into the Trapper.

Sara thought it might be working. A little, at least. Between the breaches and the power ring, the Trapper seemed to be on the ropes. Maybe they had a chance. Maybe they would survive this.

Mick roared into the void and launched a fusillade of enormous arrows at the Time Trapper, who cuffed them aside.

"That's my gimmick," Oliver huffed as he ran toward the sphere.

Barry grabbed Wally and helped him over the lip of the sphere. He hated to drag Kid Flash back to the site of so much of his torment, but Sara was right—they needed some shelter and a place to plan. If the sphere could contain a speedster's energies, it could probably weather the villains' assault for a couple of minutes at least.

A couple of minutes. An eternity to the Flash, but to his friends it was just . . . a couple of minutes. No time at all.

"Are we all here?" Sara asked as Barry and Wally hit the bottom of the sphere.

"We're missing Cisco—"

A breach opened, wobbled briefly, and Cisco fell through just before it closed. He collapsed to the ground. "I've given 'er all she's got, Cap'n. She canna take nae more."

"And Mick—" Oliver said.

Just then, a green slash of light illuminated the sky above them. Mick executed a barely controlled landing in the center of the gathering. His left arm was smoldering and most of his exposed flesh was cut, burned, or bruised. He looked like a man who has walked through a desert to an oasis only to realize the oasis was poisoned.

"How's the ring treating your head, Mr. Rory?" Superman asked with concern.

"Feels like someone's excavating my brain with a rusty, old grapefruit spoon and pieces of it are flaking off inside."

"That's . . . a very graphic simile," Barry said.

"He's a bestselling author," the Atom said proudly.

"Then someone get his editor on the phone and tell him to come up with a plot twist to get us out of here," Sara said. "Even with Mick's ring and my fancy new rope tricks, we don't stand a chance against that army out there. It's every super villain I've ever seen, plus all the ones I haven't."

"Look, most of us are disposable," said Ray, "but he needs

Cisco's powers. And he needs a speedster. And the ring can only help him."

"Volthoom and the Time Trapper, a match made in hell," Mick observed with disgust.

"We need to get the speedsters and Cisco and the ring out of here." Wally stood, leaning against Barry.

"Great idea, fleet-feet," Cisco said with sarcasm. "But the Time Trapper'll just figure out how to yank us back here again. Paradoxes being what they are, he might've already done it."

"What if we can trap *him*?" Superman asked. "Lock him up here at the End of All Time? His power means nothing if *we* go and he's left here."

"Again, Man of Die-Cast," Cisco grumped, "he could just pull us here another time."

"We need to use his own technology against him," Ray said. "Even he can't go *through* the Iron Curtain of Time. He just moves it through time so that he can reach into whatever era he needs."

Barry snapped his fingers. "Exactly! So we hack his technology and move the Curtain to this relative moment. Right now."

"And if there's a way to lock it into place . . ."

"Then we've trapped the Trapper," Cisco said, warming to the ideas. "Pinning him between this moment and the actual heat death of the Multiverse. He'll have nowhere to go. And without me, he'll have no way to punch through to the other Multiverse and complete his plan."

"Caught between a rock and a hard place," Oliver said.

"More like a quantum-fluctuating Heisenberg barrier and an

entropic collapse," Ray said with great cheer. "But, uh, why get all technical and pedantic with friends, right?" he added quickly at Oliver's scowl.

"There's one big problem with this plan," Sara chimed in. "Us. We'll end up stuck here, too."

"I think that's a small price to pay in order to save the Megaverse," Superman told her.

"Plus, I'm not sure it's necessary," Barry said. "I have an idea. All I have to do is relax my internal vibrations. We're all connected by our passage through the collider tunnel so that we're in tune, linked to me. Once I shift my internal vibrations, we'll instantly return to our own time."

"Running away?" Mick clearly didn't like the idea.

"Think of it as a strategic withdrawal," Superman told him.

"We're running low on fight," Oliver said. "There's no shame in a retreat to regroup and come back, fortified, to win the battle."

"And we'll return to this exact moment to trap the Trapper," Barry said, "so it'll be like we never left."

He took Wally's hand to help attune the younger speedster to the proper frequency, then adjusted his vibrations.

And screamed in pain.

His agonized bellow had company in the yelps, cries, and hollers of the rest of the time-traveling crew.

When the pain ended, they were all crumpled on the floor of the sphere. And when they looked up, the enormous black void within the Time Trapper's hood stared down at them.

50

THE IRON CURTAIN OF TIME STILL *stands. And from this side, you cannot breach it.*

"Once this Multiverse contracts to a single point, I will use Vibe's power to peer into the other timeline. Then I will use the superspeed energy collected by my temporal battery to hurl that primal atom into a breach."

"What? Why would you do any of that?" Barry had recovered before the others, his superfast metabolism allowing him to rebound from the shock of slamming into the Iron Curtain of Time.

The Time Trapper peered down at him. *"Why, to invade that timeline, of course. It has been weakened by its own Crisis, its foundations soft and malleable. The primal atom I fling at it will cause an explosion of universal proportions that will eradicate most of that timeline's Multiverse. The remains . . . I will rule over the remains. This timeline—this Multiverse—will be no more, its existence having served merely to create a weapon for me to exploit. The other timeline will be mine . . . And I will then be King of All Reality. This timeline, this Multiverse, serves only as my weapon. Its inevitable death powers my path to the other Multiverse."*

"Man, and I thought I was ambitious for wanting to win the Ivy University Science Department Challenge," Ray muttered, shaking his head to clear it.

"And the best part, Flash? The best part is that you and your friends brought my victory to me. Here, where everyone and everything has died, where gravity captures matter. Everything collapses. Into the palm of my hand. And then a new Multiverse, a new reality, a new timeline for my own amusement."

"Great," Cisco complained. "That other Barry Allen screws up the timeline and *we* have to fix it."

Barry grabbed Cisco and whisked him over to Mick. "Cisco is the most important person here right now, Mick. The Trapper can't execute his plan without him. You're the powerhouse—get him as far away as you can and keep him safe."

Mouth open to protest, Cisco only had the chance to say, "Heeeyyyyyy!" as Heat Wave wrapped him in a green bubble and took off into space with him.

The Time Trapper turned as the green blur painted its way across the black sky. Barry gave Oliver a nod, and Green Arrow launched a series of explosive arrows directly into the Trapper's hood. Just enough to distract him for a split second.

"You wage war to no purpose. My victory is proven. The collapse of the universe is proof of it. Entropy wins."

And then he turned away from them, growing and reaching out into the depths of space for Cisco and Mick.

"It's now or never," Oliver said. His quiver was empty, but you wouldn't know he was weaponless to look at him. He was still the steady, resolute warrior he'd been since his days on the island Lian Yu. "We need to get to the Time Sphere and get out of here, with Cisco. That's the endgame."

"You heard the Trapper—we can't get through the Iron Curtain of Time." Sara coiled up her glowing rope with but a thought, the thing slithering into her grasp and neatly wrapping itself in a circle. She looked around. They were all exhausted, wounded, depleted. Retreat was the only option—and a winning one, as a bonus—but it was also impossible.

And the Time Trapper, inexhaustible, could keep throwing enemies at them, wearing them down, until it was all over.

Which would be soon, no doubt.

Wally turned to Barry. "Do you feel it?" Wally's voice trembled, but there was a deep confidence in it. "There's something out there. Something for us."

Barry knew immediately what he meant. That sensation he'd felt ever since they'd arrived at the End of All Time. He'd ignored it in favor of the immediate problem at hand. And because he'd thought he was about to confront Thawne again. He'd allowed his own thirst for vengeance to cloud his judgment. What a fool. In such a hurry. Always in such a hurry.

Now he did what Madame Xanadu had advised him to do long ago, the day he'd met her at the Central City Pier: Slow down.

He relaxed. Despite the certainty that the Time Trapper would return his attention to him at any moment, Barry settled in and focused on his breathing. Meditation had never been his strong suit, but he'd always been good at concentrating. He did it now, focusing on his breath, then reaching out. Feeling . . .

The Speed Force. The ever-present, extradimensional source of his powers. HyperHeaven, Johnny Quick had called it.

And something else. Something similar . . .

"I can feel it," he murmured.

"What is it?" Wally asked. He, too, was in a near trance, seduced into the sensation. "It feels like . . . me. Like running. This sounds crazy, doesn't it?"

But then Barry realized. He understood what it was.

It was the vibrational energy from the Earth 27 speedsters. He could still feel it, billions of years in the future. It was not gone. It was part of the fabric of reality now.

"It's . . . it's bigger than the Speed Force," he said softly. "It's had billions of years to grow. We planted an acorn in the twenty-first century, and now it's a forest of oaks."

And there was something within that speed energy. An encoded message, pulsing with vibrational tones stretching across all of reality, permeating the fabric of the Multiverse. And only a speedster could read it.

"This was the weapon," Barry said, his eyes opening. "Madame Xanadu and Owlman planned it this way. We were just a conduit, to get through the Iron Curtain of Time. The vibrational energy was supposed to rip the Time Trapper apart. But something went wrong."

"No one could accurately calculate the impact of billions of years passing as the energy traveled," Superman said, limping over to him. "So the impact was lessened, even though the power grew."

Barry understood. "What was supposed to be a blast from a water cannon became a river instead. All the water is still there but not channeled into single burst."

Overhead, Mick came into view, hauling Cisco behind him. They alighted in the center of the sphere, and Mick quickly erected a huge umbrella overhead to shield them as the Time Trapper returned.

"Nowhere to run," Mick grunted, focusing. He reinforced the umbrella with steel and concrete and everything else strong he could think of.

"Space has contracted," Cisco elucidated. "We're almost at the end of reality. The Big Crunch. There's no room to flee."

The Time Trapper roared and pounded at the umbrella. Blood burst from one of Mick's eyes as he held tight.

"What if this isn't a Big Crunch?" Barry asked. "What if it's a Big Bounce?"

Cisco nodded. "I see where you're headed with this."

"Maybe clue in the kids who flunked science class?" Mick growled, shaking as he held off the Time Trapper.

With characteristic enthusiasm, Ray piped up. "There's a theory that says that if the universe *is* a closed system and collapses into a Big Crunch, that something called the Big Bounce would happen—the hyper-compressed agglomeration of matter and energy would *re*-explode at some point, creating another Big Bang, re-creating the universe."

"Basically, time is a circle, not a line," Barry chimed in.

"Is that supposed to comfort me?" Oliver asked. "A new Big Bang makes a new Multiverse? Where do we fit in there?"

Cisco jumped in. "Look at it this way: That Big Bang *is* the one that created our Multiverse. They're the same. Because like Barry said—time is a circle. When you go around a circle, you don't end up on a new circle. You wind up back at the beginning of the *same* circle."

"How long does it take to get to the Big Bang?" Sara asked. "And I can't believe I just asked that question."

Ray shrugged. "Once the universe—the Multiverse, in this case—collapses, there's no such thing as time anymore. It doesn't exist, because nothing exists. So the Big Bang happens immediately. Or after an eternity. They're the same thing."

"My head hurts," Mick complained, "and not just from this stupid thing." He wiggled his fist to draw attention to the glowing green ring. "But for what it's worth, Volthoom says everything you guys are saying checks out."

"Oh, good," Sara chimed in. "The evil, insane *jewelry* from another universe thinks we have a plan."

"What *is* the plan?" Oliver asked. "I don't see how Big Crunch or Big Bounce makes a difference."

Barry hesitated. "I . . . I can't run back into the past. The Iron Curtain is blocking me. But I can use the vibrational energy from the speedsters, the new Speed Force they've woven, and I can run *forward*."

"Past the end of the Multiverse," Ray whispered.

"Into the Big Bang," Superman confirmed. "Into the fires of Creation itself."

“And then keep going,” Barry said. “I can pull you guys behind me in the Time Sphere. I’ll run the entire length of history and get you back to the present.”

Ray’s lips moved as he did some calculations in his head. “Wait. At that velocity, will you even be able to stop?”

Barry shrugged, but he knew the answer, which was *Probably not.* He suspected that he could survive the moment of the Big Bang, shielded by the Speed Force and the Earth 27 speedsters’ vibrations that formed the new Speed Force. But then he would still need to run through all of history in order to get the team home. And he felt very strongly that he wouldn’t be able to stop, that his momentum would keep him going . . .

Until he got to the End of All Time again. And hit the Iron Curtain of Time moving at an unimaginable speed.

He preferred not to think about that, though. He would probably burn up from the speed of such a run long before he could hit the Curtain, in any event.

The question Ray should have asked: *Will you even survive?*

“We’re not technically on Earth 1 any longer. Johnny Quick’s formula has no upper limit here. It’ll make me even faster. Plus I’ll tap into the Earth 27 energy . . . I can do it.”

Wally stared at him. “Barry . . . That’s the craziest thing I’ve ever heard. And believe me—I’ve heard a lot of crazy.”

“I mean . . . in the moments before the Big Bang, there’s no *there* there,” Ray told him. “Nothing to run on. No oxygen to breathe. This is beyond impossible.”

“The Speed Force lets me violate the laws of physics on a regular basis,” Barry said with surprising calm and confidence. “I suspect we'll actually be translated into pure math, an encoded bolt of electrical information shooting across the universe."

"What's that going to feel like?" Oliver mused.

"Like nothing. It's the Speed Force—you won't feel any different."

Oliver didn't look entirely convinced.

"It's a moot point if we can't trap the Trapper," Superman said.

"He was using the machinery where he held me to manipulate the Curtain," Cisco revealed. "I can—"

"No," Sara said. "We need you to keep the Trapper distracted while we put this crazy plan into action. And I know your powers are tapped out. That's OK. I have an idea."

"I'll get to work stripping the Time Sphere for parts," Barry said. "Retune the chronal engines to help reinforce the Iron Curtain of Time."

"Which leaves me," Superman said.

Sara arched an eyebrow. "Last time I checked, it left Wally, Oliver, me, *and* you."

Superman offered a polite nod. "Of course. And which one of you is conversant in both alien and future technology . . . ?"

No one spoke.

"I thought so. I'll go to the other asteroid and make the Trapper's machine work for us. And then destroy it."

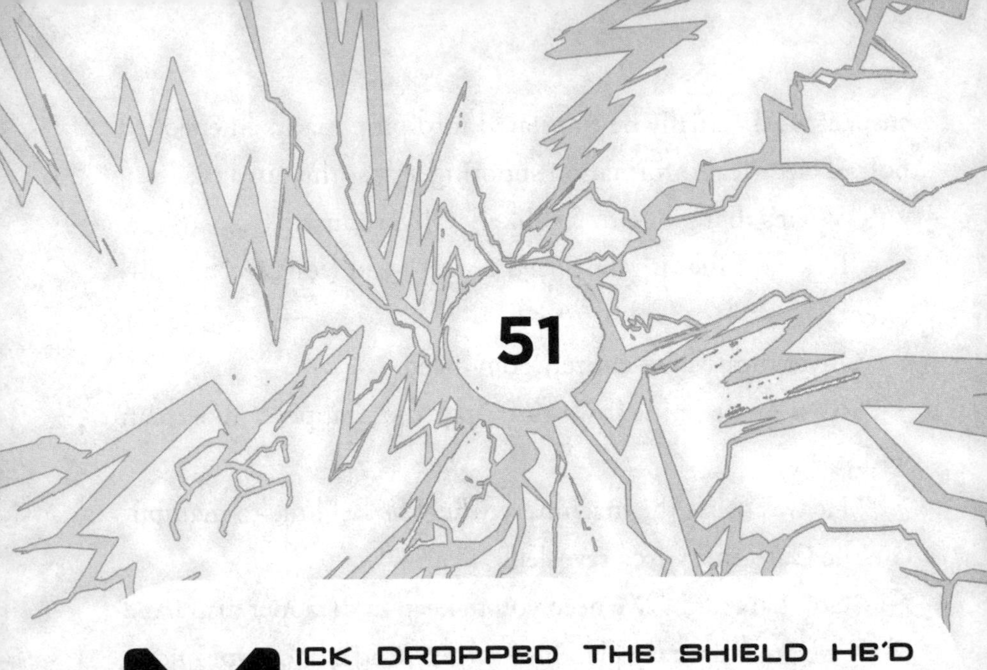

51

MICK DROPPED THE SHIELD HE'D established, letting the Time Trapper's enormous hand descend into the sphere. In the blink of an eye, Kid Flash dashed to one side, pulling Cisco along with him. Wally's speedster metabolism had finally kicked in, and with a little superspeed "jump start" from the Flash, he'd managed to get back most of his speed.

Now he and the Flash played a desperate game of "keep away," shuttling Cisco back and forth, vibrating through walls and stone outcroppings. The Time Trapper directed his legions to flank them, hemming them into an area around the broken sphere.

"How are you feeling?" Barry asked Wally at superspeed during a Cisco handoff.

"Kinda sporty," Wally rejoined, and whisked Cisco away.

If they could keep Cisco out of the Time Trapper's hands

long enough for his Vibe powers to return, maybe they'd get out of this after all.

"There's almost no gravity, so I can glide over there. I just need a push," Superman said, pointing to Needle.

Without a word, Mick conjured a big green badminton racket, which he used to swat Superman bodily from Globe's surface. The Man of Steel hurtled through space in a straight line, headed directly for his target. Without gravity or atmosphere, there was nothing to redirect him or slow him as he sped toward the asteroid. The Legends and the others were keeping the Trapper's summoned foes busy, so none of them peeled off to try to intercept him.

Good thing, too. Even though he'd studied the ancient Kryptonian martial art of Klurkor—and was rated a fifth-level headband in that school of fighting—he knew he wouldn't last long against some of the villains the Trapper had brought from the past.

With absolutely no dignity, Superman crash-landed on Needle. It hurt a lot less than it should have, thanks to the lower gravity, but he still absorbed the impact of the velocity from Heat Wave's slap.

And while pain was not new to him, it was exotic and strange, odd enough that he felt it more than he probably should have.

No time for reflection, Clark. Get up and move.

On shaky, weakened legs, he made his way to the machine he'd broken open before. Fortunately, only the part that had held Cisco was damaged—the rest seemed to be intact and functional.

"Well, well, well," said a horrifyingly familiar voice. "And here we are."

Superman turned. There, standing between him and the control console he needed to access, was none other than Lex Luthor.

52

SUPERGIRL WATCHED THROUGH THE unbreakable plexiglass as Owlman came to in a Pipeline cell. He cracked his neck this way and that, stretched his quads. As though he were in a yoga studio, not a prison.

"How long do you think it will take me to break out of here?" he asked idly.

Supergirl applauded lightly and smiled sardonically. "Well, Iris owes me ten bucks. I bet her it would take you less than five seconds after waking up to make that threat. I win. You're getting predictable, Bruce."

Owlman sneered. "Knowing I can get out of here won't make it any easier for you to stop me."

Supergirl groaned. "And now I have to give her the ten bucks back! She bet me you would say that!"

Owlman laughed and leaned against the glass. "So, you got me. Big deal."

"If you ever want to get out of there," Supergirl told him, "tell me what you're up to. What were you doing with the treadmill?"

He pursed his lips, considering. "What do I get in return for an honest answer?"

Supergirl pretended to think about this. "Food and water."

Another laugh. "You're not going to let me starve to death in here. I've already got your number, lady. You're not the kind to let me suffer."

"You're right about that," Supergirl agreed, and thumbed the pad that opened the door to the Pipeline.

Iris strode in. "I, on the other hand, have absolutely no compunction about torturing you. That's my husband in the far future whom you're messing with. I'll do whatever I have to in order to help him. And I don't have to kill you to do it. I'm more than willing to let you get within spitting distance of death before I give you to a hospital to resuscitate you." She leaned in close. "Imagine it, Bruce: Long days and nights with nothing in your belly. I bet you've trained most of your life to endure such a thing. But even training can't forestall the inevitable physiological ramifications of no food or drink. Caitlin tells me it's pretty painful. And if it goes on long enough, you'll never fully recover. Even with good medical attention, you'll still never really be at 100 percent again."

He swallowed audibly, even through the glass.

"Someone like you, someone who's spent his entire life honing his body to physical perfection . . . I bet that would drive you crazy, wouldn't it? Knowing that you'll never be at that peak again."

Owlman managed a sneer. "You're bluffing."

Supergirl whistled. "I wouldn't bet on that!"

"Possibly," Iris conceded. "But imagine how much damage will happen to your body while we both wait to find out."

She crossed her arms over her chest and cocked a hip.

It didn't take him long.

"OK, OK, you win. The truth is, I don't know *what* I was doing at the treadmill." He held up a hand to forestall her interruption. "I was just following orders."

"From whom?"

He sighed and rested his forehead against the glass. "Her. Madame Xanadu."

Iris shivered. "You're lying."

"I'm not. I've told you the truth all along. I wanted to save the world because I need a place to live, too. And I've done everything in my power to do so."

Up until that moment, he'd been calm, placid. Now, though, his temper burst through to the surface and he pounded on the glass with both fists.

"So let me out of here! I played my part! Let me go! You can't keep me in here forever! You have no right!"

Iris nodded thoughtfully. "Oh. Right. Your whole theory of *Multiversal jurisprudence*. The idea that no Earth 1 court has jurisdiction over what you did on Earth 27. I actually agree with you."

Owlman blinked a few times, processing this revelation, looking for the catch. "So . . . you're letting me out? I'm free to go?"

"Not so much." Iris grinned. "We're going to hand you over to the people who *do* have jurisdiction: the Earth 27 refugees. *They* will determine your fate."

For the first time since meeting him, Iris beheld true fear on Owlman's face.

Iris brought Caitlin with her to interrogate Madame Xanadu. Not because Caitlin was a doctor, but rather because Caitlin turned out to be a good shot with the cold gun. She stood at the foot of Xanadu's bed and took careful aim.

"Try anything tricky or witchy or magical," Iris warned, "and Caitlin will turn you into a popsicle."

Madame Xanadu showed no concern at this pronouncement. She sat up a little straighter in bed without so much as a glance in Caitlin's direction.

"There is no need to threaten me."

"You've been conspiring with Owlman."

Xanadu clucked her tongue. "*Conspire*. An interesting word. It literally means 'to breathe together.' So . . . yes, I have found it prudent to mingle my breath with his. That does not mean we share the same goals."

"I think the death of your Earth 27 counterpart drove you mad," said Caitlin. "And you're trying to bring the same fate to our world."

Xanadu shook her head. "Quite the contrary. I'm trying to save what is left of this Multiverse and the other."

"You have a funny way of showing it: sabotaging the treadmill."

"That was not an act of sabotage. We did nothing to impair your friends' run to the future. We merely . . . modified the treadmill for an alternate purpose."

Caitlin hefted the gun significantly. "No more riddles and half-truths. Tell us what you're up to."

Xanadu sighed at Caitlin's display but still did not look at her, focusing on Iris.

"Iris, I've foreseen it. We all have, the fifty-one remaining Madame Xanadus across the Multiverse. Flash and his team cannot stop the Time Trapper. As his name implies, they are running into a trap."

Iris felt a chill. "Then why did you let them go?"

"Because we needed them to breach the Iron Curtain of Time. And now Bruce has reconfigured your treadmill, turning it from an engine into a weapon. A pulse of vibrational energy so powerful that it will destroy the Time Trapper at the End of All Time and collapse the universe into its next form."

"But . . . but Barry and the others . . . They're at the End of All Time, too! What will happen to them?"

Madame Xanadu's expression told Iris everything she needed to know. "This is why I needed Owlman. His narcissism made him desperate to save the universe so that he could live. And at the same time, I knew I could rely on his ruthlessness to do what had to be done."

"No," Iris said, wiping furiously at a stray tear. No time for sadness. Only anger and action. "I don't believe you. I can't let this be a suicide mission."

"Never fear. Our plan will not work."

Caitlin groaned from the foot of the bed. "What? Then why go through all of this in the first place?"

Madame Xanadu smiled her enigmatic smile. "Because something else *will*."

"This is absolutely nuts!" Iris exclaimed.

With a soft, slow shake of her head, Madame Xanadu said, "This is how it must be. This is how it *shall* be. This has all been foreseen, including Bruce's betrayal and the destruction of the Time Trapper and the heroes at the End of All Time."

"Will I ever see Barry again?" Iris asked.

Madame Xanadu folded one hand atop the other and closed her eyes. For a long time, she said nothing. Then, with a small, placid smile, she said, "You already have seen him again."

53

LUTHOR WORE A PRISON JUMPSUIT, so the Trapper had plucked him from one of the many times he'd been incarcerated on Stryker's Island, the special airborne prison for super-criminals.

He also wore a smarmy smirk. Superman hadn't much cared for that expression when they'd been kids—he liked it even less as an adult.

"I don't have time for you, Lex. Get out of the way."

"Oh, how I've missed that confident, solipsistic tone of voice!" Lex crowed. "As though you were the only person in the world who mattered. And I'm sure you actually believe that. Which is why . . ."

Superman marched over to Lex and did what he'd been wanting to do for years but couldn't—wound up his fist and punched him squarely in the jaw with every ounce of strength in his body. If he'd done this under a yellow sun, Lex's head would have become a grayish-red free-floating mist. Without his powers, though, only two things happened: First, Lex shut up and dropped to the ground, unconscious.

Second, Superman realized he'd probably broken a couple of bones in his hand. It throbbed with radical pain.

Worth it, he decided, gazing at Lex's prone form beneath him.

Shaking the pain from his right hand, he stepped over Lex and rotated the console toward him. He knew alien and future technology, true, but this was something beyond even him. He worried at his lower lip. *Think, Clark. Prove that you don't solve every problem with your fists.*

He glanced at Lex. *Appearances to the contrary.*

The wiring and cabling of the machinery seemed chaotic at first. He blocked out the battle raging in the distance, blocked out the enormity of the Time Trapper, and focused on the task before him. Soon, it started to make sense. He began tapping at the screen. Tentatively. Experimentally. A set of concentric circles widened and a green light flashed. That didn't seem right to him. He tried another series of taps—the circles tightened on each other and the light faded into crimson.

I think this is it. I think I'm moving the Curtain closer to the present.

There was another console nearby. His own console was about as red at it could get, but the concentric circles still weren't overlapping. There was a gap there. He knew it in his gut—the circles had to meet, had to become one. That would mean the Curtain had arrived at the present moment.

But to do it, he would have to manipulate both consoles at once. And the other console was out of reach.

What was he going to do?

"I'm hope this makes sense to you," Oliver said. "Because to me it just looks like a stereo committed suicide."

Sara nodded in agreement. She and Oliver had helped Barry disassemble parts of the Time Sphere. The hull was still intact and would—theoretically—shield them as they made their lunatic dash into the future of nothing, desperate to circle back around to the past. But the guts of the Time Sphere were now arranged before them, disconnected and then reconnected in a spiral pattern on the ground.

"Trust me," Barry said. "When the Curtain hits the present moment, this device will activate and harden it. *Nothing* will get through it from this side. Not the Trapper. Nothing."

He gazed over to Needle. "Now it's up to Superman."

"What have you done?" the Time Trapper demanded, swinging a gargantuan arm at Mick, who buzzed around him like biplanes around King Kong. *"The Curtain approaches!"*

"Yeah, and the fat lady's tuning up her windpipe, you Scooby-Doo reject!" Mick knew he had to keep the distraction going. Out of the corner of his eye, he could see the Time Sphere, a pattern of circuitry arrayed around it. Flash and Kid Flash were loading everyone into the Time Sphere. It was only a matter of time now.

Mick used the ring to make a gigantic mace and swung it at

the Trapper, but something went wrong—it fuzzed and fizzled and dissolved before the blow could land.

"Your wearable thought-weapon is losing its charge," the Trapper advised. He brought one fist down with astonishing speed and power.

Mick created a brick wall overhead, interposing it between them. Then he made another wall behind that one and then a steel wall and then a concrete wall.

The Trapper's fist smashed into the first wall.

Mick gritted his teeth together and screamed in absolute agony. The ring was on fire, burning his hand. Blood seeped from ruptured blood vessels in his eyes, oozed from his ears, gushed from his nose. Volthoom cried out in his mind, begging for mercy. Something about limits to power. Something about exhaustion . . .

The Time Trapper bashed his way through the barriers Mick had erected. The feedback from the ring was excruciating, but Mick fought against it, throwing up wall after wall. He had to hold the line. They were still getting everyone into the Time Sphere. Still hooking up a pair of cables to the Flash's costume. The only things standing between the Multiverse and destruction were Mick Rory and Volthoom.

He imagined a cannon loaded with napalm, aimed it at the Time Trapper, and fired. "Eat hot liquid death, you faceless creep!" Mick shouted. He could barely see through the blood, but the ring guided him, and the fire belched out at the Time Trapper.

"Take that!" Mick screamed, and then showed off the finger on which he wore the ring of Volthoom.

54

"RAO'S SHADOWS!" SUPERMAN SWORE in his birth language. It was the worst epithet in Kryptonese, and he was immediately ashamed of himself for having uttered it. If ever there was a time for profanity, though, it was now.

"Need some help?" a small voice asked.

Superman looked around. The voice had seemed to come from the air itself. Only, there *was* no air here, so where had—

In the blink of an eye, the Atom grew to normal human height. "I hope you don't mind—I thought you might need a hand, so I shrank down and hitched a ride on your belt buckle."

Superman laughed his enormous relief.

Careening in mid-flight, Mick hoped that once the smoke and flames from his napalm burst cleared, he would see nothing but scraps of scorched purple cloth and maybe a nice, fricasseed Time Trapper corpse. He was beyond tired—his entire body felt as though it had been pounded for hours with a meat tenderizer. And that was *good* compared to the pain and fatigue pummeling his brain.

Of course, when the smoke cleared, the Time Trapper still stood there as if nothing had happened.

"You have delayed and delayed," said the Trapper, reaching out, *"thinking that to be your advantage. But it is to* mine. *All delays serve me. As your weapon's charge depletes. Entirely."*

The Time Trapper reached out to Mick, pinching the ring between his thumb and forefinger. With a near-silent *krak*, the ring crumbled into dust.

In that moment, Mick no longer heard Volthoom in his head. He had become so accustomed to the pain, the sensation of something chewing at his thoughts, that the sudden relief brought tears to his eyes.

Without the ring, he should have plummeted from the sky. Instead, with there being no gravity, he simply bobbed in space. The Time Trapper flicked him with the back of his hand, and Mick spiraled across the void, colliding with one of Globe's rocky outcroppings. He lay against it, closing his eyes.

Well, well, well. Hey, Lenny. He thought of Leonard Snart, Captain Cold, his old partner and fellow Legend. Who'd died at the Vanishing Point, at the End of Time in the Earth 1 universe. *Hey, Lenny, looks like we both get to go out heroes. Who'd a thunk it?*

Hands grappled him. Reluctantly, Mick forced his eyes open. Kid Flash grunted as he tugged Mick up. "We don't leave people behind, man."

• • •

"Now or never," Sara warned. She had been keeping an eye on the Time Trapper, who—without Mick and the ring to distract him—was now turning his attention toward them. Everyone was loaded into the Time Sphere, except for Superman and . . .

Ray?

"Cisco, you have enough in you for one last breach?" Sara yelled. The Time Trapper was now sweeping aside his own army, knocking them this way and that, reaching out for the Time Sphere.

With a squint and a grimace of anguish, Cisco fanned his fingers out, pointing. A breach opened just outside the Time Sphere, and Superman and Ray crashed through it. Leaning on each other, they crammed into the Time Sphere.

"Did you do it?" Sara asked, grabbing Superman by his shoulders and shaking him. "Did you adjust the Iron Curtain of Time?"

Superman nodded, his mouth set into a grim line. A trickle of blood ran from his hairline down along his temple. "Did it. We can go."

Barry licked his lips. The cables connected to his costume would allow him to translate his speed energy to the Time Sphere, hauling it through the time stream with him as he ran. He'd designed it so that when they intersected with their own present, the Time Sphere would drop out of the temporal zone and back into reality.

It should work.

It *had* to work.

Behind him, standing just inside the Time Sphere, Oliver put a hand on his shoulder and gazed at him with great emotion.

"I know, I know," said Barry with a forced smile. "'Run, Barry, run.'"

"No. Just . . . Godspeed, Barry Allen." Oliver paused. "And . . . we'll never forget you."

Barry whispered, "3X2(9YZ)4A." It was the only thing left to say.

55

HE RAN, VIBRATING HIS BODY AS HE did so. There was still a chance—a good chance, honestly—they were wrong about all of this. It was all theory, none of it proven. For all they knew, this was a Big Crunch, not a Big Bounce, and he was running to a place and a time that simply did not exist. In which case no one could say what would happen.

The Time Trapper's hand came down, hard. But it didn't matter. Not any longer. They were already fading seconds into the future. The last thing Barry saw at the End of All Time was the circuitry he'd laid out flaring to life as the Iron Curtain of Time solidified.

A series of bright white bursts of light erupted all throughout the void. The activated circuitry had also reversed the Trapper's latest breaches, sending the super villains back to their native time periods. Barry wondered if they would just imagine this whole episode had been a bad dream.

It's done. We did it. The Time Trapper is penned in. We stopped him.

Now the question is just whether or not we live to tell anyone.

Barry ran, his legs pumping. He felt the Speed Force. He felt Wally lending him speed along the cable connection. He felt the vibrational energy from the Earth 27 speedsters, that ripple that had grown over the eons into a tidal wave. It all propelled him forward.

Forward. Reality was blueshifting as he ran, condensing down. The distance between stars became measurable in miles, then in yards, then in feet, then inches . . .

And then the whole of reality—the entirety of fifty-four universes—compressed down to atomic size. A single, primal atom, lost amid an infinity of absolute nothing.

And still Barry ran. There was no light—photons did not exist—and nothing to run on, nothing to push against. Somehow, though, he did it. Somehow, he kept running. Converted to math, to numbers, to pure information, as he'd surmised. Shielded by the mad science of the Speed Force. He'd been bending the laws of physics for years—now he utterly smashed them to bits and trampled on the bits.

And ran.

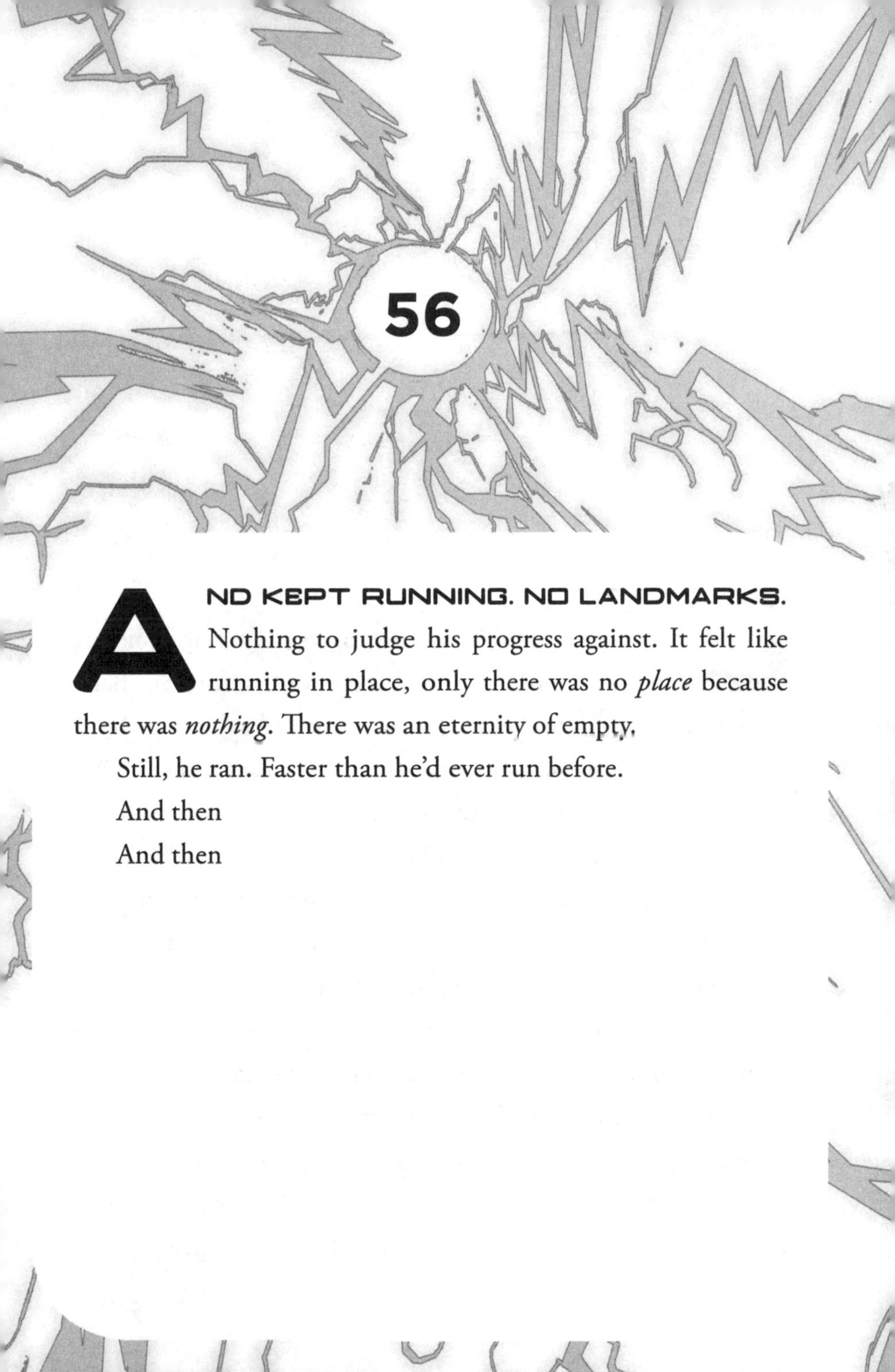

56

AND KEPT RUNNING. NO LANDMARKS. Nothing to judge his progress against. It felt like running in place, only there was no *place* because there was *nothing*. There was an eternity of empty.

Still, he ran. Faster than he'd ever run before.

And then

And then

57

LIGHT!

No sound. There was not yet anything remotely like an atmosphere to carry sound, so the Big Bang happened in absolute silence. Barry whispered a "*Yes!*" to himself as the Multiverse erupted into existence all around him, universes spinning out of one another.

He was running in the so-called Planck era, the earliest time in all of reality, the first 10^{-43} seconds in the universe, a time so small and so quick that even he could barely perceive it.

And then: cosmic inflation! The creation of the quark-gluon plasma, a "soup" made of the particles that would give rise to neutrons and protons, the very foundation of all matter and energy.

Barry kept running. He had to outrun the universe itself, the rapidly expanding, redshifting plasma flung out from the center of reality. The Time Sphere could withstand the rigors of time travel, but not the incredible heat birth of the universe.

He ran thousands of years in the blink of an eye. The universe cooled around him. Atoms coalesced; nuclei formed. Electrons whirred and spun. Reality was coming into view.

He dared not peer over his shoulder to check on his friends. He could feel the mass of the Time Sphere tugging at him, but he had no way of knowing if they were okay. Turning to look would slow him down, and he could not slow down. Not one instant.

He ran, each stride a millennium, pulling the Earth 27–generated wave with him, hyper-accelerating beyond his own top speeds.

The heat enveloped him. He outran it, but he felt it tugging at him nonetheless, wicking along his costume. The Flash uniform was designed to handle the heat of superspeed, but this was beyond superspeed. Pieces of the uniform smoldered, caught fire, peeled off, and drifted into the incipient vacuum of aborning space.

Stay strong, Barry. Don't stop. You can't stop!

You can do this. You have to do this! This is what you were born to do. To save them all. To make the world safe for the ones you love.

Thousands more years. Hundreds of thousands. Millions.

Tears collected in his eyes, then whipped away into the Speed Force. He would never see them again. He would never hold Iris again. Never feel Joe's arm around his shoulders.

It's OK, though. It's OK. The world—the Multiverse—is safe. Two timelines, protected. That's what matters. You set it right.

Lights flickered around him. The universe, coming into

being as he ran, solidifying around him. He wavered in and out of the Speed Force, stumbling occasionally. His vibrational pattern locked in on home and guided him there, pulling him along even as his strength flagged.

Almost there. I can feel it. Almost there.

His body was on fire from within. He could feel his muscles dissolving, using up their lactic acid, feeding on themselves. He'd run billions of years, passed through the fire of Creation itself.

You couldn't do such things without consequences.

Something hovered into view before him. Walls faded into existence. It was dark and he saw her, saw Iris.

It had to be a hallucination. It couldn't be real.

She was in one of the bedrooms at S.T.A.R. Labs. She sat up and turned to him, shock written across her face.

"Barry? What happened?"

He reached out to her but could not close the gap between them. The tips of his fingers fell short of her by inches. A low-pitched crackle hissed around him as she jagged in and out of sight.

"I love you so much," he said, tears streaming down his face. "It'll all be OK. I promise. I will never stop loving you."

And then she was gone.

He was seeing things. That was it. He was losing his mind. He'd run so hard. His body was cannibalizing itself now. Translating from matter into pure energy. The first physics formula he'd ever learned: $E=mc^2$.

Meaning mass converts to energy at a ratio equal to the speed of light squared.

The speed of light was nothing to him. He was faster than light. Faster than any single thing had ever been.

Something new came into his view. Another hallucination? Random sparking in his brain, summoning images to distract him from his fate?

A dirty city street. A man, distracted. Familiar.

"Joe?" Barry said.

Yes. Yes, it was Joe.

Joe snapped his head up and said, "Barry?"

Barry wept at the sight of his adoptive father. He should have been there to help Joe, too. But he had to tell him. He had to let him know . . .

"Joe, I'm sorry. I'm going to make it all work out."

"What?" Joe put his hand out to touch him, but in that same instant, he vanished.

Barry howled, the flesh around his mouth gone thin and taut. It was happening. It was all happening around him. The world turning in its rhythms. The universe expanding, redshifting, moving on.

He was in the Cortex at S.T.A.R. Labs. Madame Xanadu before him. And holding a knife to her throat . . .

"Owlman?" Barry said, his voice tremulous and thready. "But that must mean . . ."

That must mean I'm almost there. I'm almost to the present.

His body had converted partly to energy, flaming and

radioactive. If he stopped in the present, he would combust and kill everyone around him.

He had no choice—he cut loose the cables, letting the Time Sphere drop out of the temporal zone and into the present.

And he kept running.

58

SARA YELPED AS THE TIME SPHERE jerked and tumbled around her, jostling everyone inside. Mick's elbow ended up in her gut, and Wally's hand swatted her in the head.

They had been at the End of All Time. Barry had begun running and then everything was a blur. And when she said *everything*, she meant *everything*. She'd eventually shut her eyes against the mad, chaotic smear presented to them, ground her teeth together, and thought of Ava.

Now the Time Sphere felt as though it had collided with something hard. Something real. She risked opening her eyes but saw only Mick's armpit, which wasn't much of an improvement over time travel.

A sound. A voice.

". . . on fire! Put it out! Put it out!"

59

SUPERGIRL HELD A COLD PACK TO her forehead, where a large bruise was already forming. "Good thing I took most of the wall with my thick skull," she joked.

Caitlin stood nearby, examining Supergirl's head X-ray. "I don't think you have a concussion. There are some *weird* brain anomalies, but I guess that's just what Kryptonian brains are supposed to look like."

Iris clucked her tongue, irritated. "I don't know which one of you I'm more annoyed with," she said. "You both took crazy risks that—"

"Wait!" Supergirl jumped up. "Do you hear that? It's like . . . like a clock . . . ticking . . . too fast . . ."

With a harrumph, Iris said, "Don't try to distract me."

"No!" Supergirl said. "Seriously!" She grabbed Iris and Caitlin by the wrists and tugged hard. Once upon a time that would have ripped their arms out of their sockets, but right now all it did was propel them toward the door that led out into the corridor.

At the same time, she shouted, "Everyone get down!"

The Time Sphere materialized in the center of the S.T.A.R. Labs Cortex out of nowhere, steaming and burning upon reentry into the physical world. If Supergirl hadn't flung Iris and Caitlin out of the room, the Sphere would have collided with them and incinerated them in an eyeblink. Felicity, wearing earbuds and typing on her keyboard, didn't notice it at first, then yelped as the heat and light exploded nearby, and she dived under her own desk.

The room lit up instantly, shadows chased into the corners. Smoke rolled out from the Time Sphere, and flames crackled. Reflexively, Supergirl ran to it.

"Kara!" Iris yelled from the doorway. "Get back!"

Rolling, the Time Sphere shuddered along the floor, heading for Felicity. Supergirl threw herself in its path. Fire sizzled around her. The ends of her hair burned.

When she touched the metal skin of the Time Sphere, pain seared her flesh. A touch of her invulnerability and superstrength had returned—just enough to keep her from passing out from the pain. Grunting and straining, she dug her feet in and held the Time Sphere in place so that it couldn't destroy the Cortex or hurt her friends.

"Hurry!" she yelled.

"It's on fire!" Iris cried. "Put it out! Put it out!"

She wasn't asking someone else to do it—she was telling them to help her do it. She was already on her way to the emergency fire extinguishers.

Mr. Terrific dashed through the door and sent a T-sphere to the wreckage; it pumped a foam out from above, helping Iris, Felicity, and Caitlin as they hit the Time Sphere with the fire extinguishers from different angles. Soon, it was out.

Supergirl stumbled away from the steaming hulk of metal. Her hands were burned and her face was covered in soot, but she waved away Caitlin when the doctor approached her with a worried expression and a medical gleam in her eye.

"They might need help," Supergirl said, panting slightly. "Don't worry about me. Worry about them."

As she spoke, the door creaked open, then fell off entirely. Iris screamed in surprised joy when Wally stepped out. She ran to her brother and threw her arms around him.

Cisco, the Atom, White Canary, Heat Wave, Green Arrow, and Superman emerged next. Every single one of them looked wrecked, even the Man of Steel.

Iris clutched Wally and planted kisses on his forehead. "Where's Barry?" she asked.

Wally said nothing. He looked at the floor.

Iris thought of Madame Xanadu's words. *No.* "Is he hurt? Still in the Time Sphere? Wally . . ."

"Kal . . . ?" Supergirl said, her tone acknowledging what she already knew.

Superman came to her. "Mrs. West-Allen . . . Iris . . . I'm so sorry . . ."

Iris howled and swung her fist at him. He rocked with the blow, accepted it, then folded her in his arms and held her as she wept.

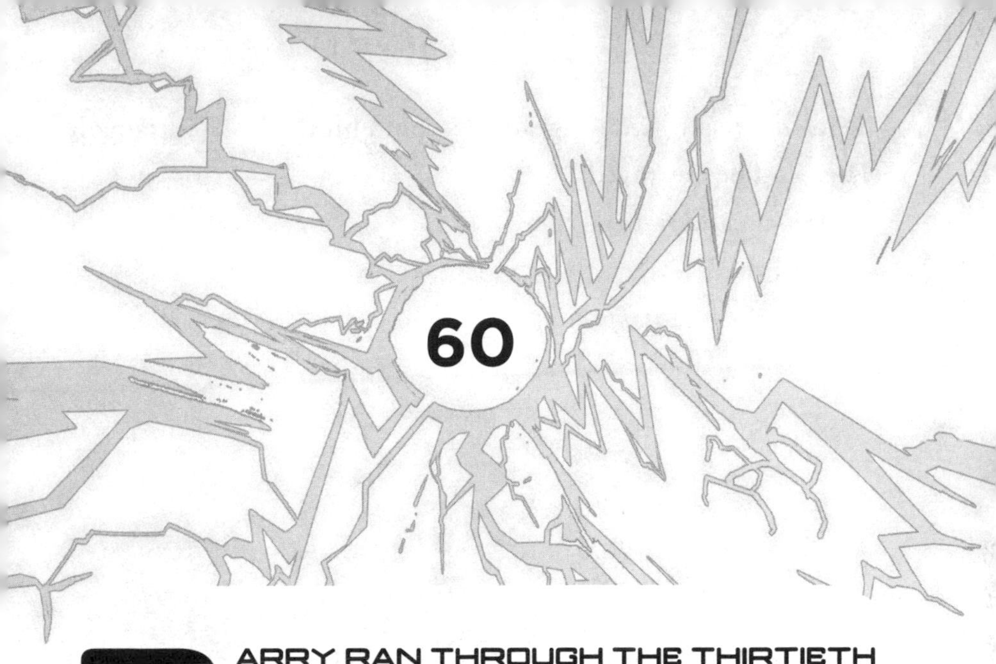

60

BARRY RAN THROUGH THE THIRTIETH century, wondering briefly and wryly if the Tornado Twins, Dawn and Don, would be aware of his passing.

He ran to the Legion, blew through the thirty-first century on a wind of tachyons and bosons. Chased the history of the future down its pathways, the only sounds his own breath and the sizzle-crack of his atoms shifting into energy.

In the sixty-fourth century, he phased back into reality for just an instant, spying a familiar face.

“ϟ !” she exclaimed, forgetting in her shock to revert to ancient English.

“Hefa!” he cried out to her. And then more. Hoping she could hear him. Knowing she probably couldn’t.

The sixty-fourth century was history now, so distant in the past that it might as well have been the Jurassic.

He ran and ran. He ran, missing them all. He ran, loving

them all. He ran, knowing that he would hit the Iron Curtain of Time and be destroyed.

He ran and ran and ran.

And then . . .

And then he *stopped*.

61

THERE WAS SUNLIGHT AND A BREEZE and cool green grass under his feet.

Barry peered around. The sky, blue, offered a single white cloud, a puffy and cheerful promise on the horizon.

It had to be morning, because the grass was wet with dew. It grew almost waist-high in some spots. With gentle curiosity, he stepped to the tall grass. Watched as it bent in the breeze.

He was not tired. He was not on fire. He was whole and intact. His breath came easy. His heart beat normally.

"Barry, you did it."

It was the voice of his mother.

"Son, we're so proud."

His father.

Dead all these years. Speaking to him now.

He had run faster than light. And then he'd run faster than life itself.

"You can rest now, Barry. Everyone is safe. You saved the world. Again."

He ran the tips of his fingers along the grass, picking up the dew. Dew was the product of water vapor condensing overnight on flat surfaces, usually when the air was calm. Determining whether or not dew would form was a simple matter of calculating the dew point, using the Magnus formula.

$$EW = \alpha \cdot e^{\left(\frac{\beta . T}{\lambda + T}\right)}$$

Everything was calm now. There was no wind.

Their arms around him. The familiar brush of her lips on his forehead, wishing him sweet dreams.

He turned his face to the sun. He smelled the air and the grass and the clean soil.

Dew was just condensation, he knew, but it had different meanings across cultures. For some, it was a symbol of reincarnation, a promise of new life with each morning.

He smiled.

Flash Fact.

62

THE LEGENDS AND SUPERMAN USED the Time Courier to travel to the thirty-first century for emergency medical aid. Iris shook off Felicity and Curtis. She needed to be alone. Her father was headed home from Star City, but she didn't want to see him, either. Not right now.

Instead, she went to the Time Vault. She called up the newspaper that predicted Barry's disappearance during some sort of "crisis." This had been a crisis, all right, but the timing had been all wrong. He was supposed to vanish years from now.

She stared at the newspaper. Everything about it was the same.

Almost everything.

The byline was the same. The date. The masthead.

The headline, though, had changed.

Iris didn't know what it meant, but it made her smile through her tears.

63

HEY, PRETTY LADY. CAN I BORROW a cup of sugar?"

Ava jolted upright at her desk. Since Sara had disappeared, she'd been spending every waking moment at her desk at the Time Bureau. Compartmentalizing. Keeping herself too busy to mourn.

"Am I seeing things?" she said softly.

Sara, leaning against the doorjamb, shook her head, grinning that self-satisfied grin she always flashed when she'd just pulled off the impossible. "Nah. You're seeing exactly *one* thing: the woman who loves you."

Ava launched herself over the desk and threw herself into Sara's arms.

Mick moved slowly as he chose a seat in the commissary at the Time Bureau. He didn't trust fancy-pants thirty-first-century medical technology, so unlike the others, he'd just let the Legion's docs put some bandages on him and that was that. He would heal on his own, the way it was supposed to be. His body hurt, but eventually it would hurt less.

In the meantime, he had a plate piled high with french fries, a nice lean corned beef sandwich with mustard hot enough to burn out his nose hairs, and a beer. Good medicine.

Ray came in, bearing a tray with a plate of broccoli and a fruit cup. Mick wrinkled his nose. "Rabbit food, Haircut?"

Ray beamed as he sat down. "Healthy body, healthy mind, Mick!"

"Meh." Mick waffled his hand back and forth.

"How are you feeling?"

Mouth stuffed with corned beef, Mick managed another "Meh."

Leaning in conspiratorially, Ray asked, "What's it like being without the ring?"

Mick chased his sandwich with a hearty glug of brew. "Just like being with the ring. Only, without it."

Ray snorted. "C'mon, man! You can tell me! You had the most powerful weapon in the universe. That had to have changed you."

Mick regarded Ray quietly and seriously for a moment. Then, without warning, he belched—loud, long. Powerful enough to muss Ray's hair.

"Kinda . . . like that?" Ray asked, combing his hair back into place.

"Kinda like that," Mick agreed, and drank again.

64

AFTER FELICITY AND OLIVER RE-turned to Star City, after her father came home, Iris sat with Caitlin and Cisco in her apartment. They held hands and said very little.

Until Superman appeared through a Time Courier with White Canary and Heat Wave. Iris glared at them, then relented and sighed, sinking into Caitlin.

"I'm sorry," Iris said. "Whatever you need, we can't help. I'm closing S.T.A.R. Labs while we mourn."

Superman smiled gently. "We're not here to ask for help. We're here to offer it."

"What do you mean?" Cisco said.

Superman exchanged a look with Mick and Sara, then unconsciously brushed a finger along his hairline. He had told the Legion's medical robots not to use healing radiation on this cut, so it had healed into a pale scar there as his powers returned and the broken flesh became invulnerable to medical lasers. He wanted it. Wanted it as a reminder of what he'd seen and what he'd lost.

With his hair brushed forward, it wasn't visible. Only when he swept it back, as Clark.

"There's still work to be done," Sara said. "We need to track down the people who've been shifted from universe to universe and get them back to their homes."

"And we need to find our missing crew members," Mick said.

"I don't see how this is helping Iris," Caitlin said somewhat defensively. Her friend had been through enough. She didn't need to be worrying about jumping through time and the Multiverse right now.

"I'm going with them," Superman said. "Supergirl's powers are back and she's taking care of Earth 38. But I need to finish the job we started. I'll be joining the Legends, in Barry's memory. To help."

Cisco whistled. "You're gonna be a Legend of Tomorrow?"

Sara shook her head. "Rip Hunter named us the Legends when he first gathered us together. He told us we were hailed throughout history. Turned out to be a lie. So then he told us we had a chance to *become* legends. But the thing is, we have to do our work in secret. It's become a sort of self-deprecating in-joke.

"But now . . ." she went on. "Now, well . . . We've been to tomorrow. And we've been beyond tomorrow."

"We're now the Legends of Forever," Superman said. "And we're going to heal the damage the Time Trapper did to the

Multiverse. And, Iris, I swear on the memory of Krypton: If there is a way to find Barry and bring him back, we will find it."

Iris sniffled and dabbed at her tears. "Thank you."

"But there is one more thing." Superman hesitated and gazed meaningfully at Cisco. "Do you want to tell her, or should I?"

Iris glared at Cisco, who ran his hands through his hair, tugging at the ends. "Oh man. Are you sure? Do you think so?"

"What?" Iris asked. "What else could there possibly be?"

"We have reason to believe that the Time Trapper sent an agent back through history," Superman said.

"*Hypothetica dominium . . .*" Cisco shivered at the memory.

"An agent?" Iris asked. "Why?"

"According to what Cisco gleaned, to take revenge if he were

to be defeated. We believe this agent will target you first, Iris."

Iris laughed without mirth. "Of course."

"But we have an answer. The Legion has established a . . . well, for lack of a better word, a safe era. It's like a safe house, but a whole time period. Where the Trapper's agent can't see or go. We can take you there and keep you safe until we track it down."

"Like a witness protection program," Cisco breathed.

"Something like that," Sara said. "How about it, Iris? You up for living in the future for a little while?"

Iris drew in a deep breath. "It doesn't seem like I have much of a choice, do I?"

"Do it," Caitlin urged her. "Stay safe. We'll be waiting for you when you can come back."

"Yeah," said Cisco. "We'll keep the lights on, coordinate with Team Arrow to keep the mad science going." He shrugged. "And Wally will keep the speedster flame alive in Central."

Iris chewed at her lower lip. "Can I have some time to say goodbye to some people?" she asked.

Sara chuckled and gestured to her Time Courier. "We have a time machine. Take as long as you need."

65

MADAME XANADU STRODE DOWN the hallway at S.T.A.R. Labs, turned at a certain door, opened it, and stepped through into another dimension.

Whorls of color spun around her. The door to S.T.A.R. Labs and Earth vanished.

A moment later, she heard the impossible sound of measured footsteps where there was no floor. Her associate, he who wore the fedora and the cloak and the medallion, known to humankind only as the Phantom Stranger, approached her and spoke with neither introduction nor preamble.

"It is resolved. Though not in the way we anticipated."

"No? Barry Allen saved the Multiverses."

"At what cost? Time has realigned. The future is in tumult."

Madame Xanadu smiled. "Ah, but at least there *is* a future, my friend."

He raised a finger to chide her, but before he could speak a word, she said, "If such as we cannot call each other *friend*, then who can?"

Miffed but also mollified, he offered a small shrug. "What now? What of Barry Allen? Do you truly believe this reality has no further use for him?"

Madame Xanadu sighed, then smiled. "He has run far and fast. He has earned his rest. And at long last, he now can finally stop running . . . and slow down."

EPILOGUE

FROM HER BALCONY, IRIS WATCHED the sun rise over the city of Metropolis in the mid-thirtieth century. Even with weather control technology, the night still often left her the slick surprise of dew on the balcony rail each morning.

Something in the dew spoke to her. She thought of Barry when she ran her fingers along it, drawing a lightning bolt or spelling his name. He would have understood the how and the why of dew.

She touched her belly. She wasn't showing (not yet), but thirtieth-century medical technology had already told her that the babies she was carrying—fraternal twins—were healthy and on track to deliver normally in thirty-three weeks.

Barry's last legacy. His children.

The sun broke through the clouds. Morning dawned and she thought again, as she so often did, of the newspaper in the Time

Vault, of the headline that had once caused dread and despair but that now—through the vagaries of paradox—gave her hope.

FLASH REAPPEARS DURING CRISIS! the headline now proclaimed.

She sketched another lightning bolt next to the one she'd already drawn in the dew. Twin bolts. In the first glorious bright light of a new day, it occurred to her: Dawn, she thought, would be the perfect name for Barry's daughter.

Yes. Dawn.

And the boy?

Well, she'd think of something.

ACKNOWLEDGMENTS

Hello, dear reader! We've made it to the End of All Time and back together, and I am so grateful that you took this trip with me.

I offer my gratitude to the folks at Warner Bros. and The CW who made this madcap story possible, especially Carl Ogawa, Amy Weingartner, Victoria Selover, and Josh Anderson, but also to Greg Berlanti, Todd Helbing, Sarah Schechter, Lindsay Kiesel, Janice Aquilar-Herrero, Catherine Shin, Thomas Zellers, and Kristin Chin. I asked for the moon and the stars, and they said, "Why think so small?"

A big thanks is also due to Russ Busse, my editor, who absorbed the craziness with aplomb and who got me to change my original ending without even asking me to. Your Jedi mind tricks are strong, Russ . . .

And thanks, too, to the rest of the hardworking crew at Abrams—including but not limited to Andrew Smith, Kara Sargent, Jody Mosley, Maggie Lehrman, Chad Beckerman, Evangelos Vasilakis, Marie Oishi, John Passaineau, Alison Gervais, Melanie Chang, Maya Bradford, Kim Lauber, Trish McNamara O'Neil, Brooke Shearouse, Borana Greku, and Liz Fithian.

My thanks as well to Shawn M. Moll, who saw us through to the end with an amazing cover.

Lastly, I would run the length of the universe for my wife and kids. You are my lightning and chemicals.